WICKED HUNGER

DelSheree Gladden

Clean Teen Publishing

Wicked Hunger

Clean Teen Publishing

PO Box 561326

The Colony, TX 75056

www.cleanteenpublishing.com

Typography by: Courtney Nuckels

Cover design by: Marya Heiman

ISBN: 978-1-940534-39-8

For Ryan

YA M

Content Disclosure

For more information about our content disclosure, please
utilize the QR code above with your
smart phone or visit us at

www.cleanteenpublishing.com.

Van

1

STORIES

*H*aving my back turned toward the empty parking lot as I lock up the dance studio is slightly unnerving. In the back of my mind, I know there's nothing to fear, but I still turn the key quickly and spin around to face the approaching darkness.

I hold myself close to the door, waiting for the feeling to leave me. Several minutes pass before I realize it isn't going away. I can either stand here all night, or start walking. It's with a show of false bravery that I take a step forward. As I walk away from the dance studio, I know I'm being silly. My brother, Zander, is constantly telling me that fear is a weakness. I know how to defend myself.

Defending myself isn't the problem. Controlling myself is.

The walk to my grandma's house where Zander and I have been living for the past year is a good five miles away. I was supposed to ask Grandma to pick me up when Zander said he couldn't, but I thought some time alone sounded better. At least, at the time, it sounded like a good idea. Now, I'm not so sure that a fifteen-year-old girl walking home alone at night is smart at all. It only invites trouble. The fading sun seems to retreat faster than normal. Within ten minutes, I am left skulking along the streets of Albuquerque in the full black of night. My pace quickens.

I know the way home, but in the darkness I feel my courage fizzle. I am practically running past shops with my feet set in the direction of the relative safety of my neighborhood, taking any shortcut available to get me home faster. I'm not the only one out on the streets. Average looking people mill about on the sidewalks, but I keep my distance.

Eyes down, I run. I'm only two blocks away from the cramped little neighborhood where Grandma has lived for twenty years. I am almost there when I lurch to a stop in front of a dank alley filled with scuffling noises and pain.

An unsettled feeling rises in the center of my body. I try to take another step, to get away, but I can't. A muffled scream sends another shot of wretched pain shooting through the air. It's too much to resist.

Dance bag abandoned, tennis shoes slapping against asphalt, my body powers down the alley independent of rational thought. Fragile bones snap and howls of pain erupt. Delicious satisfaction rushes in as agony fills the damp alley. Everything else is forgotten.

The sting of a knife pierces my thigh, the burst of pain only continuing the frenzy. Blood splatters, knuckles crack, flesh breaks. Nothing else exists in that moment.

"Hey!" someone yells out.

Suddenly, without warning, the space around me is empty. I stumble up to my feet in search of the three chollo gangsters who were just on top of me. They are racing out of the alley, with only one looking back with a terrified expression before darting around the corner.

Stunned, confused, I stand up covered in blood and bruises. My eyes flit around for an explanation, landing on a caramel-haired teen with a cell phone in his hand. I think he tries to say something to me. I watch his lips move without comprehending. The only rational thought I have is that he's holding my ballet bag. Then, I hear the word *police* slip past his lips. In a panic, I snatch my bag out of his hand and run.

Laney's elbow knocks into my head as she tries to slide into the seat next to me. The contact sends my hair into my face, and applesauce sloshing off her tray to land in a cold splat on my bare thigh. I jump in surprise.

"Sorry!" Laney apologizes. She finally manages to drop her lunch tray on the table, and grabs a handful of napkins. She passes them to me with another apology. "Sorry, Van, did I get it all over you? These new heels have been tripping me up all day."

"I told you they were too high," I say as I take the napkins and start wiping off my leg. Laney grimaces and points to my hair as well. Shaking my head at her, I wipe applesauce out of my platinum locks.

"They aren't too high! I just need a little practice," Laney says with a pout.

"If you haven't mastered walking by now…"

Laney opens her mouth to object, but is cut off by a new arrival. Two new arrivals, actually. Identically adorable, Sandra and Kari barely reach five foot, but their eclectic style—which consists mainly of as many mismatching colors and patterns as possible—makes them extremely noticeable. They sit down at the table in perfect unison. I think they practice that. Beyond weird, but they're my friends, and I don't have nearly enough of those to go tossing them out just because of a few idiosyncrasies. The banana yellow top with the flouncy green and pink ruffled skirt, fur lined boots, grey dancer's shrug, and rhinestone studded belt are quickly giving me a headache. And that's just Sandra's outfit. Kari's is even worse.

If they notice my chagrin at all, they don't mention it. Kari says, "We think your stilettos are to die for…"

"You would," I interject.

Sandra throws me a scowl and continues. "But Vanessa is right about your ability to walk across a flat surface without nearly killing yourself."

Vanessa. Why do they insist on using my full name?

"I am perfectly capable…"

"No, you aren't," Kari interrupts, "so we think you should give us the shoes. We'll make much better use of them."

They both grin. I feel like Alice staring at a double nightmare of Cheshire cats. Any minute now the rest of them will disappear—taking their bizarre outfits with them, hopefully—and leave only their too-big smiles behind. Laney sticks her tongue out at them. It completes the down-the-rabbit-hole experience for me.

I'm determined to tune all three of them out as Sandra starts talking about feather boas and rubber galoshes. Maybe I should feel left out, but the hum of craziness that surrounds my group of friends is comforting. Until Laney jabs me with her elbow and starts waving wildly at someone behind the twins' heads. All I can see is a hot pink streak against a background of short ebony hair. Friend of the twins?

"What is your problem today?" I snap at Laney when she elbows me again.

The pink-and-black-headed mystery sees Laney and changes course. Laney is too busy gesturing like a maniac to answer me, so I scoot away from her and start stabbing at my meatloaf, or whatever it's supposed to be. I'm still trying to talk myself into taking a bite when a familiar feeling courses through me. My head pops up to stare at this nightmare of a girl.

I can feel the muscles in my body tightening to the point of near-rupture. Every cell is begging me to give in again. Tears burn behind my eyes at the effort it takes not to listen. I can almost feel it…almost feel her suntanned skin dimpling under the pressure of my grip before giving way and breaking in welcome of my hunger.

Terrified by the intensity of my reaction, I scour her for some explanation. I scan the heart shaped face and subtle makeup that make her pretty, but average, the clothes that are stylish without being too trendy, and even her mannerisms, but with no success. I shouldn't want to harm her, but I do.

I want it more than anything I have ever wanted in my life. The sound of something snapping draws her's and Laney's attention to me.

"Geez, use a fork much?" Laney asks me. The girl across from me stares with one eyebrow cocked curiously.

It takes me a minute to look down at my fork. I blink in surprise at the broken shards of plastic littering my meatloaf.

"You…all right?" Laney asks slowly.

My gaze snaps over to her. Shame for my thoughts and near-actions overpower my hunger enough for me to respond. "Yeah, sorry. This food, it's so gross," I mumble.

"So you thought killing it a second time would help that problem?" Laney laughs and bumps into me with her shoulder. She's known me long enough not to be surprised by my sudden and unexplained funks. She flicks away her worry and turns back to the pink and black haired girl. I reluctantly follow her gaze.

The hunger tries to explode again when I look at her, but I do better now that I'm expecting it. A little better, at least. It's only a gnawing ache on the brink of breaking me rather than an all-consuming need. What really helps me keep myself in check is her wide-eyed expression. Laney may be able to brush off my weirdness, but this girl is staring at me like she's afraid I might take my mangled fork to her eyes. She must be psychic. Or just smarter than the average bear.

Frightened by my reaction to this girl, I sit very still, and will her to do the same. I can't mess up. I can't give in. After Oscar…one more mistake would mean leaving, at the very least. Being locked up or dying, those would be the worst, but still very possible. I can't do that to Zander. My brother has suffered so much already. Thinking of him focuses my energy. I'm the only one left who can protect him. Even knowing that, I struggle to rein in my hunger.

"This is my cousin, Ivy Guerra. I told you about her, remember? Her family just moved here from San Diego," Laney says.

I just stare at Ivy for a few seconds. It's not that I'm trying to be rude, but if I open my mouth right now the result may not be pretty. I flex and point my toes, slowly, focusing on the contracting and relaxing of my muscles. It's a trick my grandma taught me. It helps sometimes.

"Nice to meet you, Ivy," I finally manage to say. "I'm Van."

"Short for Vanessa?" she asks.

I nod, not wanting to open my mouth again.

A tray drops onto the table next to me, splashing yet another blob of apple sauce onto my body. My arm, this time. "Would people please stop spilling food on me?" I snap.

His answering grin weakens my anger as it always does. His presence distracts me from Ivy beautifully, as well. I do my best to remain annoyed, but I'm secretly grateful he showed up. The warmth behind his smile seeps under my skin.

"Sorry, Van. Who else spilled goop on you?" he asks. "Laney? I saw her fall into a row of lockers on her way to class this morning."

Laney pointedly ignores him after that, and he turns his attention to trying to wipe the applesauce off my arm. His touch is a little too much like a caress. My body softens

7

in response, savoring the contact. Ivy notices the exchange, her eyebrow rising in question. I force myself to snatch the napkin out of his hand and finish cleaning myself up without looking at either of them. It earns me a frustrated sigh from Ketchup, but he knows this is how it has to be. Knowing doesn't stop him from scooting his chair close enough that our knees touch. I resist the urge to lay my hand on his thigh, but I can't make myself move away from him.

"Ivy, this is Ketchup. Ketchup, Ivy. She's my cousin," Laney says casually.

"Ketchup?" Ivy asks. Yeah, she definitely thinks we're all crazy. "What kind of name is that?"

"Why? What's wrong with it?" Ketchup asks in mock outrage. "You're named after a vine. Why can't I be named after America's favorite condiment?"

Ivy doesn't seem to know how to respond. She takes a bite of her roll, watching him carefully. He keeps up his attempt at an intimidating glare. I know he's a big dopey pushover, but Ivy doesn't. I grab an apple slice off Ketchup's tray and throw it at his chest. Laney backs me up by chucking a piece of bread at him. His façade cracks when he jumps and tries to deflect the food missiles. I just shake my head at him and try not to regret having pushed him away. As if he knows my unspoken desire, he moves his chair even closer to me when he sits back down. I swallow hard and turn my attention back to Ivy.

"His name's not really Ketchup. It's just a nickname," I say in an attempt to appear halfway normal and ward off any awkward questions.

"How do you get a nickname like Ketchup?" she asks.

"By pulling his lunch out first day of kindergarten and having nothing but a plain piece of bread and a bunch of ketchup packets," Laney says. "He sat there squirting ketchup all over his bread while the rest of us just stared at him. And then he actually ate it." Laney shivers at the memory.

I like ketchup as much as the next person, but gross! Ketchup just laughs as he tears the corners off three ketchup packets and starts squirting them all over his meatloaf. Ivy and I both wrinkle our noses at him.

"What?" he laughs. "You're supposed to eat ketchup on meatloaf!"

"Not that much," I say.

"Whatever." He drops the empty packets on my tray and takes a huge bite of his ketchup-drowned lunch.

"What's your real name?" Ivy asks him when he finishes chewing the gloppy mess.

Ketchup stops, taps his finger against the side of his head, and says, "You know, I don't think anyone remembers."

"Really?" Ivy asks sarcastically.

He looks over at Laney and me for confirmation. We both shrug. Even the teachers know him as Ketchup. Ivy shakes her head.

"This has got to be the weirdest group of friends I've ever met. Two matching fashion catastrophes, my klutzy cousin, a guy named Ketchup, and a...and Van. You guys are messed up."

Ketchup and Laney both laugh at Ivy's apt descriptions of everyone, but I'm left wondering what she was going to

9

say about me. And a *what*? She can't possible know anything about me. Right? People knowing is dangerous. She just thinks I'm strange, that's all. I tell myself that, but for some reason, I don't believe my own words.

Something seems off about this girl, though I can't put my finger on why. I'm going to have to keep an eye on her, which is probably a bad idea given the hunger I am still struggling to control. Just thinking about subjecting myself to her presence again makes giving in that much more irresistible. My fingers grip the edges of my chair, clenching to the point of deforming the bumpy plastic seat.

I frantically try to calm myself back down. Breathing, stretching, counting down from one million. Sensing my need, Ketchup's hand slides onto my knee and squeezes. My hunger instantly drops a few notches as I focus on his touch. No one else notices the contact, but it helps immensely. I try to banish the rest of my hunger by drinking in the ambient noise of the cafeteria and letting it momentarily numb my brain.

"So, how did you all end up becoming friends?" Ivy asks, her voice ratcheting up the hunger inside me. "You guys seem like a pretty odd combination, so there must be a good story behind it."

Oh no. My insides squirm and twist in panic. My hand snaps down over Ketchup's, begging for strength. I try to find my voice somewhere amid the aching need to hurt Ivy so I can stop anyone at the table from answering and giving her any more hints that there's something wrong with me, but Ketchup is faster.

"Not just one story, but six very interesting stories. One for each of us."

"But there's only five of you here," Ivy argues.

"You haven't met Wyatt and Holly yet," Laney pipes in.

"That's seven."

"There's six, not including Van."

"Why doesn't Van get a story?"

"Because she's in all of ours," Ketchup says. "She's the one who brought us all together."

"How did she do that?" Ivy asks.

I want to stop him from saying anything. My rigid muscles won't let me. All I can manage is to look over at her and see the heat of something I don't understand held tight in her features as she waits for her answer.

Ketchup grins, sending my stomach down to the basement. "She saved our lives."

Van

2

THE RULES

I hurry away from the cafeteria in search of peace and quiet. That means my Home Economics class, a passion I owe to Grandma. A professional chef in her younger years, her mouthwatering dishes made me fall in love with cooking the first time I tasted a piece of her Black Forest cake.

I scurry into class, being sure to stay well away from Simon Dale and the hunger he inspires. After what I just experienced with Ivy, I can't handle any more temptations. Years of practice avoiding Simon lets me move past him quickly and reach my work table. I huddle in my seat, glad to be away from Ivy. I'm sure I surprised everyone by bolting up from the table before she could ask questions, but I don't care. I needed to get away from her.

Soaking up the calming scents and flavors of the room, I sit quietly with my eyes closed in hopes of blocking everyone else out. A sudden, fiery flash of hunger snaps my eyes open. My sanctuary has just been tainted pink and black.

Ivy stands before me looking rather smug, but feigning politeness. "Um," she starts, "is it okay if I sit here? I didn't see any other tables open, but if you already have a partner..."

"Nope," I say, sounding sharper than I would have liked. "I usually work alone."

Sitting down next to me, Ivy asks, "Why's that?"

I look away, not interested in explaining anything to Ivy. Some kids go through high school as outcasts because of one idiotic reason or another. Lame clothes, not enough money, unfortunate physique or skin issues...the usual. I'm not one of those people. My status as untouchable is rightly deserved. It wouldn't be the first time my hunger has gotten me into trouble. There's no unfairness about it, just plain old common sense. Stay away from Van, stay alive. Simple as that.

Mrs. Huff starts class with her overly loud voice and squeaky dry erase marker as she writes out the instructions for today's recipe on the board, repeating every word as if she thinks we aren't capable of reading it ourselves. Everyone starts rummaging around in cabinets and gathering up supplies from the pantry. I get mine. Ivy gets hers. No talking necessary. If only our work areas were a little farther apart. Being only a few feet away from her, no matter how far I push my chair away, sets my teeth grinding with the effort to keep them in check.

"So...did you really save Laney's life?" She waits expectantly when her surprising question causes me to look up at her. I look away without answering, but she continues. "I mean, Laney told me you'd helped her out of a bad situation once, but she didn't really go into details."

I don't respond.

"Laney's pretty accident prone, but it sounded like it was something more than that, and she said it was a long time ago, like when you two were little, but how young could you have been, right? How many four-year-olds go around saving people's lives?"

Five-year-olds, actually. But I don't say that out loud.

Ivy waits expectantly. She can keep waiting all she wants.

After a few minutes, she finally seems to realize I'm not interested in sharing. She goes back to preparing ingredients for the recipe without voicing any more questions. Outwardly, she seems perfectly absorbed in her work, but a hint of irritation lines her features.

Clearly, Ketchup's mentioning of the stories has her interest piqued, but she seems to already know something about Laney's story. Her irritation about not hearing the rest seems unjustified, which makes me wonder. Laney wouldn't give away what really happened—not only because she's a true friend, but because she knows anyone she tried to tell would think she had cracked like Humpty Dumpty and she'd be sent off to try and put her head back together again.

Laney knows about insanity, and where it's housed, from being friends with me. She wouldn't risk that, and telling her story would be a one way ticket to professional help. There's no way Laney told her anything about what she's seen me do. Could Ivy possibly know something about me? I don't know how. I'm just some fifteen year old girl living quietly in the middle of the desert.

Except, I'm not.

It's not exactly a secret that I'm a freak. That's why no one sits with me in class. I've grown up through elementary school with a lot of these kids, but even the ones I've only known since we were all pooled into the same high school have heard the stories and know enough to stay away from me, even if they don't actually know why.

But who am I kidding? I don't even know why. I don't understand the most basic part of who I am. My grandma tries to help, but even she is limited in what she knows. Her only knowledge comes from family legends passed down through generations of old coots mumbling scary bedtime stories to trembling little children. Half of what she's told me sounds like total crap.

I carry the filled cookie sheet to the oven, relieved to have some distance from Ivy. I slide the tray in and step back to close the oven door without paying much attention. Someone smacks into the back of me, hard. My hands spring out in front of me, palms slapping into the hot racks and oven door.

The pain that bursts through my body kills, but rouses my hunger as well. It's a battle between not reacting to the injury and lapping up the pain hungrily. Ivy, who is suddenly next to me, yanks me back from the oven. Her touch barely registers under the pain of my scorched flesh. My brain finally refocuses, and I push the oven door shut with my elbow, hoping desperately that no one saw what just happened. I shove my blistered hands down, out of sight before anyone can take notice.

My sigh of relief is interrupted by Mrs. Huff rushing over to us with a panicked expression. I guess I didn't escape everyone's notice. "Sorry," I say quickly, "I wasn't paying attention and I bumped into someone."

My eyes dart around for whoever ran into me, but everyone else seems to be working quietly at their tables. A sick, angry feeling stabs at my insides. I turn back to look at Ivy, more suspicious than ever.

"Are you both okay?" Mrs. Huff asks, her eyes darting over us.

"Yeah," I start to say, not taking my eyes off Ivy, but Ivy interrupts me.

"No, Van got burned! I saw her hands fall on the oven racks." Ivy grabs for my hands, but I yank them behind my back before she can get me. I keep my eye on her for a second attempt and completely miss Mrs. Huff making the same move. She pulls my hands from behind my back and stares at them. Then she flips them over, and back. She touches my pink, perfect skin gently, then more forcefully.

"Looks fine to me," she says with relief.

Ivy's eyes pop open wide in disbelief. "What? I saw her touch the racks! They were both red and blistered!"

"Must've been the lighting. I stopped myself in time," I say tightly. I tug my hands out of Mrs. Huff's grip and start back to my table. Our teacher just shakes her head at Ivy and stalks back to the front of the classroom.

"I could have sworn…"

Ivy falls silent as I start cleaning up the mess I made while mixing my cookie dough. She doesn't say anything else, but the smug expression on Ivy's face before she turns away stops me. What did that look mean? I'm sure she was the one who ran into me, and as I head out of Home Ec a few minutes later, I am even more convinced that it wasn't an accident.

Ivy's odd behavior follows me the rest of the day. I can't remember a single thing any of my teachers talked about in my classes after Home Ec. All I can think about is the way Ivy looked like she had gotten what she wanted after seeing my hands unburned.

Could she have been trying to burn me just to see what would happen? That is beyond sick, but something is definitely not right about Ivy. She was so quick to point out that I'd been burned. Sure, she could have been genuinely concerned about me, I guess. Or was there another reason? Did she want someone else to witness that the injuries I had definitely sustained were already healed? She looked so satisfied when my hands were fine, despite her confusion and disbelief just a few moments earlier. She was acting. I'm just not sure which part was the act.

By the time I burst out of my last class and gather my books from my locker, I'm actively looking for Laney and her bizarre cousin. I need some help, some indication of whether or not I'm going crazy, and I know just who to turn to. I need Zander. I know I shouldn't get him involved. Zander has been through enough over the last few years. Everything that happened nearly broke him, and it scared me to death.

I debate going to him for help as I walk away from my locker, but I'm positive he'll pick up on any honest to goodness weirdness. Meeting my brother may give her an opportunity to sniff out a few more clues about us, but Zander is always so careful. She shouldn't be any risk to him. Whatever this curse is, it doesn't work like that. We don't share meals. It'll be fine. Zander will know if my reaction to her is something above normal. It may just be that I'm getting too close to my sixteenth birthday, but it might be something else.

When Laney and Ivy come down the hall toward me, I force myself to put on a somewhat friendly appearance. It's the best I can manage in the face of the reaction she elicits from me. I take my place next to Laney when they reach me. That puts Ivy on Laney's other side, away from me. Even still, it isn't much of a buffer. My hunger still gnaws at me, so I step a little further away.

"Hey," Laney says, "what time do you work today? Ivy and I wanted to go for ice cream. Wanna come?"

"Can't. I've got class right after school today. It's Monday and Wednesday I don't go in until five," I remind her.

Laney purses her lips. "I can never remember what days you teach what. I really need to write it down somewhere."

"If you tried coming to a class, maybe you'd remember."

Her snorting laugh startles Ivy. "Yeah, right. You just want me to come so you can laugh at me."

"Everyone laughs at you, anyway," Ketchups says as he catches up to us. Laney rolls her eyes. He ignores her and slings his arm around my shoulder. Normally, I would throw it back off, but the comfort of having him next to me helps with my hunger.

Ketchup was obviously expecting my rebuff, and when it doesn't happen he looks down at me with a frown. I try to avoid making eye contact. That's not very easy when it comes to Ketchup. His jet black hair, baby blues, and general Superman-lookalike quality makes it hard not to stare. I meet his concerned eyes and he sees the turmoil raging inside of me.

"You okay?" he asks quietly.

No. But I can't explain this to him. Ketchup is always there for me, no matter what, but he has no idea what is really behind my strange abilities and disconcerting mood swings. I shrug and look away, wishing Zander wasn't right, wishing I could tell Ketchup everything.

"What do you teach?" Ivy asks, her eyes focused on Ketchup and his arm around my shoulders. Her scrutiny almost makes me push Ketchup away, but the hunger keeps me from listening.

"Hip hop and ballet," I say, hoping it will distract her from Ketchup.

It does.

I watch as her eyes take in the surprise of me being in anyway rhythmically inclined. That's the reaction I usually get. People who don't know me well think I'm a moody, dark teenager. I'm really just trying not to kill them.

Ketchup takes offense to Ivy's disbelief. "Van's a great dancer. Best in her class."

A small smile creeps onto my lips. I snuggle into Ketchup's embrace for a brief moment before remembering myself and putting a little distance between us. Ketchup frowns, but doesn't comment, given that I still haven't pushed his arm away.

"Where do you teach?" Ivy asks as we head to the parking lot.

"All Star Dance, over on Candelaria. It's not a very big studio, but we compete all over the state. It's a lot of fun." I smile honestly for the first time today. Dancing is more than fun, it's my only release. It is the only time I get to take hold of my emotions and hunger and channel them into something beautiful. I can hide everything that is wrong with me when I dance.

Ivy's mouth turns up along with mine. "I used to dance. I haven't taken a class in a couple of years, but I've wanted to get back into it. Maybe I'll try out one of your classes."

"Yeah…great," I say, trying to hold onto my smile. The last thing I want is her ruining my hunger-free time.

Ketchup's arm tightens around my shoulder. "I've gotta go pick up my brother. See you tomorrow."

Laney and Ivy mumble their goodbyes, but I panic. My sudden stiffness gives Ketchup pause. He turns just enough to get away from Laney and Ivy. His voice is filled with concern as he asks again, "Is everything okay?"

"Yeah, sure. It's fine."

He frowns at me, not taking my lame answer at face value.

I sigh. He won't back down. "It's…family stuff. I'm just worried. No big deal."

Ketchup's gaze goes from probing to compassionate. Talking about my family is generally off limits, and he respects that. There's just too much I can't explain to him. But he knows enough to understand that my family is precious to me, and that we're all walking a fine line to stay together. I don't know how he has stuck by me all these years not knowing our secrets, but his support means everything to me.

"If you need to talk…"

Tears singe the inside of my eyelids. "Thanks, Ketchup."

He walks away, then, leaving me at the mercy of my hunger. It takes monumental effort to turn around and face Ivy without launching myself at her throat. I have to force myself to remember why I wanted to follow them outside to begin with.

"Hey, Laney, I have that khaki skirt you wanted to borrow in the truck. You wanna come grab it?" When she nods, I turn away and start walking before Ivy can get too close to me. I know I'm not wrong about her.

When I see the familiar silver truck, the outrageously gigantic one I'm forced to be driven around in, I pick up speed. He's only a few steps ahead of me. My brother's height matches the truck, and so does his build. Zander always reminds me of a tree…tall, massive, and immovable. That's not the only tree-like thing about him. His expression is as interesting as bark. Nothing affects him, good or bad. I think a nice way of putting his emotional blandness would be even-tempered. The only time anyone ever sees any kind of emotion out of him is when he plays sports, when he channels his own hunger into pounding his opponents into the ground.

Zander sees me coming and pauses. His eyebrow crooks up at my approach. I must look like a lunatic half running toward him, but I don't care. I push forward and nearly burst when I make it to his side.

"In a hurry?" he asks flatly.

"There's someone I need you to meet," I say in a rush.

Before he can ask any questions, Laney stumbles up behind me. "Good grief, Van, I wasn't in that big of a hurry to get the skirt. You didn't have to run like that. My feet are killing me bad enough already."

"Sorry, I…"

Ivy moves from behind Laney and I never get the chance to finish. My body convulses with the renewed urge to hurt. I'm shocked when I feel Zander react as well. Nobody else can ever feel the hunger rising inside of us, but we can feel it in each other almost as strong as within ourselves. It ripples over me in a massive wave that combines with my own burning desires and makes me stagger forward. I don't even realize his hand has clamped around my arm until he jerks me back to his side. The throbbing pain in my arm barely even registers in the face of our combined urge to rip Ivy apart. Suddenly, I realize Zander wasn't just pulling me to his side, he's holding me back, still.

Laney is staring at the both of us with wide eyes. "Uh… Ivy, this is Van's brother, Zander."

"Hey," Ivy says. The uncertainty is clear in her voice and expression.

The pain in my arm spikes. I look down to see Zander's fingers turning white under the force of his grip. Suddenly, he releases me and storms away, around the truck to the driver's side. He yanks open the door without a word to anyone and climbs in. The slam of the door makes me jump. I just stare at him for a moment. His reaction is completely unexpected, frightening even. Ivy affected him enough to break his indomitable cool, but the really scary part is that he shouldn't have reacted to her at all. I am stunned. He felt it too. That's not supposed to happen.

My fear of Ivy's real intentions amps up even more. If Zander is reacting to her, there is definitely something wrong. She didn't leave the sand and ocean behind for just plain old desert sand for the heck of it. I'm more convinced than ever that she came here for a reason. She came here for us.

Determination to stop her steels my resolve. Whatever she wants with us, she's not getting it. I've lost too much already to let some pink haired freak take anything else.

Voices from behind pull me out of my plotting slowly. I can't seem to take my eyes off Zander's hulking form sitting in the truck, staring dead ahead at nothing, his fingers slowly strangling the steering wheel. My ears, though, manage to catch a few bits of their conversation.

"I don't know, Ivy. He doesn't usually act like that," Laney says. "I mean, he's always kinda quiet and standoffish, but that was just weird. I don't know what was with Van, either. I'm really sorry."

"No," Ivy says, her voice carrying a tiny tremor, "I should have expected it."

Expected it? What does she mean by that?

"Expected what? For them to both give you such a bizarre welcome?" Laney asks.

"No, uh, I just meant..." Ivy suddenly sounds like she's trying to backpedal. "You told me Van was a little different. I should have expected it to take a while for her to warm up to me. That's all I meant. Her brother's probably the same. They just...surprised me."

When they both quiet and fall into an awkward silence, I finally manage to get my mind and body back on the same page. I open the door of the truck and grab the skirt without looking at Zander. I make a quick exchange of the skirt with a hasty apology for Zander and use work as an excuse to ditch them both.

I turn back around to get into the truck and freeze when I catch sight of Zander's eyes drilling into me. An involuntary flinch runs through me. I got what I wanted out of this plan, but I broke the rules to do it.

3

NO HAPPY ENDINGS

watch as Van, my little sister who is always getting herself into trouble, climbs into the truck with her head hanging. She looks plenty ashamed already, but I'm not about to let this slide. "What were you thinking?" I demand through gritted teeth.

"You felt it," she whispers.

She doesn't say it in the form of a question, but I answer anyway. "Yeah, I felt it! Why on earth would you bring her around me if you knew I would react like that? I could have hurt her! I could have killed her, Van! I was this close," I say, holding up my first two fingers bare millimeters apart from each other. "I was so close to grabbing her and tearing her into little pieces. You know better than to bring someone like that around me. Do you want me to end up like Oscar?"

"No!" Tears start dripping down her cheeks. "Of course I don't want you to end up like Oscar. I'm sorry, Zander, but I had to. I had to know if you felt it, too."

Another string of threats and fury are about to slip out

of my mouth when her words sink in. "Too?" I ask slowly. "What do you mean you had to know if I felt it…too?"

Van sniffs and wipes her nose, still refusing to look at me when she talks. "When I met Ivy at lunch today I almost jumped over the table at her."

My stomach churns at the mental image. Van has always had much bloodier tastes than I have. More dramatic, too. Her hunger craves blood and gore just as much as pain. The messier the better for her. I know all too well that the girl's throat would have been removed with Van's teeth, like a predatory animal. Van is predictable in that way, fast, adrenaline driven, and deadly. My hunger has a totally different taint to it. Just thinking about what I wanted to do to that girl makes the steering wheel crunch under my hands. My whole body is shaking with the desire to jump out of the truck and follow her. I can still see her walking away from me, the pink stripe in her hair bouncing lightly with each step.

I shake my head and try to clear my thoughts of the girl so I can focus on what Van is telling me. "Your hunger wanted that girl, and so did mine. It's never worked like that before."

Van trembles and hugs herself. "I know."

"What made you even think to bring her to me then?" I ask, my body finally starting to relax.

"I've never felt such a strong desire to kill anyone before. That was the worst it's ever been for me. She's different. Something's wrong with her. I thought I was losing it, but I thought that if you could feel me respond so much it would at least mean it was real. I never expected you to react to her.

26

I'm so sorry, Zander."

I manage to get one hand off the steering wheel and rub it against my forehead. Was seeing that girl, Ivy, a worse reaction for me than usual like it was for Van? I shiver at the mere memory of it. The hunger for her is going to stay with me for a very long time. Van is always looking for something more, something to explain what's wrong with our family. She wants our problems to be bigger than us. She wants an explanation. I do too, but I came to face the reality that we are alone a while ago. There is no secret behind our disastrous existence. We're freaks, mistakes, oddities. No one is going to come and explain the purpose behind our design. I understand that, but Van doesn't. That's why I'm not about to admit to her how much Ivy affected me.

"It's probably just because you're getting closer to your birthday. You know the hunger gets worse once you hit sixteen."

"No," Van says shaking her head, "this was different. I've felt it all day. She knows something, Zander. She's been acting really strange. There's something off about her."

My frustration with her bursts out of me in a growl. "There's nothing wrong with her, Van. There's something wrong with us! Or haven't you figured that out by now?"

I don't wait for her to answer. I jam the gearshift into reverse and plow out of my space without checking for cars or pedestrians. The truck powers out of the parking lot and into the busy afternoon traffic like a bulldozer. Everyone gets out of my way.

The quiet roar of the truck's engine is the only sound

as we drive. Van sits quietly, tugging at a loose string on the hem of her shirt. Part of me wants to put my arm around her shoulder. I'd like to tell her that everything will be okay. I would give anything to be the comforting big brother I know she's desperate to have. But I can't. Not after Oscar. I learned my lesson with him. Van needs to grow up, and the sooner the better. She needs to accept that if she doesn't figure out how to control her hunger now, it's going to change her into something neither of us will recognize.

I pull up to the dance studio and turn off the engine. Usually, I just hold the brake and wait for her to jump out. She looks over at me with a question in her blue eyes.

"I want you to stay away from that girl," I say.

"But she's Laney's cousin. I can't avoid her without doing the same to Laney."

"Maybe that's just how it has to be, then. When you turn sixteen and your hunger really wakes up, it will be too intense and you'll have to give up all of your friends anyway. You know that, even if you won't admit it." Giving up friends, it's something Van should get used to, now, because it isn't going to stop any time soon.

Van shakes her head. "No, Zander. She's my best friend. I'm not going to bail on Laney like that, no matter how bad my hunger gets."

"You think she'll be happy you stayed friends with her when you kill her pretty little cousin?" I snap.

Her head drops down, but I can still see the corner of her mouth twitching. "I can control it. I won't hurt her."

"You can't guarantee that."

"I won't live like you," she says quietly. "I won't live alone for the rest of my life because I'm scared of hurting people."

I sigh and close my eyes. "It's not about being scared, Van. It's about being smart. Stay away from her."

For a long moment, she doesn't say anything. Deep down, I'm hoping with everything I have that she'll listen to me. I can't go through it again. Oscar nearly broke me. She can't expect me to go through that with her. I won't make it. Please just listen to me, I beg.

When she finally speaks, her voice startles me. "She knows something."

It's just a simple sentence, but it ignites my anger like a match to a fuse. "She doesn't know anything! Nobody does. Get that through your head and quit looking for answers, Van!"

My sister's head snaps up and my hands tighten into fists at the determination in her eyes. "She knows something, and I'm going to find out what it is."

Then she throws open the door of the truck and runs away.

A pair of little girls, who can't be more than four years old, bounce into the studio behind Van with their tutus and ballet slippers. The urge to run in after my sister and shake her until she changes her mind dissipates as the tiny ballerinas start pouring into the building. She's not going to escape me, though. I still have to pick her up when she's done working, and take her home, and drive her to school tomorrow. I'm going to crush this out of her eventually.

Since my crusade is going to have to wait until at least

eight o'clock, and football practice starts in twenty minutes, I pull out of the parking lot and speed back toward the school. When I burst into the locker room, it's almost empty. Only a few stragglers are still pulling on pads and practice jerseys.

A quick look around confirms to me that Carson Davis isn't one of them. Carson is the only one of my teammates that stirs up my hunger this year. Last year, two of the seniors nearly made it impossible to control myself on the field. Luckily, Carson plays on the offensive line, opposite my usual starting position, and we have very little contact. Carson is the least of my problems today.

Curses run through my mind as I rant at both myself and my sister. Outwardly, I'm calm and controlled. My movements are efficient as I shrug into my gear. As quickly as possible, I am stalking out of the locker room.

As soon as my feet hit the turf, the other players come alive. I never join in their rowdy behavior and general excitement, but my team's enthusiasm to see me makes me smile inwardly. They all know their chances of winning double as soon as I step onto the field. When I finished my freshman tryout, Coach Benson walked up to me and simply asked what position I wanted to play. It didn't matter that the team already had a senior playing quarterback, another one at wide receiver, and juniors at most of the other key positions. I could have my pick, no questions asked.

I think my answer surprised him. Safety isn't the most glorious position in football. Coach Benson didn't seem to appreciate my choice, and all but refused at first. He wanted me in a more active, gaming determining position. His suggestion was runningback. I wasn't thrilled about the idea of playing runningback, and it took a deal with Coach Benson to finally make me agree. I got to play safety on defense as long as I tore up the field as a runningback on the offense. Offense doesn't interest me that much, because I'm always running away from the other person, but as long as I get to be where I know I will get to hit a lot of people on the other side of the ball, I don't mind as much.

Nobody gets by me, which is how I ended up the team captain as a junior instead of the senior playing quarterback. We all pile out onto the field together, the others jogging excitedly, me walking with my thoughts more focused on Van and Ivy than football. It's almost impossible to stop thinking about my sister and the effect that strange girl had on me until the first real play kicks off. The massive bodies of the offense charging down the field reaches down inside me and grabs onto the hunger I keep so carefully hidden.

Hitting people hurts. The person getting hit feels it the most, but the person doing the damage gets a piece of it as well. It's nothing compared to willfully and maliciously causing pain to another human being. Nothing can replace the all-consuming feeling of stripping away life, but this is a substitute that keeps me from indulging in things I shouldn't.

Samuel keeps the ball tucked under his arm and against his chest like he's supposed to. He's got guts. I keep my eyes on him as his body speeds toward me, judging my position and trying in vain to get around me. The hunger I felt at the sight of Ivy rebuilds inside of me. It's so hard not to let it fill me, to carry me over the limit of my endurance. My vision tints red as I burst forward. Samuel's eyes widen as his body turns slightly to prepare for the impact he knows is coming. The strength in my arms wraps around Samuel to the point that I can feel all the breath rush out of him. Whatever air was left comes bursting out as I fling him to the ground with me.

We roll a couple times across the grass before coming to a stop. There's still so much hunger left that my fingers dig into the grass in an effort to keep them from acting. It takes me a moment to realize Samuel hasn't gotten up yet, either. The familiar feel of panic pulls me up from the ground. I crawl over to my teammate in a rush. I let myself drink too deeply. My hunger will take me on a ride I can't control if I'm not careful. I touch his shoulder gently, praying to a god I have no belief in, desperately asking for him to be alright.

I sigh in relief when Samuel coughs and struggles up to a sitting position. "Crap, Zander," he says, "that was worse than usual. What'd you eat today?"

It's not what I ate, but more of what I didn't get to consume. I shake that thought away fiercely. "Sorry, man."

"No, problem, just promise me you'll do that to Los Lunas next week." He winces as he pulls himself back up to his feet.

"You okay?"

He claps me on the back and nods. "Overheard Coach Benson telling Coach Falk to work you hard the next couple weeks. Couple scouts are coming to the season opener next Friday, I guess."

"I'm just a junior, Samuel. I've still got another year here."

"You should be a senior. If it weren't for all the stuff last couple years that put you behind, you'd be out of here at the end of the year."

"Well, things are what they are. They're probably interested in Thompson or Sanchez."

"Right," Samuel scoffs. "How many scholarship offers do you have already? Five? Six?"

There's no jealousy in his voice. Samuel is a tough kid and he loves the game, but he has no delusions of making a career out of it. He just hopes that when I go pro I'll get him season tickets. He's the closest thing I have to a friend.

"Twelve," I say in answer to his question, "but some of those are for basketball."

He just shakes his head. "The scouts aren't coming for Thompson or Sanchez."

"Where are they from?" My curiosity gets the better of me and a hint of excitement slips through my mask. Samuel sees it and grins.

"LSU and Alabama."

The two top college football teams in the country. I can't contain my smile any longer. I've got for sure full rides with a dozen colleges, promises of scholarships and more from twice that number if I commit now. But most of those offers are from my home state colleges UNM and NMSU and the surrounding states, which are good schools, but not the best. I want a top college. It's not that I care about the prestige or the fame that goes with playing for teams like Alabama or LSU. I want the carnage. Teams like that play other top teams. They go at each other with bone crushing force born from a need to be the best. I'll help them out with that, but I'm after the pain, not the record.

Coach Benson's whistle calls our attention back to practice, and I'm forced to put on hold my dreams of inflicting maximum damage on other college players. I'll have to settle for my own teammates for now. I throw myself back into practice, although I tone down my enthusiasm a little in order to keep from maiming my teammates before the scouts get here. Most of the offense that comes in contact with me still walks back to the locker room feeling the residual ache, but it's not too bad. As for me, I find myself almost happy as I follow the rest of the team into the locker room.

The feeling lasts through my shower, through getting dressed, all the way until I get out to the parking lot and see her.

4

NOT OVER

*J*ust the sight of her pink and black hair sends fire racing through my entire body. The chin length cut with the ends fraying out in a pixie-like style make her defined cheekbones stand out, the pink wisp matching her full lips in a way that makes them look even sweeter. Her smoky eyes watch me carefully, on guard. Every inch of her is beautiful, I realize for the first time, but it's only a small, unimportant thought in the back of my mind, about to be swallowed up by the aching need to wrap my fingers around her neck.

For several excruciating minutes, neither of us moves or speaks. Ivy holds perfectly still, but I can see the fear in her eyes. She doesn't move because she's likely afraid of looking aggressive. I don't believe for a minute that Van is right about her knowing something about us. This girl is simply smart, level-headed enough to realize that I am more dangerous than I look. Running only incites a predator's drive to conquer. Even with her standing still, I am the first one to take a step.

My other foot follows, picking up speed as they go, and carrying me over to her before I can form a thought coherent enough to stop my body from taking control. Ivy's eyes are big and bright when I finally pull myself to a halt less than two feet in front of her. She draws in a slow breath as her blue eyes sparkle with panic. Her bottom lip trembles so slightly I would never have noticed it if I weren't staring at her so intently. I want to touch her rose petal pink lips, but whether to see them turn scarlet with blood or simply to feel their softness against my mouth, I don't know. I just want… to touch her.

"Z-Zander," Ivy says quietly, her lips barely able to form the single word.

I can't respond. If I move a single muscle, my hunger will take control. She'll be dead before she can even start to cry out for help.

She bites the corner of her lip, looks at the ground, and then back up at me. "I'm, um, sorry, if I, uh, did something to offend you earlier," she manages to say.

Ivy bites her lip again, which does absolutely nothing to curb my desire to make her suffer, and waits for me to say something. All I can do is watch her canine dimple her flesh and beg it to keep going. My hand moves from my side, toward her. Ivy flinches at the movement, and I pull myself together enough to bring it back.

"I…should go," Ivy says suddenly. She starts to turn, but my hand snaps out and grabs her arm before she can complete the movement. Her eyes fly to mine. I can see the tears forming. The glassy affect they cause makes her eyes melt into liquid sapphires.

We are frozen like this, with her about to cry and me holding her arm, when Samuel and a couple of the other guys walk around the building and see us. All three of them slow to a halt as they take in the scene.

"You okay, Zander?" Samuel asks. "Is she bothering you?" The three with him square their shoulders in my defense. Ivy only blinks in disbelief, dislodging a single tear.

"No," I say, "we're fine."

"You sure?"

Samuel scrutinizes Ivy. Her average height, maybe five foot seven, is nothing compared to mine, and our weights are an even bigger discrepancy, but these guys know me. Thanks to my careful control, they only see me as a quiet, calm guy who never raises his voice or shows any kind of aggression off the field. They know, too, that I've had trouble with persistent girls before. None of them have ever asked why I don't date, and no one has ever been brave enough or stupid enough to insinuate that I might be gay, but they are aware of the fact that status-hungry girls have no place in my life. They've run interference for me before, and they must all think this is just another one of those times.

"We're fine, Samuel," I assure him. "Go ahead. I'll see you guys tomorrow."

The three of them nod reluctantly and head toward their cars. I don't let go of Ivy's arm until they leave. Fear that she'd run away isn't what made me hold her until we were alone again. It's the bruises. My hand springs away from her skin and blood rushes to the injured tissue, discoloring it instantly. She sees the finger-shaped splotches and her other hand reaches up to cover them. Her touch must hurt, because a few more tears fall down her cheeks.

I don't know why, but my fingers are suddenly on her cheek. Her gasp makes me pause. Another tear falls, and I watch as my fingers glide across her silky skin and brush it away. It is by far the strangest experience I have ever had. Not just touching a girl's face, but touching Ivy's skin and feeling something other than the desire to crush and disfigure it. Those feelings aren't gone, not even close, but battling with the urge to dig my fingers into her skin and strip it away is the desire to simply run my hands over every inch of her. It's almost as strong as my hunger.

"I'm sorry," I say quietly.

She just stares back at me.

"About your arm," I add.

My gaze is drawn down to the hand that is hiding the damage I did to her. My fingers follow. Ivy doesn't stop me from peeling her hand away and revealing the bruises. The mottled purple spikes my hunger to the point that nothing else matters. It takes all my effort to keep my hands still. Pain ripples off her arm. I can almost see it. I *can* taste it, warm and luscious on my tongue. The most decadent desserts have nothing on the taste of suffering for me. My tongue runs across my bottom lip, begging for a deeper draw.

Without warning, Ivy jerks her arm out of my grasp. She stumbles back a step and bumps into her car. "I have to go," she mumbles, turning and stepping further away from me.

I panic. She can't leave. "You didn't do anything," I blurt out.

She stops, but doesn't turn back around. I should let her leave, get her away from me as soon as possible and make sure she never comes near me again. Just let her walk away.

But I don't.

"Earlier this afternoon, you didn't do anything to offend me. You didn't even say anything. It wasn't you."

Ivy's body stays turned, but her blue eyes peek back at me from over her shoulder. "It wasn't me?"

I shake my head, a lie, but one that will keep her from walking away from me like she should.

"You seemed pretty upset." She turns around to face me slowly.

"Just having a bad day," I say honestly.

"Oh."

We stand there in awkward silence. I don't know what to say now. The only girl I ever talk to is my sister, and that usually involves arguing. I don't want to argue with Ivy. What *do* I want to do with her? No, strike that. What *can* I do with her that won't involve getting arrested or locked up somewhere worse than jail? I can say goodbye, I tell myself.

I can't seem to get the words to leave my lips, though. Frustration spins me away from Ivy, and I stalk over to my truck without another word to her. A collection of sounds drift past me, but the blood pounding through my body doesn't let me hear them clearly, let alone understand them. My hunger screams at me to turn back. Desperately, I want to give in. My truck door slams shut behind me and the tires squeal as I tear out of the parking lot. In my rear view mirror, I catch sight of her pink striped hair as she stands in the middle of the parking lot staring after me.

Keeping my truck on the road consumes me. More than once, I find myself slowing down, signaling to exit the freeway, only to speed back up and get into the far left lane, away from the exit ramps. In the middle of rush hour, my fellow drivers hardly appreciate my struggle. Their honking and angry gestures roll off me. Their problems are so insignificant.

I drive. And drive.

I can't understand the intensity of my attraction to Ivy. Yes, she is beautiful, and there is an edge of something captivating in her eyes I can't quite pin down, but I know this isn't a normal reaction to a pretty girl. It's as if my emotions are trying in vain to beat out my hunger, pushing me to lose myself in her before I kill her. That thought sticks with me. The truth of such a simple idea wedges itself into my consciousness.

Eventually, the traffic thins. It's the lack of people flipping me off and blaring their horns that actually makes me notice. When I realize I'm through the never ending construction on I-25 and approaching the exit to Bernalillo, I finally let myself jet across the lanes to the exit and take it. It's a small town on the outskirts of the Albuquerque metro area, miles away from Ivy. Instead of turning toward Bernalillo, I take a right and head past the Sandia Mountains.

Two hours until I have to pick Van up. It's more than enough time to give my hunger what it wants. It will take me at least that long to burn away my encounter with Ivy. A random dirt road that looks to be heading out into the plains catches my eye. I speed through the high desert in search of something that will sate the hunger still pulsing inside of me. The sight of a herd of Pronghorns moving through the scrub and grasses grabs at my hunger viciously. Seconds after sighting them, my truck is abandoned on a dirt road, my feet silently carrying me toward the herd as my hunger swells in anticipation of being fed.

Van would launch herself straight into the thick of the deer-like creatures and let her hunger take over. I have no desire for chaos. Instead, my hunger becomes increasingly unbearable as I stalk forward silently. A deliberate noise made by me kicking a rock spooks the herd. Their black, pronged antlers perk up, bringing images of Ivy to life and fueling my hunger even more. The animals scan the area cautiously, but they don't run. I can taste their wariness as it hovers on the verge of full out fear. The memory of Ivy's wide eyes and racing pulse slips through my control. Any thought but fulfilling my hunger is shoved away.

I creep forward, making enough noise to frighten the animals, but not enough to scare them away. Their quivering muscles, poised to run, drip with panic. I drink it in. Nearly close enough to touch one, I stand to my full height. The second they see me, they flinch, but remain locked in indecision. This is the ultimate moment of fear for them. The musk that fills the air is thick with terror. I crave this moment just as much as the pain that will follow.

In an instant, the moment passes, and every Pronghorn

in the herd jumps into action. Completely overtaken by my hunger, I have no ability to resist. I lunge after them in a mindless need to consume. It only takes mere seconds to reach one, to pull it down and succumb to my hunger completely.

I don't know how long it takes for me to shake off my hunger-induced haze. Only the sound of my phone ringing snaps me back to reality. Van's face staring back at me from her contact picture sends my eyes to the time. Eight-fifteen. I snap the phone open as guilt piles on top of my shoulders.

"Van, I'm sorry, I'll be right there," I say as soon as I get the phone to my ear.

"What the crap, Zander? I've been sitting here for fifteen minutes. Where are you?" she asks.

"Uh, hiking. I'll be there in half an hour. Sit tight."

"Hiking? What on earth…?"

She's just going to rant at me, so I end the call and start booking it back to the truck. I push myself to get back to the road as fast as I can. I make it in less than fifteen minutes and jump into the truck. When I finally make it back to the dance studio, the sun is almost completely gone. My baby sister sitting in the shadows of the building looking scared and angry kills me. She knows it, too.

Van sits there staring at me with her narrowed eyes and huddled posture for a full minute before picking herself up off the ground and stomping over to the truck. She turns to glare at me as soon as she sits down, but her fierceness falters when our eyes meet.

"Zander," she says quietly, "are you okay?"

"Great," I say. "Sorry I was late. Let's go home."

I move to shift into reverse, but Van stops me. "Zander, you're never late. And you're sunburned." She stops to wrinkle her nose. "And you smell weird."

She waits for me to say something. I opt for silence.

"What's wrong? Did you slip up?" she asks, her voice shaking.

"No," I snap. She flinches at my sharp tone and I sigh. "Almost."

"What happened?"

I almost tell her. So badly, I want to tell someone. Van is the only one who will really understand what I'm going through. But I can't. When she told me how much she wanted to kill Ivy, I passed it off, blamed it on her hunger maturing. If I admit how close I came to ending her life myself, not once but twice now, she will be furious with me. Even worse, she'll be more convinced than ever that this singular girl holds some kind secret to our release.

"It was nothing," I say with a sigh. "It's over with."

"Zander…"

"Leave it alone, Van."

She doesn't say anything else, so I pull out of the parking lot and drive home. Crickets fill the warm night air as we walk up to our modest home where our grandmother waits for us. The only sound that joins their serenade is the second wooden step that creaks on our way to the porch. I have hopes of making it inside and up to my room wrapped in the same silence. That dream is dashed when Van lightly touches my shoulder as we reach the door. I freeze, fearing what she has to say.

"It was Ivy, wasn't it?" she asks.

I don't answer, but I'm sure she can feel the way my body tenses at the mere mention of that name.

Van sighs. "Then it's not over, Zander. You'll see her again. You'll have to fight off the hunger again and again."

"You don't know that," I say, hating how quiet and fearful my voice sounds.

"Just trust me on this one," Van says. "Ivy is here for a reason."

That's the last thing she says before slipping past me and into the house. It takes me a few minutes to follow her in. My grandmother's voice follows me, letting me know there is dinner in the kitchen. I mumble my thanks and walk past without going in. I'm not hungry. Not hungry for food, anyway. All I can think about is Ivy. I still don't believe there is any design behind her appearance, but I do agree with Van on one thing. Today wasn't the last time I'll have to battle my hunger because of Ivy.

She's pure, unadulterated Kryptonite to me, but I want more of her. As much as I can get. No, it isn't over yet. I won't let it be over.

5

RUMORS

On my way to the cafeteria, I am surprised when Zander appears beside me. I look over at him in question. "Is everything okay?"

"That's what I wanted to find out," he says. "Have you seen Ivy today?"

I shake my head, and bite back the desire to ask him the same question. If I pry, it will only inspire another argument. I decided last night that the only thing I can do to protect Zander is watch as carefully as I can and find out what Ivy is before anyone gets hurt.

"How are you doing with everyone else?" Zander asks, the conversation becoming more normal. Checking in on each other is a regular habit.

Grandma wanted our parents to homeschool us to limit our contact with people who elicit our hunger, but Mom and Dad knew we would need to learn to control ourselves in the real world. Outside of school, though, we tend to avoid crowds, just in case.

"Being around Ivy seems to make everyone else a little harder to deal with," I admit, "but I'm doing okay. It helps that Evan Conners moved last week. I don't think I could handle having three classes with him right now."

Zander nods in agreement. "If you need me…"

I wave him off. "I'll be fine. The only class we have together is Home Ec. Being around her when I'm cooking helps. There are lots of distractions."

"Don't you eat lunch together?"

"Sure, but I don't sit right next to her or anything, and Ketchup's there."

The grunt that slips out of Zander's mouth makes me look away.

"It helps to have him around," I say quietly.

Zander shakes his head, but doesn't argue. "Just be careful, please."

"Yeah, you too."

His shoulders bunch, but he doesn't say anything else. He turns to leave, but something makes me stop walking. A sound? I pause, trying to figure out what exactly it was. My nose wrinkles as I realize it wasn't a sound or something I saw, it was a taste. Without making it obvious I'm scoping out the hallway, I try to figure out where it's coming from.

"Van, what's wrong?" Zander asks looking very anxious. "Is it your hunger?"

I shake my head, still scanning. "No, it's this weird taste. I can't figure out…"

Turning to face my brother, the taste intensifies. Zander? Then I notice his wide eyes and tense posture. I'm about to question him, when it suddenly vanishes. I test for the taste again, but it's gone. Maybe it was nothing. "Huh, that was weird. Has that ever happened to you?"

"What?" Zander says, flinching at the sound of his own voice. He looks away from me as if the hallway suddenly holds something more interesting than milling teenagers. "Hey, I better get to class. See you later."

And then he takes off.

I stand there for a few minutes totally confused. That seems to be happening a lot lately. Now, I am sure I didn't imagine the strange taste, or that it was coming from Zander. He obviously knew what I was talking about, too. Why wouldn't he tell me? As close as Zander and I are, the idea that he might be keeping a secret from me is not only surprising, it's frightening. Keeping secrets when lives are on the line never turns out well.

The familiar feeling of fear begins creeping up my spine as I walk toward the cafeteria. I balk at the open double doors, unsure if I can handle seeing Ivy right now. I begin to wonder if the strange taste is somehow connected with Ivy. Two oddities appearing at the same time seems more than coincidental. It's a logical jump, but something seems wrong about the idea.

Trust is a hard thing when you're constantly looking over your shoulder for someone who is ready to betray your secrets. Even within my own family, trust is difficult. Grandma tries to help, but I've often had the impression she holds back more than what she shares. I think there are things Zander doesn't tell me, too, in hopes of protecting me.

One thing I have learned to trust are my own instincts. They are the reason I have any friends at all. If my instincts are pointing the finger at both Ivy and Zander, I'm going to listen. I'm going to find out what is hiding behind their lies.

I plan to start with Ivy.

That's why when she walks up to the table with her tray of nasty cafeteria food, I don't run. Pushing my hunger away requires putting a little distance between us, namely moving away from her and closer to Ketchup. He doesn't object, but he does throw me a questioning look. It causes me no end of guilt to use him like this. The last thing I want to do is give him false hope, but having him near me is so mind-stealing, it makes even my hunger a little woozy.

I have no idea what Ketchup is thinking, but he doesn't try to further anything between us. I let his nearness distract my hunger, and try to think of something to say to Ivy as I take a bite of my pizza. I want to ask her how she ended up running into Zander yesterday, but I can't think of how to do that without sounding like I am attacking her. Laney saves me from having to figure it out.

"So, Ivy bumped into Zander again yesterday afternoon."

I try to look surprised. "Oh really?"

"Yep," Laney says, obviously leaving the floor open for Ivy to finish explaining. Ketchup interrupts before she can.

"Please don't tell me you're already chasing after Zander." He rolls his eyes at her. "I'll tell you right now, it isn't going to happen. Zander does not date. Plus, I don't know what girls see in him. He is the definition of boring. Try talking to him for more than five seconds and you'll see what I mean."

Laney glares at him. "Shut up, Ketchup. The only reason Zander doesn't talk to you is because you're annoying and beneath his notice. He's perfectly talkative to other people, just ask Ivy. She talked to Zander yesterday for quite a while."

That catches my attention. "Oh really?"

"It was just a few minutes," Ivy clarifies. "I ran into him by the football field."

"What were you doing at the football field? Did you watch practice?" I ask. It's a pretty direct question, but a reasonable one. I'm not into football a ton, but practice is pretty exciting to watch, especially when Zander is out there. It's not unusual for there to be a small crowd at the team's practices. It surprises me when Ivy stumbles over her answer.

"No, I wasn't. I, um, wasn't there to watch anybody. I just needed to find someone. The track coach. I ran track at my last school, and I wanted to see about getting on the team here."

I'm not sure if I believe her, but I say, "Oh, I've heard Coach Holland is pretty good. You think you'll try out?" Too many questions or doubts might spook her and make her stop talking to me. I pack her words and reaction away for later.

"Yeah, I think so, but training doesn't start for a while," Ivy says. "I've got a few months to get back into running shape, so I was thinking maybe I'd try out one of your dance classes."

"Really? Ballet or hip hop?" I ask, not exactly thrilled with the idea, or the fact that she's distracting me from the conversation about Zander. I let my focus slide before, but not this time.

"Ballet would be good conditioning for your legs, but

49

hip hop would help your endurance."

Ivy nods, and looks like she's about to say something, but I have one more suggestion.

"Zander likes hip hop better, thinks ballet is too boring."

Ivy's body tenses. I hadn't noticed her unseasonably long sleeves before, but I take notice of them when she tugs them down. My fingers bite into the table. Zander said he'd *almost* slipped up. Just how close did he come? I suddenly want her to come to one of my classes despite the risk. For ballet she'll need a leotard, hopefully a sleeveless one, but even for hip hop her long sleeved shirt will be too hot. She'll have to bare her arms either way. I want to know just how close my brother came to killing her. Bruises can tell stories better than most people. Hers will tell just how much danger Zander is in. If I have to take Ivy out of the picture to protect him, I will.

"Ooh, do the hip hop, Ivy. It's so much fun," Laney says. "I totally suck at it, but I still have a blast doing it. When's your next hip hop class that's not for your teeny weeny dancers?"

"Tonight, actually. It starts at six." I can't tell whether Ivy looks eager or unhappy. Just to make sure she doesn't try to back out, I say, "Or I've got ballet tomorrow at five. You're welcome to try either."

Ivy looks oddly relieved. "I wouldn't be able to come tomorrow, family thing. So I guess I'll try hip hop tonight."

"Cool," I say. "The air conditioning isn't the best at the studio, so make sure you wear something…breathable."

"Yeah, sure," Ivy says. Her eyes drop noticeably.

Needing to breath in air not contaminated by Ivy, I

make up an excuse about forgetting something in my locker and bail on the rest of the lunch hour. Once in the hall, I lean against a row of lockers and take a deep breath. The plunk of Ketchup's body hitting the locker next to me opens my eyes. Fear that he has indeed mistaken my behavior lately makes me pull back. His hand reaches out and grabs my arm before I can escape. He doesn't try anything more than that, and I feel the tension in my body slipping away.

"Van, what's going on?" he asks. "You've been acting kinda weird the last couple days. Is something going on at home?"

I sigh, knowing I can't refuse him. "No. Well, not exactly. I don't know."

Ketchup chuckles, "Thanks. That was illuminating." He's quiet for a few seconds, but eventually bumps his shoulder against mine and asks again if I'm okay.

"It's…complicated, Ketchup. I think something might be wrong, but I'm not sure. More than one something, actually."

"And you can't tell me about either one." It's not a question. He's too familiar with these types of conversations to ask.

"I'm sorry. You know I would explain if I could."

Ketchup nods, but I get the feeling he isn't done with his questions yet. The important ones are still burning in his eyes. I wait. When he speaks, I wish I hadn't waited.

"You've been acting different…with me. Has anything changed?"

My fingers start twitching. They want Ketchup. I

want him. Slowly forcing my hands into my pockets, I say, "Nothing's changed."

"Then why...?"

"Ketchup, I'm sorry." My head drops in shame. "I wasn't trying to tease you. It's just...I need you to be there for me." I shake my head. That's not fair. I can't ask that of him. "Never mind. Forget I said anything, okay? I'll deal with this. I won't ask..."

Ketchup's fingers close around mine. "Whatever you need," he says quietly. "You know I'm not going anywhere."

He doesn't say anything else before letting my hand fall from his and walking away. It takes me a long time to start breathing again. Wiping away my tears takes even longer. I don't deserve him. He gives me everything, and all I do is turn him away. I am the one holding him back. It was my choice. He says he'll always be here, but I know one day he'll get tired of waiting and walk away for real. That is every bit as terrifying to me as the thought of losing Zander.

As the herd of students begins spilling out of the cafeteria, I pull myself together. Ketchup's touch and promise linger in my heart, but I have to focus on Zander and Ivy right now. I drag my feet down the hall to the Home Ec lab and make my way to my table. When Ivy wanders in, the battle to control my hunger renews. It is an hour of torture. I don't have to take any extraordinary measures, like mangling a piece of cast iron cookware to avoid breaking Ivy's bones, but I manage to hold my hunger in check by sheer force of will and lots of spices to cloud the air and distract myself.

I'm still glad Home Ec is the only class we have together,

though, because my will is only so strong. By the time the bell rings, I am dying to get away from her. As soon as Ivy's pink striped head disappears around the corner, I make a mad dash to the empty boxing gym and lock the door behind me. The strong history of boxing in our area spawned the boxing gym, but it's really only used after school when the team practices. I'm the only one who ever slips in here during the day. It's one of the few places on campus I can be alone to deal with my hunger.

My bag gets ditched against the wall and I take up position in front of the heavy punching bag, knowing that if Grandma ever finds out about this, I will be dead. Guilt for that, and for willfully satiating my hunger plagues me. If I were stronger like Zander, I wouldn't need this. My weakness screams at me, but I have to do something. The first hit thwacks into the leather and makes the bag lurch.

Just looking at me, most people wouldn't think my five-foot-four height and slender build would be able to move this bag more than a few inches. They would be wrong. The frustration at not being able to hurt Ivy puddles in my fists. Frustration at Zander for not answering my question earlier sends another fist into the bag. The day's torture bursts out of me in a rush. Bare-knuckled, my hands slam into the bag over and over again. It swings wildly, the chains groaning under the abuse. The leather cracks with each hit, and blood smears across the bag, but I don't stop. The pain burns up my arms and into my chest, but I can't escape the animalistic thrill of destruction. It hurts like hell, and I love it. It's sick, but I love it.

Another hit to the seam, and the bag ruptures. Sand spills out of the gash, rushing out to meet the floor. My chest is still heaving with wild adrenaline when my hands fall still. Satisfaction fills me at the sight of inflamed and bloody knuckles, of bruises and torn flesh, but I stare at the ruined bag in a panic. I try to focus on how to fix it, but my hunger is still lapping up the traces of pain, keeping my mind captive. Standing still, I give my body and mind a few minutes to calm back down as I watch my hands change.

As twisted as it is to hurt myself in order to keep my hunger in check, watching my hands incites a strange sense of amazement. The ruptured skin fuses back together slowly. Bruises and burst vessels fade, all the way back to pink right before my eyes. Deeper down, a crack in one of my fingers stiches itself back to one solid piece, and the last hint of scars vanish. I stare at my healthy hands, disappointed in myself, scared that my control will never be as tight as I claim it is.

I look at the bag with no idea of how to put it back together. I stare at it for several long seconds before admitting to myself that there is nothing I can do but wipe off the blood and slip away, hoping no one saw me come in here. Eyes downcast, I step back into the now empty hallway with shaking hands.

Despite what I just did, I'm not invincible. Far from it, actually. Given time to rest, I can heal some pretty serious wounds, but it costs me something. I stumble a little going around the corner. The strength to heal myself comes from inside of me. It uses up my stored energy and saps my strength. The bigger the injury, the more it wipes me out. And there are some things I can't recover from, like losing a limb, my heart stopping, or my mind breaking like a cracker. By far, my mind is the most fragile part of me. Oscar is a perfect example of that.

By the time I get to class, my teacher is already a good ten minutes into his spiel about Shakespeare's *Much Ado about Nothing*. I pretend I don't care as he flicks an annoyed little mark next to my name, and sit down behind Wyatt and Holly who are glaring at each other like they're the ones with the hunger problem instead of me. That makes me smile.

Mr. Littleton made the monumental mistake of pairing them up for the midterm drama project. They were given the topic of romantic tragedy and expected to write a ten minute scene to perform for the entire class. That's a problem because Wyatt thinks the greatest thing he could ever do in life is become a championship rodeo rider, while Holly has her road to the White House planned out down to the exact date and time. Wyatt claims to be allergic to any kind of chick flick, and Holly has made it perfectly clear that romance is the absolute last item on her To Do list. Their scene is going to be a spectacular disaster. It's a little over three months before they have to perform for the class, but I'm counting down the days. I think the whole class is.

As for me, I'm just glad we have an odd number of kids in this class. It left me without a partner for the midterm fiasco. I get to demonstrate a monologue. Not terribly exciting, but it's safer for everybody that way. Clearly, Mr. Littleton knows what he's doing. I had feared for a brief time that he would pair me up with Cody Hansen or Estella Cordova, both of which draw out my hunger, but like I said, Mr. Littleton knows what he's doing. Deciding I probably ought to pay attention to what he's saying up at the front of the class, I settle into my chair.

Mr. Littleton is discussing the different speech patterns of the various characters, Beatrice's constant stream of insults, or Don John's sullen and bitter phrases, and how their words and tones make them who they are. He takes a side trip into how we should be aware of this so we can use the same devices when writing out midterm scenes. He starts to head down another rabbit trail of thought when the door swings open. Mr. Littleton pauses mid-sentence and looks at the stranger in the doorway expectantly. So does everyone else, including me.

As soon as I see him, my whole body goes rigid. A little taller than average, caramel colored hair with lighter highlights that are definitely fake, eyes the color of early spring grass, and an uncertain expression that makes him look gorgeous and fragile all at the same time are immediately recognizable to me. He's the guy from the alley!

Immediately, I slink down in my chair and hope he won't notice me. Fear that he will expose me dips my head.

"Do you need something?" Mr. Littleton asks the guy at the door.

"Sorry, to interrupt, but I guess I'm in your class now," he says. He offers Mr. Littleton a slip of paper and continues. "I got put in a junior level English class by mistake and it's taken the office forever to get it straightened out. They had to rearrange a bunch of my classes."

Apparently, the note checks out, because Mr. Littleton

nods and hands it back. "Alright, Mr. Harbach, go ahead and take a seat."

Harbach. That names sounds familiar, but I can't seem to place it. I risk a furtive glance at the guy, but still have no idea where I might know him from, other than the alley. He starts to look in my direction, forcing me to scrunch down even more and pray for spontaneous invisibility.

"I've already assigned partners for the midterm project," Mr. Littleton says, "but if I remember right, I had an odd number of students this year."

Mr. Littleton walks over to his desk, and my entire body freezes. As he shuffles through his notebooks, I stare at my desk like it might hold the secrets to the universe. He can*not* pair me with this guy. The second he meets me, he'll recognize me, realize what a freak I am, and tell everyone about what happened—if he hasn't already. I really don't need any more bad press right now.

Mr. Littleton finds the right notebook, and I swear I can hear his smile stretching his tanned skin. "Ah, that's right. Vanessa Roth doesn't have a partner. Looks like she does now. That worked out nicely, but I suppose I'll have to change her topic from monologue to…hmm, I think I'll go with a battle scene."

My head pops up to spear Mr. Littleton with my glare. If it bothers him, he doesn't let it show. His smile only gets bigger. I can't believe he's doing this. He knows as well as most of the students about my reputation. It wasn't a big mystery why he didn't give me a partner the first time around. Now he's changing his mind? What is he thinking? Sure, I don't get hungry when I look at Mr. No First Name Harbach, thankfully, but if I get riled up there's no guarantee I won't hurt him. And with Cody and Estella in class to fuel my hunger, things could go bad very fast! My glare goes from fiery to a laser aimed straight at his head.

"Van, why don't you raise your hand so Noah knows who you are?"

I don't move a muscle. Mr. Littleton refuses to back down. He keeps his eyes fastened on me until I am forced to give in. I raise my trembling hand just high enough to make the motion noticeable without taking my eyes off my traitorous teacher.

"Oh look, Noah, there's even a space next to her," he says cheerfully. "Why don't you go sit down so I can get on with my lecture?"

Noah nods reluctantly and starts heading toward me. Reflex drops my gaze back to my desk, but I catch sight of his expression before I can look away completely. Wary. He looks nervous. Yeah, he definitely recognizes me. He's probably afraid to even sit by me. On top of the stories I'm sure he's heard, he's had the added misfortune of seeing me firsthand. My head sinks all the way down to my desk with a thud, trying to disappear.

If I just refuse to do my midterm, will I fail the class? Or can I make it up with my other grades? Even if I do fail, it's just one class. It won't really matter that much, surely. I'll still get into college.

I don't listen to another word my annoying teacher says. I'm too absorbed in being irritated and being terrified that

Noah will freak out and tell everyone. Zander is constantly telling me that I'll end up alone. When I really press him about it, he admits that my little circle of friends works for now, but he's adamant that it won't always be that way. It scares me to think of my birthday coming up and my hunger getting even worse. I'm afraid I'll realize he's right and I'll have to give up my odd assortment of friends in order to protect them. That doesn't mean I still don't pretend I'll have a normal life.

If I were a normal girl, I'd be ecstatic about being paired with the handsome new guy. I'd go all gooey at the thought of him accidentally brushing up against me or asking me to get together to work on our project. I'm not normal, and I know I'm about to face another round of recrimination. This project is going to be a miserable experience of him wanting to keep as far away from me as possible, and me wasting time wishing things could be different. I hate Mr. Littleton.

The bell blasting through the school jerks my head up from my desk. I just want to get out of here, and maybe kick Mr. Littleton in the shins on my way out. Everything on my desk gets swept into my bag and I zip it up with my eyes on the door. I'm about to stand up and bolt when someone taps my shoulder. I spin around in surprise, and Noah takes his hand off my shoulder quickly.

"Hey, Vanessa."

"It's Van," I interrupt out of habit.

"Sorry," he says. "Are you okay?"

I stare at him, completely dumbfounded.

"I mean, after the other night." He stares at me, his eyes flitting over my body, and suddenly looks confused. "I thought..."

Not daring to utter a single word, I grip my backpack strap tighter and look for an escape route.

Noah shakes his head. "Sorry, it's just when I saw you the other night you were pretty hurt. I was really worried when you ran off without waiting for the police. But you look fine, now. Even that cut on your leg."

He pauses, his eyes dropping to my bare thigh where one of the chollos in the alley did actually cut me pretty badly.

"Your leg's perfectly fine. Weird." He looks back up. "It must not have been as bad as it looked."

"Yeah," I finally mutter.

"You're okay, though?" he asks again.

The genuine concern in his eyes is just plain weird, but hard to ignore. "Yeah, I'm fine. Thanks."

Noah smiles, looking slightly embarrassed. "Can I ask you something?"

"Uh, sure," I say, surprising myself. I'm positive it's going to be about the injuries, or what I was doing trying to kill three grown men. I can't answer any of those questions, but for some reason I don't want Noah to walk away just yet.

"Why didn't you stay and talk to the police? I mean, I don't know what made them attack you—you don't have to explain that, or anything—but what if they come after you again? Didn't you want to press charges?"

My brain has a complete meltdown at that point. I almost start laughing. He thinks those guys were attacking me? He was trying to save *me* from *them*? I am at a total loss for words at the idea that someone else, someone who doesn't owe me anything, who barely even *knows* me, was actually trying to rescue me. He has no idea that he was actually saving me from myself, from killing those men, but that's hardly the point. I am so shocked and amazed I can barely even form words to answer him.

"It's, um, complicated. Reprisal, you know? They might come after my family if I tried to press charges." It sounds like a really stupid explanation, but I can't think of anything better.

"Sure, I guess," Noah says.

I'm relieved when he doesn't ask any other questions, but when he turns to the project, I'm still wary of this whole situation.

"So, can you explain this project? I have no idea what he was talking about."

Knowing that Noah's concern can only last so long before his logic catches back up, I decided to put an end to this for both our sakes. "Look, he's probably got a handout or something. I've got to get to algebra."

"One or two?"

"Two," I say as I head for the door.

"With Ms. Collins?"

"Yeah. Why?"

"That's who I've got next, too. Mind if I walk with you? I'm not sure where it's at," Noah says, "and you can tell me about the project on the way."

Great. "Come on."

I don't really make much of an effort to wait for him, though. Unfortunately, Ms. Collins' class is clear on the other end of the building, so Noah has plenty of time to catch up with me. His long legs do most of the work. I swear he takes one step for every two of mine.

"So, what project are we supposed to do together?" Noah asks.

"Write an original scene five to ten minutes long and perform it for the class before Christmas break," I say. "I was supposed to do a monologue, but now I guess we have to do some kind of battle scene."

"Battle. I can do that. There isn't much speaking in battles, but that's fine with me. I don't like talking in front of a crowd."

I look over at him and slow down. I can't help it. "But you don't mind fighting in front of a crowd?"

"Do it all the time," Noah says.

"Huh?"

"Jeet Kune Do. I compete. You ever tried martial arts?"

I have to lick my lips to keep a handle on the way my mouth suddenly starts watering. My grandma encourages us to find outlets for our hunger, but any kind of combat training is strictly off the table. It's a little too good of an outlet. People get hurt. Zander had to fight her to let him play football, thanks to the violent nature of the sport.

It took him forever to convince her that he could absorb the other players' pain without putting himself at risk. He claimed the continuous small burst of pain actually helped him keep control. Eventually, he won her over, but she'd kill me if she ever found out about my boxing forays because she knows I don't have the same level of control that Zander does. I know it, too. The idea of actual combat-based exercise sends a chill right through me.

"No," I say, sounding a little strangled. "I dance, though, so I'm not totally uncoordinated."

Noah smiles. I kick the back of my foot on accident and stumble forward. Red flushes my face. Yeah, I totally look coordinated. Noah's smile brightens some, but he doesn't say anything. I remind myself not to take his talkativeness at face value. He may think he saved my life, but at some point he'll realize what really happened and bolt. I can't let myself believe he really wants to be my friend. That kind of delusion will only end up in me getting hurt, again.

In a moment of sudden paranoia, I wonder if Noah's interest has anything to do with Ivy. Before I let myself get carried away on that unlikely train of thought, I remember why Noah's last name seemed so familiar. He has an older sister that's Zander's age. She was friends with Lisa before…I shake my head and try not to think about that. Noah's family has been here for years. I push away imagined connections and make a decision to end this conversation. Before I can say anything, Noah speaks again.

"I can show you a little about martial arts sometime. I'm not really sure how to make a whole scene out of it, but we can get started at least."

It would almost be sweet, if I believed his motive weren't born from saving me and now feeling responsible in some way. That will wear off soon enough. We're right in front of Ms. Collins' door when I stop and turn to face him.

"Look, Noah, you don't have to be nice to me just because of what happened in the alley. You don't even have to work with me. I'm sure if you tell Mr. Littleton you want to do something on your own, he'll let you. I know you've heard about me. Regardless of what happened the other night, I'm still the same girl everyone tries to avoid. Thank you for helping me, but you and I both know this isn't going to work."

"I…what?" Noah looks rather taken aback.

I sigh, frustrated by this whole conversation. "I just don't want to be the subject of your curiosity, or pity, or whatever it is that's making you talk to me."

"It's not any of that stuff," Noah argues. "I just want to talk to you, get to know you better. What's wrong with that?"

"Because nobody ever just wants to get to know me," I admit. "You have to have heard the rumors about me. Everyone has."

Noah shrugs. "Sure, I've heard them, but they're just rumors. I don't believe everything I hear in the halls."

My sigh startles me with its profoundness. Just like in the alley, he's blind to the truth. Sadness I wasn't prepared for brings tears to my eyes. I turn away from him and say, "Well you should believe the rumors. They're true."

6

ALMOST DYING

I must have shocked him pretty good, because Noah doesn't follow me into the room right away. He's a good fifteen or twenty seconds behind me. There are two empty desks on the opposite side of the room. Those should be his goal, but Noah surprises me by slipping into the desk next to me. He doesn't say anything, but he does look over at me when he sits down. A few more students file in, and class gets started. I find it completely impossible to focus with Noah looking over at me every few minutes with his crisp green eyes. Eventually, I settle for hunkering down in my chair and pretending I can't see him.

Normally, I'm pretty happy to get out of math class, since algebra isn't my favorite subject, but as I watch the clock wind its way toward the bell, a nervous flutter starts growing in my stomach. What is Noah going to say...or do? His possible reactions are all I can think about as the last few seconds tick by.

When the bell rings, I stay seated half a second longer

than everyone else. It feels like I'm moving on autopilot when I finally stand and sling my bag onto my shoulder. The sound of Noah's voice almost makes me jump.

"What do you have next?"

"PE," I say, risking a look at his expression.

He seems disappointed. "I've got history."

"Okay." I'm not really sure what he expects me to say to that. I'm not even sure why he's still talking to me.

"I guess I'll see you tomorrow, then."

I stare at him, confused. "Really?"

"Yeah," he says, and heads for the door.

It takes me a minute longer to start walking. That was so weird. I have no idea what was going on inside his head. Did he not believe me? I spend the next class thinking about him. He seems to be stuck there. Even Zander notices my preoccupation as he drives me to the dance studio after school. He tries to ask me what's wrong, but I shrug off his concern. I'm not actually sure anything is wrong.

When we roll to a stop in front of the studio, I hop out still thinking of Noah. My confusion over him sticks tight until I hit the studio door. That's when my focus shifts completely. I can't think about Noah and his odd behavior. Ivy will be here tonight. I spin back around to look for Zander's truck. I have to warn him not to come in, but he's already gone. My phone is in my hand as I hurry into the studio.

My thumbs start tapping out a message, but I pause, not sure what to say. If I come out and say Ivy will be here, that might pique his interest and draw him in. That would put him and everyone else in danger. There would be witnesses if anything happened. Witnesses mean Zander being taken away from me. I decide against mentioning Ivy. The message I send simply says that I might be getting out of class late and he should just wait for me in the truck. That should keep everyone safe. I stuff my phone in my bag and rush to get set up for my first class, thoughts of Ivy stomping around my head.

This will be my chance to find out what happened yesterday. Ivy is smart, and sly. It's going to take all my focus to get her to slip up. If I'm right about Ivy, exposing her could mean everything for Zander. It could mean his sanity, his freedom, even his life.

My first class passes quickly, a hurricane of miniature tutus bounding around the room. It always seems like they don't actually learn anything during classes, because they're always more interested in being silly and playing with each other than doing what I say, but they always surprise me the next class by remembering the new steps I taught them.

A dozen hugs later, I hand the last little ballerina off to her mom and take a deep breath. I know I have a few minutes to get set up for the next class before they all start filing in, but I leave the ballet bars in the middle of the room and peek out into the lobby. Ivy was true to her word. The mere sight of her instantly revives my hunger.

"Van," someone calls, drawing my attention down the hall. I flinch when I see the mother of a little girl I moved out of my class last week.

"Mrs. Earl, how nice to see you. How is Bella liking tap?"

"She's just loving it! Thank you for suggesting the move.

I think it was the right call," she says happily.

"Great. I'm glad to hear that." I make an excuse and hurry back to class, feeling a little guilty.

I didn't move Bella from ballet to tap because she wasn't enjoying ballet. I moved her because my hunger couldn't handle having her in class. Unfortunately, that happens fairly often.

As I move the free standing bar out from the middle of the room, I glance out the door at Ivy again. She sits on a folding chair looking more than a little bit nervous. She's not the only one. I feel like I'm going to either throw up or lose it. Just looking at her is torture. Even after my pit stop in the boxing gym earlier today, I feel like I am starving.

The only thing I can think about besides hurting her is that she's wearing a tight workout shirt with sleeves that go down to her elbows. She's definitely hiding whatever Zander did to her. I desperately want to see her injury. Thank goodness class is about to start, because it's the only thing that's going to keep me from going for her throat.

Rushing over to the stereo, I change playlists on my iPod to something less Nutcracker and more Shakira. The bass beat of the dance music thumps against the walls, a clear signal for the next class to come on in. Which they do. Most of them are teenagers and college students, but there's a few middle aged moms who bravely come shake it on a regular basis. They're pretty good, actually. I greet most of them with a grin and a comment here or there. When Ivy walks in, though, all I can do is wave at her from a distance and head to the front of the class.

"Alright, ladies. This is the last week we're working on this routine. You've all learned this one really well, so we should be able to get through without stopping very often. We'll have a new routine and music next week, so let me see you put everything you've got into class tonight."

They all smile and start bouncing back and forth in time with the music. The last few weeks of a routine are always my favorite. There's very little stopping and demonstrating. They've spent two months learning this dance, and finally being able to bust it out without stopping is a great feeling. It's going to save me with Ivy tonight. If I had to spend a lot of down time going over steps, I'm not sure I would be able to leave her alone.

Speaking of Ivy, though…. "We've got a couple new people with us tonight. Just follow me or the person in front of you, and do your best to keep up. If you get lost, just keep dancing. The steps aren't as important as staying active."

Ivy knows I'm talking to her, and nods. That's really the last I think of her. I crank the music up as loud as I'm allowed to go with ballet classes down the hall, and face the mirror. I can see everyone behind me take their places as well. My knee pulses in time with the music as I listen for the beat. When I find it, I signal the group behind me and count up to eight. The next beat after I say eight, everybody's knees pop up, a nice high stepping march that leads right into a series of low hops and arm movements. It's a low energy start and I quickly find it hard to keep myself from losing the beat and speeding up the dance. It's torture to lead them through the warm up phase with so much energy and hunger trapped inside of me.

As we near the end of the first song, I say, "Alright, it's time to pick up the pace. Keep your kicks in check, I don't want anyone hyperextending anything, and don't forget your arms. The more your body's moving, the more calories you're burning. Here we go, five, six, seven, eight!"

The tempo jumps from a modest one-twenty up to a faster one-forty as we take the first step forward. My chest drops into a curl and rolls back up like a whip that's been snapped. My arms swing left to right then pump back and forth as my hips swivel with the music. The music seeps into me and draws out my hunger and craving in a way nothing else can. I'm completely lost in it. I push my body, exhausting the muscles that are constantly screaming at me to use them for more than walking. Sweat is dripping down my back and chest, but I love it because it takes a little of my curse with it as it rolls away.

When the music finally starts to drop back down, I let my body come back to normal as well. I find my voice again and start leading the class through a cool down routine. The high I've been riding begins to dissipate, but at this point I'm too spent to worry about it. I even risk a glance back at Ivy to see how she's doing. Sweat is beaded across her forehead as well, and she looks exhausted, but she actually manages to keep up with the steps pretty well. We finish up with a few basic stretches and everyone claps happily at the end of the class.

Physical exhaustion doesn't erase my hunger, but it makes it much harder for my body to respond to its call. It's the main reason Grandma pushes Zander and I to participate in sports year-round. Drained enough, now, that I can safely approach Ivy, I walk toward her. I stop a good five feet away just as a precaution, however.

"So how'd you like the class?" I ask. The buzz of hunger wriggling under my skin forces me to take another step back despite my weariness.

"It was great," she says with a smile. "I haven't danced in ages. It felt really good."

I can't see any way to get her to pull her sleeve up, but I'm still as determined as ever to find out more about her meeting with Zander. I can't take being around her for too long, though, so I need to come up with something fast. If I can't see the damage, I at least want to know how bad it was. As a plan begins to form in my mind, I take a risk and move closer.

"You never said what kind of dance you used to do."

Ivy blushes faintly. She seemed to avoid the topic earlier, so I suspected she was either lying or didn't want to admit her hobbies. "I did clogging, actually. My friend got me into it."

Finding the opening I had hoped for, I flick my hand against Ivy's arm—cringing away right after when my hunger spikes—and say, "Are you embarrassed?"

She flinches, something I don't miss. She didn't cry out, so it can't be too bad, but it has had a day to heal. I'm a pretty good judge of pain. Bruises, none to the deep muscle, but Zander left a bad enough mark that it's still stinging today. If it were me, that wouldn't have been a big deal. I mess up on that level all the time. For Mr. Master of Control, this is a *huge* deal.

"Well, clogging is kind of unusual," Ivy says.

"It's not that weird. I've known people who've done clogging before." Ivy stands up with her bag, forcing me to inch a little farther away to maintain my buffer.

"Sure, whatever." Ivy laughs. "I liked this a lot better. I think I'll keep coming, if that's okay?"

I have to swallow a chunk of panic blocking my airway. Keep her close, find out her secrets, expose her to Zander. I have to do it. Somehow. For now, I take a few more subtle steps back. "Sure. Glad you liked it."

Ivy gathers up her gym bag and shoulders it. I take the lead and start walking toward the lobby. "So, is this the only hip hop class you teach? I'd like to come more than once a week if I can. I really enjoyed it," Ivy says.

"No," I say through my thinning control. My eyes are fastened on the door, begging for escape at this point. I have to find a better way to deal with her before the next class. There has to be something that will help. "I teach a class on..."

"Van?" a voice calls out. The single word, and vaguely familiar voice, tramples on my focus and I lose my train of thought. I glance around and stop, completely dumbfounded when my eyes land on Noah holding a little girl clad in tap shoes on his hip. I know my mouth is open, but I can't seem to close it. Noah laughs.

"I thought that was you. What are you doing here?" he asks.

"Uh, I work here. What are you doing here?"

He points at the little girl with the same caramel hair as his. "Picking up my little sister, Amelia. She takes tap with

Miss Bethany."

"Did she just start?" I ask. I'm sure I would have remembered seeing Noah here before.

"No, she's been coming for about a year and a half, but my mom usually picks her up," Noah explains. "She and my dad went out tonight, so she asked me to do it instead. I had no idea you worked here."

"I, um..."

I can't think of anything to say to him. Ivy elbows me, sending a bolt of hunger through my body that nearly doubles me over. I take a hurried step away from her. My body isn't tired enough to ignore that much contact. Her jab did jumpstart my brain, however.

"Well, it was nice seeing you, Noah..."

Ivy walks past me, obviously trying to give us some privacy, but not before grinning and mouthing, "He's hot!"

I notice she doesn't go far. The five feet she moved keeps her well within hearing range, but thankfully cuts down on my hunger. I just wonder whether Ivy is lingering out of curiosity, or hope of gathering a little more information about me. Either way, at least she's not standing next to me anymore. I turn my back on Ivy, hopefully blocking Noah from her view.

"So," Noah interrupts, "we still need to get together sometime and figure out what we're going to do for our English project."

I look down, honestly confused by him. Does he really want to be around me? The hope that he is being honest is too much to bear. Knowing I may be making a big mistake, but suddenly lacking the will to walk away, I say, "Uh, I guess."

"Cool. Maybe we could get together this weekend."

I watch Noah carefully for some sign of deceit. Could he really mean what he says?

If he really intends to complete this project with me, we'll have to work on it eventually. His interest seems honestly genuine, and it does help that he really is hot. Guilt for such a thought pokes at me as Ketchup's image forms in my mind. I push them both away quickly.

"This weekend?" I say to Noah. "I guess that would be okay."

I can always back out later if I need to.

"We should exchange numbers," Noah says. When I wrinkle my nose at him, he backtracks. "I mean, I know I'll see you in class tomorrow, but just in case something comes up, I could call you."

"Already planning to cancel on me?" I ask, my suspicion growing.

Noah doesn't get flustered. He just smiles back. "Not at all, just trying to make sure I have a way to get a hold of you in case you try to back out."

That actually makes me laugh. He's quicker than I gave him credit for. I don't understand his willingness to work with me, but I find myself willing to give him a chance. "Give me your phone."

He hands it over willingly. I put my number in his phone and hand it back to him.

"Now yours," he says, holding his hand out for my phone.

I shake my head and give it to him. When he sets it

back in my hand, he takes the extra step to close my fingers around it. I can't seem to feel my hand at all. In fact, when Noah takes his hand away from mine, my fingers refuse to hold onto my phone. It starts to slip, but Noah catches both the phone and my hand.

"Thanks," I say, embarrassed.

Noah looks like he's about to say something, but his little sister speaks first. "Noah, I'm hungry. Can we get pizza on the way home?"

"Sure, pickle. Give me just a minute."

Seeing my way out of this encounter, I say, "I'll see you in class tomorrow, Noah. Enjoy your pizza."

Then, before I can be pulled in by Noah any more than I already have been, I head out of the hallway and into the lobby. Ivy is right on my heels. My hunger surges, but as long as she doesn't touch me again, I think I'll be able to make it to the door and escape. I have my eyes on the entrance, but I don't get very far before Ivy starts talking. "He's gorgeous, Van! Why on earth aren't you thrilled about hanging out with him?"

"It's complicated," I say.

"Does it have something to do with Ketchup? I've noticed how he stares at you during lunch."

"No!" I blurt out, hurrying toward the door. The topic, as well as my hunger, is overwhelming me now. "Ketchup has nothing to do with this. Ketchup is…there are reasons I won't date Ketchup."

"Such as?"

I completely ignore her and pull the door open. I

wasn't looking where I was going, so when a well-muscled chest barrels into me, I trip backward over my feet and nearly fall on my butt. The familiar feel of Zander's hunger blasting over me scares me into finding my footing. I throw my hands against his chest and force him to a stop. I look up, trying to catch his eyes. All he can see is Ivy, though. I look back at her, and am equally startled by her pleased expression. What on earth? Zander presses against my blockade, and I forget about Ivy.

"Zander," I beg. He doesn't answer. I twist a chunk of his skin. "Zander!"

The pain, more than hearing his name, snaps his eyes down to me. I have no idea what Ivy looked so happy about. He looks positively homicidal. Pushing against him as hard as I can, I force him back a step. His eyes dart away from mine, and I know I'm losing his attention. Desperate, I whisper a word I never thought I would say to him.

"Sicarius."

The single word hits him like a slap across the face. He pulls back from me and stands up straight. Then, it is my turn to be surprised when that same strange taste I experienced before saturates the air around me. I stumble back, choking on the foul odor. Looking up at Zander for an explanation, all I see is him storming out of the studio.

Completely shaken, I take several deep breaths to calm myself before turning around to face Ivy. She actually looks startled. About time. Then my eyes drift past her to Noah and his little sister standing in the lobby doorway. Poor little Amelia looks terrified. Noah's eyebrows are up as high as they can go. Great. Good thing he has my number, because he's definitely going to want to break that study date now. Thankfully, nobody else is in the lobby with us. Part of me wants to try and explain, but it's a pretty small part. The majority just wants to run. So I do.

"Uh, sorry. I've gotta go."

Noah looks at me expectantly from behind Ivy, but I just duck my head and run out the door. Please just let me get home without anyone else almost dying.

7

OTHER HUNGER

think Van expects me to say something to her when she gets in the car. Any kind of explanation or apology I could offer refuses to make it past my lips. I take the familiar route home with very little thought, the pressure of my hands just short of snapping the steering wheel in half. Not once do I look directly at my little sister, but I can see the way her head hangs and the frown on her face that almost reaches her toes from the corner of my vision. What is worse, though, is the fact that she sits very still and only moves when absolutely necessary. I know those precautions all too well.

She is scared. Of me.

Sicarius. That word rings over and over again in my head. It chimes like the bells of Notre Dame inside my skull, so loud they shake me to the core. Never, *never*, did I think Van would have to use it on me. I've used it on her…and Oscar, but I'm not like either of them. I can control my hunger. I've suffered and given up everything for that control. It's the one thing that really keeps me going. If I lose that, lose faith in myself, I don't know what it will do to me. I don't want to turn into Oscar. I don't want to end up like him.

One tear slips from the corner of my eye, but my quick reflexes brush it away before Van can see it. A second later, I pull into the driveway. Van hesitates, probably hoping I'll talk to her. My door slams behind me as I stalk up to the house. Sounds from the kitchen pull me in that direction, leading me to my cheerful and petite grandma. Dinner sits on the table, everything ready except the roast she's carrying in her hands. She's about to set it down when I walk in.

She freezes, her eyes widening, but she manages to set the heavy dish down softly before looking back up at me. "Zander," she says slowly, "what's wrong?"

"Van had to use the code word on me tonight."

That's all the explanation she needs. A few strands of wispy grey hair that have fallen out of her barrette start to quiver. So do her hands. "Did it work?" she asks quietly.

"Yeah, barely, but I need...I need to go."

"Of course." She nods and takes a plastic container from the cupboard so she can fix me a plate to go.

"I'm not hungry for that," I snap. Her eyes pierce me for my tone, and I back down. "I don't want to eat. Don't bother with that, Grandma."

"You do want food. You just can't feel it under your other hunger. Trust me, this will help. Go wherever you need to go, eat, take some time to calm down. You'll feel better."

"I don't think that will work this time," I say. My head drops at the last word as shame ripples over me. I don't notice my grandma has moved until her hand reaches up and touches my shoulder.

"What do you mean, Zander?"

Sighing, I shake my head. "I don't know. It's just so much harder with her than it's ever been before. I don't think I can control myself around her."

"Her?"

"Ivy Guerra."

"If…if we need to leave…"

I don't let her finish. "We aren't going anywhere. I won't leave Oscar here by himself."

"If I have to make the choice for you, I will," my grandma says. "I won't lose anyone else."

Her words dig up anger that almost outweighs the hunger I still feel coursing through me. Grabbing the container of food, I turn my back on her and rush out of the house, blowing past a startled Van as I do. I toss the food onto the passenger's seat and tear out of the driveway. I don't care where I go. I just need to get away. Away from my grandma and her all too true words.

It would be best to go. We've always known that might have to happen. Keeping us safe and in check is more important than friends and opportunities we might leave behind. The way Van and I both react to Ivy, it would definitely be best to pick up and leave before someone ends up dead. I used Oscar as an excuse, but he isn't the only reason I don't want to move. There's Ivy, too.

"I don't want to leave her," I whisper to myself.

Hearing those words come from my own mouth, it

terrifies me. Everybody sees me as this guy who is always in control. They don't know the truth, though. Van has no idea, and I'll never tell her, but I think my grandma suspects. When I came home that night, I fell into my grandma's arms and cried. I had never done that before, and I've never done it since. She knew something was wrong, but she didn't press me. She didn't bring up her suspicions tonight, either, but I know they were close to the surface when she said she'd make the choice if she had to.

My shoulders start shaking as I realize she doesn't just wonder, she knows. She must know. My foot leaves the accelerator. I'm too numb to keep driving. The truck rolls to a stop and I sit there staring through the windshield at nothing. Modest sized houses with neatly kept lawns line the streets. The sun is starting to fade behind the rooftops, stretching out the tame shadows into something more sinister. Fence posts become long, spindly fingers trying to close around my neck. Mailboxes morph into executioners' axes that have come to claim their rightful prize. Even the street signs...

Dark thoughts trail off as the collection of letters printed on the sign sink into my brain and form actual words. "Vista Monte," I say to myself in disbelief. "No. I didn't."

Light is fading fast, now, but I can see well enough to catch a house number. 1736. My chest constricts. Go home. Turn around. Don't even think about it. I practically scream at myself to abandon any thought of pursuing my subconscious GPS. I don't seem to have any control over my body or hunger, though, because my foot presses on the gas pedal and my hands keep me pointed in the wrong direction. No, in the right direction. I don't want to turn back. But I should. I argue with myself as I scan the house numbers- 1753 looms on the house in front of me before I finally wrangle myself into stopping. I can't pull right up to the house. She'll see me.

So I stare at her driveway, wondering if she's home, what she's doing, what she would say if she saw me outside her house. That last question really plagues me. Van is wrong about Ivy, but there is definitely something intriguing about her. I was a jerk to her, yet she seemed to be waiting for me yesterday. I hurt her at that meeting, but she was glad to see me tonight. Until I almost killed her. I don't know how I can say this, but even though she very nearly died tonight, I don't think I scared her off. Maybe that makes her brave, or psychotic, or too trusting. I have no idea, but I'm glad for it.

I've been sitting, staring at her house for half an hour when a green sedan pulls into the driveway and parks. Instantly, my hands are on my seatbelt, one trying to unbuckle it, the other trying to keep it on. My hunger flares back to life and comes very close to winning the battle. I'm far enough away from her that I hold out, though my truck suffers for it. The creaking of the brackets holding my seatbelt in place makes me grimace. I tell myself I can't be sure it's even her, but I know her car. I saw her standing by it yesterday. I also looked up her license number in the parking permit logs in the office when I was working there today. It wasn't the only thing I looked up. That's how I got her address.

It's sick, I know. I feel like some kind of twisted stalker. Ivy's black and pink hair emerges from the car, followed by her fragile looking, but beautiful body. She's still dressed in her workout clothes, and I can't stop myself from letting my eyes wander up and down her legs. They look delicious. I want my hands on her body. I want to twist her flesh into fresh bruises, or stroke it softly. I've hurt her already, and I am desperate to do it again, but it kills me to think of causing her perfect, supple body even one second of pain. My heart breaks and races at the same time. Watching her hips sway back and forth as she walks to her door unhinges me.

My seat belt is off, my hand on the door handle. It barely breaks the seal when Ivy freezes. Her hand is extended toward the door, but she doesn't grab it. Reflex saves me, because my mind certainly wasn't going to tell me what to do. I crouch down in the seat and hold my breath until I hear the sound of a door closing a few minutes later. Even after I'm sure she's gone, I stay in that position. My heart pounds against my chest, but for once, it's not out of desire to demolish her pretty face. Fear that she would catch me here outweighs everything else in that moment.

To be honest, it is a strange feeling. I'm not afraid of her finding me and getting me into trouble. There is nothing Ivy could do that I wouldn't be able to stop. Physically, it wouldn't even be a contest. I could crush her before she even had a chance to yell for help. In a battle of "he said, she said," well, I would win that, too. My reputation is impeccable. I've worked hard to make sure that is true for just this kind of situation. If Ivy tried to tell someone I had hurt her, no one would believe the pink-haired new girl over me. Plus, I'm big and intimidating, and people don't mess with me.

No, what I was afraid of was that Ivy would see me,

sitting outside her house like a total creep, and finally realize she should stay as far away from me as possible. That is what scared me into ducking. I can't be around her without wanting to kill her, but I can't stay away from her either. Even now, after almost being caught, I don't leave. I wait and watch.

I watch for any sign of her coming back outside. I wait for the lights in the house to slowly darken. The downstairs goes first. The lights on the east side of the house follow pretty soon after, first the front, then the back. The back west corner, that room's lights stay on the longest. From where I am on the street, one house down, I can't see anything happening behind the curtained windows. All I can see is the light.

It stays on past midnight, which makes me smile. Ivy must be a night owl, like me. I don't mind getting up early, but I'd much rather stay up late than get up before the sun. It's always so quiet and calm at night after everyone else has gone to bed. I don't get a lot of that any other time of the day. Ivy must feel the same way. It's a quarter to one when her light finally goes out.

Before I really know what I'm doing, I'm out of my car and quietly making my way toward Ivy's house. The neighborhood is serene, with nobody about to see me slip over their fence. I have no plan. She's on the second floor. I'm a lot more physically capable than most people, but that is too high of a jump, even for me.

When I reach the back corner of the house, I realize I won't have to jump to get to her. The covered porch that stretches the length of the back end of the house and wraps around the sides provides a railing for me to step on and lever myself onto the roof of the porch. Her window isn't even as high as my waist once I make the small climb.

The ends of the curtains billow out of the window in the breeze. They brush against my shoulders as I sit to the side of the window. Silence filters out along with the breeze, but I know she probably isn't asleep, yet. It only took me a few minutes to get up here after the light went out. Once or twice, she shifts or rolls over. I hear the rustle of her sheets as she moves beneath them. After a while, even her body goes still. I don't dare take out my phone to see what time it is by then because the light may wake her. I don't care what time it is anyway. I'm not leaving yet.

Silently, I move in front of the window and peer through a break in the curtains. Ivy's back is to me, but the pink stripe in her hair is unmistakable. My eyes slide from her hair to her shoulder and follow the curves of her body all the way to her toes peeking out from under the pink sheet. My hands ache to follow the same path. For maybe the first time tonight, I make a conscious decision. It's undoubtedly the wrong one, but I make it anyway.

My leg slips through the window first, followed by the rest of me. I make very little sound as I intrude on her solace. The brush of my feet on her carpet, the slight creak of the window sill as I press my hand against it, are so subtle Ivy doesn't even stir. She lies perfectly still. As I stare at her, I realize that my hunger isn't raging to the point that I can't control it. It isn't absent, but it's amazingly calm. I can't understand it at first. Only when Ivy shifts and my hunger spikes do I realize what is happening.

I'm a predator. I love a challenge, a chase, fresh meat. Van sat so still on the ride home tonight, trying not to accidently provoke me. Ivy is unknowingly doing the same thing. Quiet and still on her bed, she could be dead. Dead holds no interest for me. Not for my hunger, anyway. It seems to have its own mind, one separate from my consciousness. It still aches for nourishment right now, but it's just a general need leftover from earlier. The other part of my brain, the more sane one, knows Ivy isn't dead. It knows she is warm and soft and beautiful. That part of me wants to crawl in bed next to her and drown itself in the illusion that I could actually have her.

Luckily for both of us, I have a lot more control over my conscious mind than my hunger. I settle for sitting on a chair next to her bed where I can still see her clearly. At first, I don't dare even move, but eventually, the desire to touch Ivy wins out. My fingers reach across the distance and touch a strand of her short hair. It feels like silk, slipping through my fingers and falling back to the bed with the slightest movement of my hand. A smile forms on my lips as I watch how the moonlight hitting her hair shifts and swirls each time I touch it.

There is no warning before she suddenly rolls over. Her peaceful face turns right at me, and her hand lands on mine. Her movement arouses my hunger. Every muscle in my body tenses, and I close my eyes against any further movement. The heat of her hand on mine is a constant reminder that she is only sleeping. It does so much more than that, too. The only time I've substantially touched her is when I grabbed her arm in the parking lot. This is so much better.

I don't risk opening my eyes. It's easier to pretend she can't do anything to fulfill my hunger if I can't see the flutter of her eyelids as she dreams, or the way her chest rises and falls with each breath. Even more, I'm glad my eyes are closed when her fingers suddenly tighten around mine. I take a deep breath and squeeze her hand lightly. I can hear her shift, pulling her hand in more tightly, but I don't see it. My hunger reacts, bringing my other hand straight to her neck. The desire to press down and deprive her lungs of oxygen threatens to overpower me.

For the longest time, we stay like that. Hand in hand, on the verge of death, though only one of us is actually aware of it, we share the perilous night. Time seems eternal as I fight my hunger for control. Only her absolute stillness eventually gives me the edge I need to withdraw both my hands from her and sit back.

Despite my weakness, I never want to leave. I'm not like Van. I can't imagine and pretend that one day my life will be fixed. I have no illusions that I will ever be safe enough to let someone share my life. Dreams of a wife and family do not belong to me. I won't ever experience that side of life. Sitting next to the bed of a girl who is asleep and has no idea I'm here is the closest I will ever get to having a romantic relationship. This is it for me, and I loathe the idea of going home.

As my physical need for sleep starts overpowering everything else, my eyelids start to droop. I'm right next to a bed, but if Ivy were to wake up next to me...well, that would obviously go very badly. More likely than not, she wouldn't wake up at all.

I have to leave. More reluctant than I can ever remember being, I stand up. I know I shouldn't, but I can't resist Ivy in more ways than one. Careful not to disturb her, I brush my fingers against her cheek. The resurgence of my hunger the touch costs is well worth the feel of her skin against mine. The slight contact affects Ivy as well. Her frown is replaced by a smile. I can't help doing the same as I back away, regardless of my burgeoning hunger.

The smile stays with me all the way home. My own house is dark and quiet when I arrive. I walk to my room with extra care, not wanting to wake anyone and have to explain where I was, or why I'm getting back at three in the morning. I make it all the way to my bed and lie down before the fear hits me. One second, I'm smiling like an idiot, the next, my entire body is trembling.

There was a chance, before, that I could have convinced myself to stay away from Ivy because of my hunger. After tonight, that small hope has disappeared completely. For a few precious moments, I was near her without wanting to kill her. I touched her silken skin, breathed in her scent, memorized every curve of her body. She has captured my hunger and soul alike, and I have no interest in escaping. I won't be able to stay away. I'll go after Ivy, and I won't be able to stop myself from killing her.

8

NOBLE

I don't have to wait long to see Ivy again. As soon as I pull into the parking lot, I spot her car. She didn't drive to school with Laney. That strikes me as odd since teenage girls seem generally incapable of doing anything solo, but I push any thoughts about why that might be out of my mind. Instead, I look for a parking space. There is one at the end of the row, and one two spaces down from Ivy. I know which one I should take. Van glances over at me nervously when I pull into the one near Ivy. Her hands clench around the strap of her backpack, and I scramble to avoid having to answer any awkward questions.

"You don't want to stop hanging out with Laney, then you better get used to seeing her," I say.

Van looks over at me. The doubt in her eyes is hard to miss. "Are you sure this is about me?"

"Get to class, Van."

"Zander, about last night..."

"I don't want to talk about it."

"I know, but…"

"I said I don't want to talk about it!" I snap at her.

She shrinks back and turns away from me. "I just wanted to apologize."

"What?" I ask after taking a slow breath.

"I…I knew Ivy was going to come to class last night. I texted you to wait for me outside. Didn't you get my text?"

"I did."

"Then why didn't you wait outside?"

"I did, but you were taking a long time. I got worried something was wrong." I look over at Van, suddenly angry at her. "Why didn't you just tell me she would be there?"

"I didn't know if telling you she'd be there would keep you away…or make sure you did come in. I guess I should have told you either way," Van says quietly. "I'm sorry."

My hands finally slip from the steering wheel and fall limp at my sides. I sigh, but I don't look over at her. My little sister sees so much. She was always the one being protected, but not anymore. "It's okay. Thanks for stopping me."

"Sure," she whispers. Van's hand moves to the door handle, but she doesn't get out. "Ivy's going to keep coming to the dance class. I'm pretty sure I'll be okay with that, but I wanted to make sure you knew. Grandma can pick me up from work if you need her to. She'll understand."

"No," I say a little too quickly. We turn to each other at the same time. I blanch at the worry and curiosity in Van's gaze and struggle to explain my quick response. "Same goes for me, I guess. I have to get used to her, too."

Van nods, but hardly seems convinced. When she

doesn't reach for the door right away, I worry she has more to say about Ivy. She does have another question, but it's not about Ivy.

"Hey, do you remember the other day when I said I tasted something weird in the hallway?"

My fingers cinch closed around the steering wheel in panic. I would have preferred another accusing question about Ivy over this one. The effort it takes to answer her is not small. "Sure. Why?"

"The same thing happened last night at the studio." She stares out the window pensively. "Do you have any idea what that was?"

The shake of my head is slow, grinding. "Who knows," I manage to say. "The closer you get to your birthday, the more odd things you'll experience. Just forget about it."

Van's face scrunches up, but she holds back whatever she's thinking and opens the door.

"Don't be late today." I remind her. "I want to leave right after school."

"I know, Zander. It's Friday. You always want to get there as early as possible. I won't be late," Van assures me.

After that, I let her get out of the truck. As soon as the door closes, my attention redirects to the opposite side. It catches me off guard to find Ivy looking right at me. Hunger simmers along with the desire to touch her. Laney is standing next to her, and by the looks of her animated expression and waving hands, she is regaling Ivy with the tale of another klutz-induced mishap. Ivy nods at one point, but her eyes don't leave mine. They watch me, her head tilting to one side, seeming to pierce through me. Sweat beads on my forehead. It makes no sense, but I am almost certain she can see more of me than what is visible.

The feeling passes as soon as her lips turn up in a smile. Suddenly, she is the one who looks like someone has glimpsed her true thoughts. A faint blush turns her cheeks a lighter shade of the pink in her hair. When Van reaches the pair, Ivy turns. For a few moments, I watch them walk away. Van keeps her distance, not enough to make it obvious, but enough to keep her hunger from tasting too much of Ivy. It's only when my little sister tucks her hand behind her back that I realize she's holding something.

The sight of the tattered bit of purple flannel makes me frown. I haven't seen any piece of the blanket our mom made for her when she was little in years. She made one for each of us. They were made especially to help calm our hunger. Not that there is any special power imbued in them, they were just simple fabric, but they were filled with our mom's love and compassion for her children's curse. I haven't seen Van's blanket in a very long time. I sleep with mine every night, though.

When Ivy is far enough away from me, I get out of the truck, lock it up, and follow her. And that's pretty much what I do all day. Along with her address and license plate number, I looked up her schedule. At the time, I had memorized her classes in order to avoid her as much as possible. That should still be my goal. It's obviously not, though, when I skip my lunch hour in order to get some help on my calculus homework.

When I walk through the door, most of the eyes in the room peer up at me. I focus on my favorite teacher, and leave the rest to stare all they want. Mr. Dalton grins and gestures for me to come in.

"Zander, what brings you to my homeroom?"

"Got a minute to help me with my calc homework?" I ask.

Mr. Dalton was my trigonometry teacher last year, and aside from being a likable guy, he was one of the few teachers who believed I wasn't just another brainless jock who expected to get passed because of my athletic abilities. First test, he nailed me for screwing up a bunch of problems. It's not so much that I'm not smart, it's more that I've got a lot going on with sports, my hunger, family issues, and such that I don't always find time to study. The last two years have been especially hard for several reasons, and Mr. Dalton really helped pull me through it.

He gestures me over to his desk. "Of course I've got time. All I do in homeroom is keep the delinquents from doing anything too stupid. Isn't that right, Arnold?"

Some pimply, angry-looking sophomore sitting by the window pops his head up long enough to glare before hunkering down in his seat even further. Mr. Dalton laughs and shakes his head. "So, what are you getting stuck on?"

"Derivatives of continuous polynomial functions. It's just not making sense to me."

"Who do you have his year?"

"Raeburn."

Mr. Dalton winces. "No wonder you're struggling. She

is all theoretical, never bothers to put a problem into real world terms so kids can understand why they're doing what they're doing. Here, let me get a different book."

He stands up and wanders into the tiny shared office situated between his room and the next. I really do need help with my calc homework, but the desire to turn around and scan the room for her has my foot tapping. I can't resist. Attempting to look casual, I note each face, and am disappointed when I don't find Ivy's. I want to check again, but Mr. Dalton reappears with a book in hand.

"Here," he says, "this should help."

I stare at the book doubtfully. "This looks like a college textbook."

"It is. Calculus for business and economics. I teach it at night over at UNM. It isn't any harder than what you're doing now, but it's put into practical terms, like finding the optimal price for movie tickets. It explains why you're finding a derivative or doing integrations."

"That sounds great, but I'm still struggling with *how* to do it, not just why," I argue.

Mr. Dalton shakes his head. "I worked with you all last year. You'll understand the how better if you understand the why. Let's go through a few problems together, and then you can try some on your own."

I'm not convinced, but he saved me last year, and I trust him. So we get to work. The minutes pass slowly as he runs through the basic instructions for me and tries to apply them to a real situation I can understand. I won't lie and say I latch onto it right away, but it does start to make a little more sense. He's pointing out a small error I made when I hear the classroom door open. Instantly, I can feel her on my skin. My muscles bunch up and battle me for control.

"Hey, Zander, what are you doing here?" Ivy asks.

My tension-bound muscles make it difficult to move, but I manage to look over at her. Actually speaking takes a few seconds longer. "Just getting some help with my calculus homework."

Do I imagine that her mouth turns down in disappointment? Was she hoping I was there to see her, or is she upset that I might still be here for a while?

"Oh, really? I'd offer to help you out, but I'm sure Mr. Dalton has it covered," she says.

Her response surprises me enough to let me focus more on her than my hunger.

"You've taken calculus already?" Most kids don't take it until their senior year, if they take it at all. I'm only taking it my junior year because I tested out of geometry when I was a freshman. Don't ask me why shapes make much more sense to me than numbers, they just do.

Ivy shakes her head, her cheeks darkening to pink again. "No, it's just a hobby."

Even Mr. Dalton raises his eyebrows at that comment. Ivy blushes even deeper.

"My dad's an actuary. He loves math. It's super nerdy, but he used to teach me about math rather than reading me bedtime stories. I guess it kind of stuck with me. I like math, too." She closes her eyes and bites the corner of her mouth. "Sorry, I should let you get back to work. I didn't mean to interrupt you and admit what a dork I am."

Ivy doesn't wait for a response. She walks over to her desk, slides into it, and promptly puts her head down. I'm so off balance, my hunger can't even get a good grip on me. Every conversation I have with her becomes a new exercise in odd.

"Huh," Mr. Dalton says, "I'm going to have to pay closer attention to her homework assignments. If she really knows what she's doing, I may recommend her for AP next year."

I hear him, but I don't respond. I'm still staring at Ivy's ducked head, wishing futilely she would look up at me. It's not until Mr. Dalton swats my shoulder that I look back at him. "What?"

His eyebrows rise expectantly. "How do you know Ivy? She just transferred here this week, and let's face it, Mr. Social you aren't."

"She's Laney's cousin." I don't generally talk to people much, especially not about my family or friends, but like I said, Mr. Dalton helped me through a lot the last few years. He nods with understanding.

"You like her?" he asks.

My head starts nodding before my brain can catch up. "What? No."

"Zander..."

"I said no, Mr. Dalton. Don't push me."

He shakes his head and stares past me to Ivy. "I'm not trying to push you, Zander, but you obviously like her. Why not ask her out? She seems nice enough."

"You know why not," I say.

"What happened to Lisa...you can't let that stop you from getting close to people."

Hearing her name sends a spike of guilt and self-hatred through me. My shoulders hunch inward and I can feel myself starting to shrink away to nothingness. Mr. Dalton's hand on my shoulder halts the inevitable descent. "Hey, calm down. Don't let it get to you. You have to let it go."

"That isn't the kind of thing you can let go," I argue.

I'll never forget, never rid myself of seeing her face when I close my eyes, never be free of nightmares of that night. My fingers wrap around my pencil and squeeze it in an effort to vent the raging emotions that are threatening to rupture.

"Zander, it wasn't your fault."

A shiver races through me like burning acid. That's what he thinks. That's what everyone thinks.

"Hey, man, I was just making a suggestion. Don't get upset. You're a good guy. It would just be nice to see you with a smile on your face once in a while. You've been through a lot. You could use some good in your life," Mr. Dalton says.

"Yeah, I could," I say, half to myself.

"Then ask her out."

"It's more complicated than that," I say with a sigh.

"Teenagers. You all think everything is way more complicated than it is. Just wait until you have pensions and 401Ks and income taxes and student loan payments. That's when things will actually be complicated. Right now, it's all so much easier than you think."

If only. But that's one thing I won't discuss with Mr.

Dalton. So I settle for halfway appeasing him and say, "I'll think about it."

That seems to be enough for now. He settles back into helping me, and the rest of the hour passes quickly. When the bell rings, most of the bored students fly out of the room like a pack of wild dogs that just spotted their next meal. My next class is only two doors down, so I make no effort to rush as I pack up my books. At least, I tell myself that's the reason. Ivy seems to be taking her time as well.

"Hey," Mr. Dalton says to me, "come back any time you need a hand. I'm happy to help. And I think someone else might be, too." He follows his comment up with a grin and makes for his cramped office. He's not the most subtle guy in the world.

"So, did you get everything worked out?" Ivy asks.

The hunger that has been gnawing at me since she walked in flares. I have to take a deep breath and clench my jaw several times before I can face her. I remind myself that I made the choice to come here. If I can't control myself around Ivy, sneaking into her room at night will be the only relationship I'll ever have with her. Play nice, pretend I'm normal. When I do turn, I'm careful to keep my distance. "Yeah, mostly," I say.

"That's good."

I feel stupid standing there staring at her, but I'm not sure what will happen if I move. I might try to kiss her. I might do something worse. Just to be safe, I opt for not moving at all. She doesn't move either. In fact, she seems happy to wait for me to say or do something. The silence is starting to weigh on me. I say the first thing that comes into my head.

"Did your dad really teach you math at night?"

Ivy blushes, a look I'm starting to find extremely attractive on her. "Well, it was more like any time we were together. It's hard to get him to talk about anything *but* math, actually."

"You don't mind?"

"No," she says, shrugging away her embarrassment. "I think it's fun figuring out the answers to problems. It's like a game."

Talking to her occupies my mind enough for it to distract me from my hunger and let me move away from her to a safer distance. I head toward the door, and Ivy follows. When we get out to the hallway, I stop again, relieved to be amid dozens of rushing students. The more people there are around, the harder it is for my hunger to focus on one person. I'm sure there are at least a few others in the crowd that my hunger wants, but right now, Ivy overpowers anyone else.

"Math is like a game," I repeat. "Not exactly the way I would put it, but okay."

Ivy starts to take a step closer to me. She seems to think better of it, and steps back instead. "How would you put it?"

"Bamboo shoots? Hot pokers?"

Ivy laughs. It's a full, beautiful sound. No one would ever accuse me of being a funny guy, but I suddenly wish I were. I want to hear Ivy laugh again. If it were the only sound I could ever hear, I would be perfectly happy.

"That's awfully dramatic. Why not throw in some water boarding as well," Ivy says, a smile still playing on her lips.

"Okay, maybe math isn't that bad, but it doesn't come naturally to me."

Ivy's head drops down self-consciously. "Well, I'm happy to help if you need it."

"Really?"

I can't help asking. After the way I've treated her, I honestly don't understand why she doesn't run every time she sees me. Could Van possibly be right? Is there some ulterior motive to her interest in me? Maybe if I take Mr. Dalton's advice, I'll find out.

"Sure," Ivy answers.

She watches me like she did this morning, holding me in her gaze so intently I can't look away. It is an experience I both love and hate. I want her to look at me and see through the façade I wear for everyone else, but I'm also terrified that is exactly what she will do. I don't want her to see inside me and find out what I am and what I've done. I lose my nerve and drop my gaze.

Ivy leans against a row of lockers and says, "It was mostly my fault Van was late getting out of class last night, you know? She asked how I liked the class and I started talking about the type of dancing I used to do. I feel like every time we meet, I do something that makes you upset. I hope you weren't too mad at Van last night."

"I…"

Was that what she thought last night, that I was mad at Van for making me wait? Everyone else in this school thinks I'm the most pleasant guy in the world. Thanks to how I've acted like a lunatic every time we've met, she must think I fly off the handle about things as small as being late. It's much better than her realizing I was two seconds away from killing her last night, but it still bothers me that she thinks of me like that.

"I wasn't mad at Van." I pause, struggling to find some kind of excuse that won't lead her to the truth. I fall back on yesterday's argument. "I mean, I was mad at Van. We got in a fight when I dropped her off. I thought she was being a jerk and making me wait because she was still mad."

Ivy eyes me thoughtfully. I know I still don't come off as some stellar guy with that lie, but she's been willing to overlook my supposed short temper so far, so I hope she'll do it again.

"Well, I promise not to make Van keep you waiting, if you promise not to jump to conclusions. She really was just trying to be nice to me. She didn't seem upset about whatever you two argued about at all. Besides, getting so upset all the time isn't good for you."

"It isn't?" That may apply to other people, but I'm not exactly other people.

"No, it isn't," she says. "So, do we have a deal?"

I ignore the fact that this is absurd and say, "Yeah, sure."

"Good." She smiles up at me, then, a strip of pink hair falling in her eyes. On some instinct I didn't even know I had, my hand moves to brush it back. Whether Ivy acts like my "temper" is something that can be overcome by a deal made in a school hallway or not, she flinches. My hand freezes and falls back to my side.

Ivy lithely tucks the stray hair away behind her ear

and I decide it's time to go. I'm too…embarrassed, frustrated, angry…I don't know. Whatever it is, I turn away without saying anything to her and fix my eyes on the door of my next class.

"Zander, wait," Ivy calls after me. I don't stop. I hope desperately that she'll just leave me alone and walk away. She doesn't. She does something much worse.

Her fingers touch my arm. The all-consuming fire that blossoms under her touch spins me around. My body lurches toward her. Somehow, I stop short of actually grabbing her. I think it's the panicked expression on her face that reigns in my reaction. "Ivy," I gasp, drawing in a breath to try and calm myself. "I'm sorry. You startled me."

"I…I didn't mean to. I'm sorry."

"It's okay." Even as I say it, though, I take several steps back. "I…I have a thing about people touching me. I didn't mean to scare you."

"No, it's fine. I thought you heard me call out, but I guess you didn't."

"It's kind of noisy out here," I say, grateful a good majority of the students who have lunch right now are standing around eating in the halls rather than the cafeteria. It's not a great excuse, but it's semi-plausible. Ivy seems to take it at face value. I fold my arms across my chest to minimize any chance of accidental contact and say, "Did you need something? I must have missed…"

"Yeah," Ivy breaks in, "well, kind of. I just wanted to say that maybe we could get together this weekend. I could help you with whatever math homework you still have, and since

Van is going out with Noah anyway, I thought you might have some free time."

"Oh, uh, maybe," I start. Her last sentence sinks in and I falter. "Wait, what? Van is going out with who?"

"Noah," Ivy says uncertainly, "her English project partner."

"I thought she was doing that solo."

"She was, but Noah moved into her class and they got paired up. Is that a problem?" Ivy watches my reaction carefully, no doubt worried I'm going to freak out on her again.

"No, of course not. I was just surprised. Van didn't mention it to me. She's not usually one for study dates or things like that," I say.

Ivy offers me a timid smile. "Is that some kind of sibling thing? I thought you might need some help still, but if you don't, that's okay."

Now she's the one to take a step back, eager to turn away and leave it at that before I have another chance to reject or attack her. My hunger takes a backseat to the pain it causes me to think I've hurt her feelings, or made her think I don't want to be with her every second.

"No, it's nothing like that," I say, stopping Ivy from leaving. "Van is just, well, she's not really into dating right now."

"That's what Ketchup said about you, too," Ivy says, her eyebrows rising in a silent question.

I roll my eyes at the mention of his name. "Ketchup says a lot of things."

"Things that aren't true?"

I hesitate. "Things he doesn't understand very well. Some things are more complicated than his little brain cares to figure out."

"Oh," Ivy says.

"But with Van, it is true. She's more focused on getting into a good college than dating."

"I've seen her brush off Ketchup," Ivy says, thankfully letting me change the topic from myself back to Van, "but she seems to really like Noah."

I don't have any clue about Van's feelings for Noah, but I know exactly why Van won't date Ketchup or bring him around the house, and it has nothing to do with how much or little she likes him. I realize Ivy is waiting for me to say something. "I'll have to ask her about that later."

Ivy nods, but I'm not really sure whether she's agreeing with me or just doing it to acknowledge I said something. It drives me crazy that I find it so hard to talk to her. I can't read her at all, either. I feel like I'm constantly floundering every time I get near her, something that has nothing to do with hunger.

"Well, I guess I better get to lunch. Your class already started, I'm sure," Ivy says. She starts backing away, toward the cafeteria.

"This weekend," I say without thinking, "you really want to get together?"

There's a moment of hesitation, but she says, "Yeah, give me a call."

"Does Van have your number?"

"I'm not sure, but Laney does. You can get it from her, if you want." Ivy turns, then, and disappears around the corner.

The relief I feel at her leaving and giving my hunger a reprieve is hard to quantify, but along with it comes confusion. It would have been a simple thing to exchange numbers. I have my cell phone in my pocket, and I'm sure she had hers. What teen doesn't have their cell phone with them at all times?

For a moment, I wonder if she's playing some kind of hard-to-get game, but that doesn't seem like her. She's the one who's made the effort to talk to me, not the other way around. Understanding hits me when I sink into my seat in my calculus class. She's giving me a way out. If she'd given me her number directly, I wouldn't have had an excuse not to call her. This way, I could say Van didn't have her number, or I couldn't get a hold of Laney to get it from her.

Ivy is leaving it in my hands. She talks to me regardless of how I've acted around her, but she must see the risk of being near me. Apparently open to the idea of hanging out, it would seem she doesn't want to be the one to actually make the choice. Deniability in case things go wrong? I shake my head. She doesn't know just how much danger she'll be in. Only I know. Keeping her out of harm's way would be easy. Don't call her. It would be the noble thing to do.

Noble, hah.

People around here may think that word describes me, but I have them all fooled.

9

DREAMING, DREAMING

walk toward the cafeteria still stewing over Zander's response to my question about the weird taste. I don't believe him. His odd reaction to my questions, and generally ridiculous answers, has been under my skin all day. Zander is probably right about this having something to do with getting closer to my sixteenth birthday. The part he's lying about is what he knows. That was pretty obvious.

The problem is, if I keep asking him about it, he'll avoid the questions even more, maybe even start avoiding me. I wouldn't want that on a normal day. With Ivy around, I can't let that happen. I huff in irritation, completely stumped on what to do.

"Hey, what's going on?" Ketchup asks as he falls in step with me.

I glance over at him, unsure of what to say, but glad he appeared. In my head, I know this isn't something I should discuss with him. Words that will brush off his concern form on my lips, but I can't say them. There is so much banging around in my head that if I don't let at least some of it out, I am going to explode.

"I think Zander is lying to me about something," I blurt out before I can change my mind.

Ketchup looks a little surprised that I actually told him, but he doesn't let that stop him. "Lying about what?"

Now I balk. How on earth do I explain this without sounding like a total nut job? "I, well...um."

Ketchup stops walking, his hand on my arm forces me to stop as well. I can't meet his eyes. I knew it was stupid to say anything. A gentle hand under my chin pushes me to look up. Ketchup's stern expression is both surprising and welcome.

"Van, I know you've got some weird stuff going on. I figured that out a long time ago." His hand softens as he slides his hand to rest on my cheek. "If I wasn't good with weird, I would have bailed already. You can tell me. I can handle it, okay?"

He seems so sure. I'm not nearly as confident, but my earlier argument wins again. I need someone to talk to. "Okay," I say slowly.

Ketchup smiles, looking quite pleased with himself.

"I keep tasting this weird taste, and I asked Zander about it and he acted really weird and gave me some lame answer about it being normal, or whatever, but I knew he was lying because he got all tense and shifty, which made it pretty obvious he didn't want to talk about it with me, and that's really freaky because we don't keep secrets from each other *ever*, and if he won't tell me it must be really bad and I don't know what to do about it," I say all in one breath, too scared Ketchup will walk away before I can finish.

I breathe in slowly and wait for Ketchup's reaction.

Frowning, he asks, "What kind of weird taste?"

It takes me a moment to speak after his mild reaction. In my head that sounded like a whole string of random, crazy crap. He doesn't even bat an eye.

"Um, it's kind of...well, it's hard to explain. It's not really any one taste I can identify. It's like old socks and water that's been sitting around for too long, like gross puddles mosquitos like to lay eggs in. And rotten food. It's just gross."

Ketchup thinks a moment before responding. "And you've only tasted it around Zander?"

"So far," I admit, "but I have a feeling it's not just about him."

"And he won't explain it?"

I shake my head. "He basically brushed me off when I asked. That's not like him at all. That's what makes me think it means something bad."

Before Ketchup can say anything else, the hallway goes completely silent. Given how many students are hanging out in the hall right now, that's really creepy. What's even freakier is that Ketchup slips his arm around my waist and pulls me under his arm, but not in a romantic way. It's more like he's trying to protect me. Concerned, my eyes sweep the hallway for the source and land on one of the scariest guys I have ever seen. It isn't his clothes or hair, or even the way he stalks through the crowd. His cold, dead eyes are what scare me. I can't help but draw closer to Ketchup as he nears us.

I have every intention of looking away, but I freeze when the familiar taste forces its way into my body. My stomach heaves and I panic. Spinning into Ketchups embrace, I bury my face against his chest, breathing in the scent of his cologne in an effort to get away.

A few seconds later, the world goes back to normal. Sound returns, as does the normal smell of teens chowing down on concession stand grub. Still, I don't trust it. It takes Ketchup pulling back and forcing my chin up to convince me to rejoin the rest of the world.

"Hey, are you okay? What happened?"

"Who was that guy?"

Ketchup looks at me like I'm crazy. "That guy? That was Alonso Vega. He's been all over the news for months. How do you not know who he is?"

"Grandma doesn't let us watch the news, remember? Too many violent stories."

"Right, sorry," Ketchup says.

"Why has he been on the news?"

Before speaking, Ketchup pulls me closer to the lockers. "Vega is a member of the Westsides. He was supposed to be involved in all those gang shootings last summer. He's been on trial for the past few months, but they couldn't pin him down and the jury let him loose even though everyone knows he's on the gang's cleanup crew."

"That guy's a hitman?"

"A pretty good one from what I've heard. Why?"

"When he walked by, I tasted that same taste again."

Ketchup's face scrunches. "So…what does that mean?

Zander and Vega have something in common?"

"Oh, no," I say. "I really hope that isn't what it means."

Neither of us knows what to say after that. We walk to the cafeteria in silence. I'm not entirely sure what might be running through Ketchup's mind, but I am on the verge of losing it.

"Van! What took you so long?" Ivy says in a rush, surprising both me and Ketchup with her sudden appearance.

Even my hunger takes a minute to roar to life. I practically jump back in hopes of getting away from her, but she follows me. In a moment of panic, I grab Ketchup's hand for strength to resist my hunger and yank it behind my back where Ivy can't see it. Either Ivy doesn't notice, or just pretends she doesn't. Either way, she rattles on.

"You meeting up with Noah this weekend wasn't supposed to be a secret or anything, was it?"

"What? No. Why?" What on earth made her think of that?

"Who's Noah?" Ketchup demands.

"Are you sure?" Ivy asks, ignoring Ketchup's question entirely. "I mentioned it to Zander and he got kind of weird about it."

All the fear and confusion I've been carrying around today suddenly gets ten times worse. Mixing with my hunger, I begin to feel lightheaded. "You talked to Zander? When?"

"You talked to Zander?" Laney repeats, popping into the conversation as well. "Ooh, tell us all about it. What did he say?"

"Uh, can we go sit down first?" I beg as my hunger

begins to escalate. I need a little more separation as soon as possible. Thankfully, everyone agrees and scurries over to the table.

Sitting a good five feet away so my hunger only simmers instead of rages, I focus on Ivy. I want details. "You talked to Zander?" I ask as casually as possible.

"Yeah," Ivy says slowly, watching me just as closely as I am her. "He was in my homeroom class. I guess Mr. Dalton was helping him with some homework."

Dalton. It's plausible, but I'm not real big on coincidences. If it wasn't by chance, Zander was the one who sought Ivy out. This screwed up day is getting worse by the minute.

"Who cares about homework?" Laney says. "What'd you two *talk* about? And what did you say about Van going out with Noah? Who's Noah?" When her waterfall of questions finishes, she stares at me and her cousin eagerly.

Her questions about Noah dredge up a pretty heavy dose of guilt. Suddenly, I can't even look in Ketchup's direction. "Noah's my new English partner, and it's nothing," I say with a shrug. "We *might* get together this weekend to start working on our project."

"We'll discuss Noah more later," Laney says, turning back to Ivy.

Ketchup seems to be echoing that same sentiment when I risk a glance at him. I shrink down in my chair even more.

"Now what about Zander?" Laney asks.

"Nothing," Ivy says. "We just talked for a few minutes

in the hall. I asked him if he needed any more help with his homework. He said he might, and I offered to help him with it this weekend. That's when I brought up Noah. He seemed... not upset, but really surprised. I thought maybe I wasn't supposed to mention him."

I wave away her concern, and hopefully Ketchup's as well, with only half my attention on them now. The rest of my mind is scrambling to make sense of what she just said. The idea of Ivy and Zander simply talking in the hall is laughable. Whether she saw it or not, he would have been fighting his hunger the entire time. If that had been me, I would have needed to go demolish another punching bag. Zander has way more control than I do, but I bet he's suffering right now, which makes me bite my lip with worry.

He can't possibly be planning on letting Ivy tutor him. I know he doesn't believe me that there's something up with her, but his hunger for her is reason enough to stay away. It would be insane to purposely subject himself to that. Which I guess is what he thinks I'm doing by not ditching Laney, but at least I have friendship and protecting family as a reason behind my choice. What does he have? Does he want to screw up? Doesn't he understand what that would mean?

I don't get it. I want to crush Ivy every time I see her. That's pretty hard for me to ignore. Zander's more developed tastes are even harder to push away, especially the way his hunger leans. If he doesn't stay away from Ivy, he's going to end up killing her. He'll end up just like Oscar.

Laney's elbow bangs into my ribs, jarring me from my thoughts. "What?" I snap.

"Did you hear anything I just said?"

"Um, no."

She rolls her eyes. "Movie. Seven o'clock. The three of us, plus whoever else wants to come. You can even invite this Noah guy if you want."

I can feel Ketchup stiffen next to me.

I shake my head right away. "Laney, it's Friday. You know I can't go. Besides you know how Grandma feels about us going to movies."

"It's a tame enough movie. Come on, you'll be back in time to go with us," Laney argues.

"It doesn't matter. You know Fridays are hard. I won't want to go anywhere."

"It might make you feel better to go out and do something afterward."

She tries over and over again to get me to go somewhere on Friday nights. I don't know why she doesn't give up. It never works. "No, Laney. Leave me alone about it, okay?"

Surprisingly, she does. Her bottom lip pushes out in a sulky pout, but she doesn't say anything else. That doesn't mean nobody does. Ivy pipes up instead.

"Where do you go on Fridays?" she asks.

I debate ignoring her, but if I don't tell her someone else will. Taking a deep breath, I say, "We're going to visit my brother, Oscar."

"Oh, where does he live?"

"Peak View Hospital."

Ivy's eyes grow sad and wide. "Oh my gosh, is he sick? I'm so sorry, Van. What does he have?"

"No," I say slowly, "it's not that kind of hospital. Oscar is in a psychiatric ward."

For the rest of the day, I battle between not being able to stop thinking about Noah, and Ketchup's reaction to him, and worrying about Zander. Now, as I stand in front of Peak View Hospital, Oscar is all I can think about. I want to go in and see him, I do, but I can't force myself to take the first step. I love Oscar, despite the things he's done. Seeing him locked up and raving never gets any easier. I always walk in expecting him to get better. All he ever gets is worse.

Zander hides his emotions most of the time, but during our visits to Oscar, we are equally overwhelmed. He doesn't even try to hide it. His hand slips into mine and squeezes tightly. Having him close reassures me, but not enough to keep a shiver from running through my body.

"You don't have to go in if you don't want to," Zander says. "He won't even…"

I flinch, even though he doesn't finish. I know what he was going to say. Oscar probably won't even notice if I'm not there. He may not even remember us coming at all. So what if he doesn't? I'll know.

"No, I want to go in," I say. "I'm ready."

Even still, Zander has to tug on my hand to get me to take a step forward. We make it to the front doors, and as soon as we step in, the gloom of the place presses in around me. It affects Zander, too. The way his shoulders drop and his expression pales betray him. He always handles these visits better than I do, but he is the one who has the most reason to never want to set foot in this hospital. He's the one who found out what Oscar did. I shudder at the thought and fight to keep tears from falling. Before I'm ready, the visitation room is standing before me.

Of course, it's not the regular visitation room with couches and rocking chairs and people playing checkers and reading books. Only the non-violent residents get to use that room. Zander pushes the door open and tows me into the room where Oscar waits for us. I close my eyes to the sight of the plain metal table with shackles bolted onto the top and legs, against my oldest brother being attached to those chains. I can't stand seeing him like this. I have to shut away everything else and picture myself dancing. Ballet. In my head, I run through my favorite dance, *The Red Shoes*, a piece that is very technically difficult and requires absolute control. I work through the skills and elements one by one until I feel my emotions calm and settle. Only then do I open my eyes.

Oscar used to look a lot like Zander, fit, handsome, tall, and magnetic. Most of that is gone, now. The sallow tone of his skin and sunken crags in his face have aged him and stolen any hint of the good looks he once had. His muscles are flaccid, though I know they still contain more strength than most people have. Although his height hasn't changed, the way he hunches and hides from the world makes him look small. "Oh, Oscar," I whisper quietly.

It takes Oscar several minutes to even realize we're in the room. When he does notice, his whole body jerks against the chains. Fists slam down on the table and his eyes rise to meet Zander's. At first he doesn't say a word, but his nose wrinkles in disgust. The sneer isn't normally something I would scrutinize. Given Zander's lies lately, I wonder for a moment if Oscar tastes it, too. I wish I could ask him, but Zander's presence isn't the only thing that holds me back. I doubt Oscar could even answer a question like that judging by the way he's acting today.

The purplish color around Oscar's eye sockets make his blue eyes look so much darker than they used to, but they pierce Zander all the same. He shivers under his brother's glare and says nothing.

The quiet twists Oscar's features. His head tilts to one side and a hideous smile that shows strangely white teeth appears as his lips turn up. "I know you," Oscar says slowly. The harsh edge to his voice makes me step back. His eyes slither from Zander to me. "I know you, too."

Neither of us responds. I can't make my mouth work in the face of his disturbing voice and appearance. Zander doesn't seem to be having any more luck than I am.

"I know your faces," Oscar growls, "but they've changed." He shakes his head viciously. "They've changed from what I remember."

The sharp ping of his hands slapping down on the table startles me into jumping.

"Younger, happier, hopeful, that's how they used to be. No more young and innocent for us. No more happy, no more hope. No more happy, no more hope," Oscar chants. "No more happy, no more hope. No more happy, no more hope."

"Stop it," Zander finally says.

"No. I won't stop. I won't stop until you admit it. No more happy, no more hope, especially not for you," Oscar hisses at him.

"Shut up!"

Oscar's eyes widen and fixate on Zander. His finger waggles back and forth in front of his face. "Shame, shame, I know the truth. You can't hide it from me. I know."

Zander's fingers crush mine in their grip. I have no idea what Oscar is rambling about, but Zander is shaking next to me. I want to ask him what is going on, but I'm afraid of this getting out of hand. My frightened and distraught mind struggles to find something to distract my deranged brother. "Oscar, did you like the CD I left you last time we were here?"

I don't have a lot of hope that he'll actually answer me. Hope that he even remembers me giving him the music, let alone him actually listening to it, is even slimmer. So when he turns to look at me and speaks, I am caught off guard.

"Tchaikovsky was never my favorite. I like Beethoven better. The madness in his music makes me feel less alone."

Following up such a lucid comment from Oscar is completely impossible. I'm too shocked to respond. I can't remember the last time he spoke to me in such a clear way.

"Alone...alone," Oscar sing-songs. "I am all alone. Hopeless and forgotten, I'm alone now."

"No you're not, Oscar," I say quickly. "We're still here. You're not alone."

"Have you come to take me home? Home to our broken home?" He says it mockingly, but there is hope in his eyes. My lips break into a frown that threatens to split my face in two.

"Someday," Zander says quietly, "but not today."

"Promises." Oscar closes his eyes. Then he suddenly slams his head against the table. The crack of skull on metal twangs through the room. A man at the door moves to come in, but Zander holds him back. Slowly, Oscar lifts his head back up. The unfocused quality of his eyes makes his sneer even worse.

"Someday isn't a real day. It will never come. I'll be stuck here forever, getting poked with needles and fed drugs and being broken even more than I'm already broken. Promises are nothing. I won't believe you. It's all fake!" he screams. Red in the face with anger one minute, he's back to normal a moment later. Well, he's back to the way he was when we walked in today, glaring and maniacal. Somehow, he seems to focus on both me and Zander at the same time. "If you believe I'll ever leave here still alive, you're crazier than I am."

"You'll get better soon," I say quietly.

Oscar's hyena laughter fills the room. "Better?" he trills. "Are you stupid? There is no better. You know that. You've got the same thing I do. You're sick, too. You're one slip away from landing in the room next to mine. You both are." He breaks out in psychotic laughter again.

"That's not true," Zander says forcefully.

Snickering like he's heard the funniest joke in the world, Oscar rocks his body back and forth. "Alec-zander and Van-essa. Baby brother changed his name. Little sister changed hers too. Neither one can stand to hear their given names. They hate who they are, try to hide their true nature and hope reality will just go away. Zander and Van pretend they're normal. They're delusional, insane. I'll wait here in my personal hell until they join me. I'll wait and wait. I know they're coming. It's the only thing that keeps me from losing it completely. Baby brother and little sister come hoping they will one day take me home. I let them come with their foolish dreams, knowing the hope belongs to me. One day they'll come and they won't leave, and then *my* dream will come true. Baby brother and little sister dreaming, dreaming, building their nightmare one visit at a time."

The room falls silent and I hate the sound even more than Oscar's voice. In the quiet, I can hear his words whispering their way into my head and taking root there. The absence of sound lets me hear his insanity digging into my brain and settling in. We're given half an hour to visit, but I've had all I can take for today.

"Zander, I want to go," I whisper.

"Go?" Oscar asks. "You can't go, silly little sister. You belong here. There's no home for you to go home to anyway. Nobody left to love you."

"Yes there is," I argue.

"No. There. Isn't."

"Zander loves me. Grandma loves me. Even you love me, Oscar."

That part of him has to be there still. He can't have completely forgotten playing tea party with me when no one else would, or walking me over to Laney's house when I was too little to go on my own. He's my big brother. He has to see that still.

"I don't love you anymore," Oscar says. "I don't love anyone anymore. All I am is hate and anger, pain and destruction. I don't love you anymore. I don't love you! I don't love you anymore! Get out! Leave and don't come back. Don't come back or they'll keep you here forever. Get out! Get out! Get out!"

On the last sentence, he pounds his fists against the table and doesn't stop. Over and over again the metallic bashing washes over me. He takes up the chant again at some point, but my eyes are closed and my hands are over my ears by then. Suddenly, I am moving, but I don't open my eyes to see where I'm going. I don't even realize Zander has my arm until the door closes behind me and the noise stops. I open my eyes at the sudden lack of screaming and banging. Zander stands in front of me pretending to be stoic and calm, but the twitch at the side of his mouth gives him away.

A sob breaks out of me, and a second later Zander's arms are around my shoulders. I don't miss the fact that he's shaking as much as I am, but I pretend he isn't crying and he does the same for me. Standing in the hall of the building we hate more than any other, we hold each other and wish... wish things were different, wish everything Oscar said to us wasn't true.

10

WORTH THE RISK

As soon as we get home and shake off the disturbing experience of visiting Oscar, Zander corners me about Noah. Zander is always pretty protective of me, for good reason, so his reaction doesn't surprise me. His questions range from whether or not my hunger reacts to Noah to why I didn't try to get out of working with him, and just to be safe. It takes a while to convince him that working on an English project won't put either me or Noah at risk. Not mentioning the Jeet Kune Do is key to making that argument work. I feel a little guilty leaving that out, but I figure Zander is hardly the one to judge me about keeping secrets right now. The last question Zander asks is whether or not I actually like Noah.

His last question is hard to answer. Already strung out after seeing Oscar, not to mention angry at Zander for seeking out Ivy, I can't really say how I feel. If Noah honestly wants to hang out with no hidden agenda, well, that's pretty hard to resist. He's certainly handsome and he seems like a nice guy, but every time I think I might be starting to like him, Ketchup pops into my head. I just don't know yet.

Before leaving, Zander warns me to be careful. His reminder that my birthday is only a few months away is hardly needed, though. It's been on my mind constantly. I remember all too well both him and Oscar reaching their sixteenth birthdays. Emotionally, they were wrecks. Hunger-wise, they were even worse off. Their desires would be manageable one moment, then flaring into an inferno the next. They were dangerous to be around.

I wasn't allowed to see them during that time. Even Mom and Dad tried to stay away as much as possible. Oscar had to be sent away for a while after our dog and several of the neighbors' dogs went missing. Dad slipped on the stairs and twisted his ankle shortly after Zander turned sixteen. Even such a small amount of pain was too much for him to handle. It took me and Oscar to pull him off of Dad.

After that, Zander locked himself in his room and refused to see anyone. He became a total recluse until things calmed down. Oscar handled the changes differently, but I push those kinds of thoughts away before they can really develop.

I spend the rest of the night in my room thinking about everything I don't want to deal with right now. Noah is a problem, not only because of my confusion over him, but because he expects me to try something I was expressly forbidden to participate in. I know my limits, and this may well be beyond them. The only reason Grandma ended up agreeing to Zander playing football was because of the way his hunger leans. Zander enjoys the chase. He feeds off the fear that leads up to the pain. His hunger can be patient. Mine can't.

My sixteenth birthday scares me even more than thinking about Zander and Oscar because my hunger is by far the least controllable. I crave total pandemonium. The messier, the better. If I lose control, I really lose it. If I can't handle practicing with Noah…I know the results won't be good.

My phone sits on my desk patiently. It waits as if expecting me to use it, to call Noah and cancel. Logic begs me to do it. The allure of having a friend that I didn't have to save in order to earn, one that wants to be around me just because, is too much. The phone remains unused for the rest of the night while I dream horrible dreams of losing control and mauling Noah as Ketchup looks on in fear and disgust.

Hours later, as I sit in the living room trying to focus on my homework, the images from my dreams keep popping back into my head. Tearing Noah apart is disturbing, but watching Ketchup turn his back on me is heartbreaking. It doesn't help that no one else is around to distract me. Grandma is grocery shopping, and I have no idea where Zander went. He was gone when I woke up this morning. That is more than a little worrisome.

I called Laney the second I realized he was gone to ask her what she and Ivy were doing. Used to my occasional weirdness, she told me they were swimming and asked if I wanted to join them. I dodged that invitation quickly, as I have done frequently of late, and hung up. He isn't with Ivy, but my anxiety is still riding high. He hasn't answered any of my texts today. That is unusual, and infuriating. Where is he?

I can't seem to focus on anything but the disturbing dreams and frightening images of what Zander might do to Ivy. I stare at the words of my history book, tapping my pencil against the coffee table. They make no sense, blurring, turning blood red, leaping off the page to bite at me. Sick of trying, I toss my pencil at the book and slam it closed. I'd call Ketchup to come distract me, but he isn't allowed to come over, and I can't drive. If I asked him to pick me up, I'd be at his mercy for the rest of the day. He wouldn't let me go until he absolutely had to either. I don't think I could handle that much time with Ketchup. The temptation would be way too great. Stuffing my phone back in my pocket, I wander into the kitchen in search of something to eat instead.

Usually, I'm pretty particular about what I eat, but when I find a box of lemon cookies hidden in the back of the pantry, I pull it out. I stick a couple of cookies between my teeth to hold, and reach in for another one. The sudden ringing of my phone in the dead quiet of the kitchen startles me so badly I drop the box, bite down on the cookies I was holding in my mouth, and spray crumbs all over the place. Including down my shirt. Spitting and swallowing to get the rest of the lemon and powdered sugar mush out of my mouth, I pull my phone out of my pocket and answer the call before it goes to voicemail.

"Hello?" My voice comes out loud and I'm breathing way too hard.

"Uh, Van?"

My hands fly over my shirt in an attempt to get rid of the lingering crumbs at the sound of his voice. There's some part of my brain reminding me that Noah can't see me, but I keep brushing regardless. "Noah? Hey."

"Did I call at a bad time? It sounds like you're busy."

"No," I say a little too eagerly, "I just practically dumped a box of cookies down my shirt."

Noah laughs. "Why did you do that?"

"It was an accident."

"Sure, sure," he teases.

I roll my eyes at him and smile as I try to get the rest of the crumbs out of my bra.

"So," Noah says, "I was just calling to see if you still wanted to get together and work on our project this weekend."

Zander's warnings and my own fear come zipping back into my mind. I told him it wasn't a big deal to hang out with Noah, that he was just my English partner, nothing more, but standing in my cookie covered kitchen, knowing he's waiting for me to respond makes it very difficult to take Zander's advice. Noah's interest seems so genuine. That's a pretty rare thing for me outside my little circle of friends. The lingering doubts in my mind are pushed away when I remind myself that Noah did save me. Don't I owe him something? I'm more than a little familiar with the debt that saving a person's life incurs. Backing out on him seems impossible.

"Um, yeah, I guess. If you want to."

"I do. You busy right now?" Noah asks.

I glance down at the mess I just made. "Right now?"

"Sure. The gym I take Jeet Kune Do at has open gym

hours on Saturday afternoons. I could show you some of what I know, and you can tell me if you want to use it for our project or not."

It's a simple request, but my hand starts shaking. If my grandma finds out, she'll ground me for the rest of my life. If I agree, something worse may happen. Physical activity helps calm my hunger, but dancing is way different than fighting people for fun. I don't know how I'll react to that. What if I hurt Noah?

I won't, I argue with myself. If things get too intense, I'll tell him I don't like it and want to try something else. He'll understand. It won't be a big deal, and if it is, maybe we just won't work together. That would certainly solve my problem of getting too close to him, although it would rob me of the chance to have a normal, uncomplicated friendship.

I'll only try it this once. If I can't control it, I'll never do it again.

"Uh, Van?" Noah asks.

"Sorry, I was just trying to remember if I have to do anything this afternoon." Cookies down my shirt, long odd pauses, the way I accused him of basically being a jerk the first time we talked, Noah must think I'm a nutcase.

"Did you come up with anything, or should I come pick you up?" he asks.

I take a deep breath, and a huge risk. "Sure, I can come, but give me half an hour to take a shower, okay?"

"You may want to wait to shower until after we go to the gym."

"I'm covered in powdered sugar from the cookies, and I

probably taste like lemons," I say with a laugh.

"Hmm."

That's all Noah says, but the way he says it, slow and thoughtful, makes me wonder what he's thinking about. A shiver runs down my spine, something that has never happened with anyone but Ketchup before. To be honest, it kind of freaks me out. But I also kind of like it.

"Half an hour?" I ask.

"Huh? Oh, yeah, that sounds great. Is your brother home?"

"No. Why?" I ask.

"Just wondering. I'll be there in half an hour."

After giving him my address, I run upstairs and take the fastest shower of my life. No way do I want him showing up before I'm ready. I can only imagine wrapping a towel around my wet body and hearing the doorbell ring. There's no chance of me answering the door in nothing but a towel, so he'd be forced to stand out there like an unwanted salesman until I finished getting dressed. I already act like a total spaz every time I see him, so I rush through getting ready with the hope that, for once, I can have a normal interaction with him.

Still wet from my shower, my normally platinum hair almost looks like it has some color to it as I twist it into a ballet knot on my way down the stairs. Wet hair bugs me big time, but faced with a choice between blow drying my hair or putting on my makeup, makeup wins out pretty easily. I dash into the kitchen to find a notepad so I can leave my grandma a note, and step on an already broken cookie before remembering the mess I made. I brush off my bare foot with a grimace and reach for a broom.

The broom is right where it should be, but I can't find the dustpan. I'm rummaging through the closet where we keep the cleaning supplies when the doorbell rings. The sudden noise makes me knock my elbow on a shelf and bump into a wire rack as I try to untangle myself from my search and hurry to the door.

In an attempt to look semi normal, I pause, take a deep breath, and then open the door casually. Noah, dressed in running shorts and a plain white tee, bursts into a huge grin as soon as he sees me. At first, I think he's super excited to see me, which seems a little extreme, but nice. When his grin turns into a snicker, I get worried.

"Am I dressed wrong?" I glance down at my black leggings paired with simple black shorts and my pink tank top. It seemed like a decent choice, but maybe I was wrong. "I, uh, didn't know what to wear, so I just put on some dance clothes. I can change if I need to."

Noah's laugh deepens as he steps toward me. I flinch back, but he brings his hand up and reaches toward my head anyway. I'm a second away from slapping his arm away when I feel something move in my hair. Noah's hand comes away bearing a small sea sponge. He smiles again and says, "Your clothes are fine, but you might want to leave the dried up sea creatures at home."

"I couldn't find the dustpan."

It's a perfectly ordinary statement, but Noah starts laughing. "I'm sorry, but you say the weirdest things sometimes. What does a missing dustpan have to do with a sponge in your hair?"

"I was looking for the dustpan in the closet, and I bumped into a shelf. The sponge must have fallen off. What is so weird about that?" I ask, embarrassed once again.

"Nothing, nothing. It makes perfect sense now." Noah offers me the sponge with an apologetic smile. "Did you need help cleaning up?"

"No, just give me a minute. I'll use the vacuum instead."

Noah tries to follow me into the kitchen, but I insist he stay put in the living room. I've said and done enough stupid things today to leave me red in the face for days. No need to make him think I'm a slob, too. I suck up the crumbs and write Grandma a note about where I'm going, leaving out certain details, of course. I could text Zander easily enough, but I don't. Not in the mood for a lecture or more questions, I skip over his name and stop on Ketchup's.

I open a message, but knowing what to say is not as easy. Thanks to Laney, he knows about Noah and that we were supposed to get together this weekend, but his reaction to that information wasn't happy. I don't want to hurt him even more by flaunting who I'm going to be with today, but I don't know who else to tell. Laney can't drive yet. The only other one of my friends with a license is Wyatt, but he's out of town visiting his grandma.

Ketchup is the only one who could actually help if things go badly. Plus, I know he'll be home today. His mom works six days a week, so he's left to fend for himself most weekends, and his dad lives out of state and rarely bothers to visit his son. I know he'll be able to come if I need him. I feel like a jerk using him as my backup when I know how he feels, but I have no one else to trust with this. Praying Ketchup will understand, I open a text message to him.

Trying something new. Not sure how it will go. I may need help later. I'll be at 724 Alameda.

Keeping my fingers crossed that Ketchup won't hate me for asking his help on this, I tuck my phone into my pocket and walk back to the living room. Noah asks if I'm ready. I nod and follow him out to his car. I'm buckling up when my phone chimes at me. I open the message and finally manage to breathe.

Call if u need me. I'll B there.

No questions asked, even though I'm sure he made the connection and knows I'm with Noah. Gratitude for his unrelenting loyalty fills me to the brim, along with a pretty severe stab of guilt. I hate that I had to involve him in this at all.

"Ready?" Noah asks.

I nod my head because my throat is too closed up to speak.

A short ten minutes later, we pull into the parking lot of the gym. A new emotion takes up residence then. Fear. Somehow, I push my door open and follow Noah across the parking lot. As we walk in the front door, I feel like I have to revise my description of the building. Gym doesn't quite fit. The only pieces of exercise equipment I see are racks of free weights along one wall. The rest of the gym is open space with perfectly square blue mats dotting the area. Four of the six mats are occupied with people ranging in age from elementary school kids to older than my grandma. This isn't at all what I was expecting. Of course, I didn't have a lot to go off, either. My grandma not only forbids us to participate in combat sports, but movies and TV shows on the same topic are taboo as well. She wouldn't even let us see *The Karate Kid.*

"So, you ready?" Noah asks.

A teen sparring on the mat nearest me snaps his foot into his partner's leg and knocks him to the ground. My hunger yearns to get a little closer as the fallen boy groans. I should go. I should really, really go.

"Yeah, I'm ready," I say. Nodding, Noah gestures to the far mat and I follow. The fallen teen gets up as I walk past him and rubs his leg. His lingering pain floats off his body and skims through the air to reach me. A fight starts a little further away from me and the air is tainted with their minor injuries. It's such a small amount. The air is filled with it, though.

We pass by another mat and I stop, trying desperately to control the sudden urge to leap into the fight I am watching. Two boys, no more than eleven or twelve, are pelting each other with jabs and kicks. One of the boy's pain leaps out at me, rushing in to stoke my hunger happily.

"Cool, huh?" Noah says with a smile. "Let's go get a mat before someone else snags it."

I grab Noah's extended hand, not caring if he interprets it the wrong way. I just need to get as far away from those boys as possible. By the time I reach the mat Noah picked out, I'm feeling a little lightheaded.

"So, you're going to want to take your shoes and socks off first," Noah says. He slips his tennis shoes and socks off and sets them to the side of the mat. Shaking my head to clear it, I follow his example and step back on the mat with bare feet. The impression that I should run only gets worse.

"Nice toenails," Noah says, eyeing my glittery purple nail polish.

I'm so nervous about being here that I can't even laugh at his teasing. The best I can dredge up is a faint smile. "Are you going to show me what I'm supposed to do, or what?" I say lightly, trying to hide my nervousness.

"Sure, I've just never fought anyone with sparkly toes before," he says.

Another round of his playful teasing eases my anxiety a little. I throw him a more meaningful smile, and he continues.

"So, Jeet Kune Do isn't a set of patterned movements like some other martial arts. It's a more free flowing, reactionary style."

"What does that mean?" It seems to me like all fighting should be reactionary. If someone's about to hit you, you have to stop them, and probably hit them back. Zander probably wouldn't agree with me on that one, but it certainly seems like the logical way to fight.

"Well," Noah says, "with Kung Fu, if your opponent strikes you with a certain attack, you would answer with the appropriate response move. Attacks and counterattacks follow a pattern in those methods, but in Jeet Kune Do the idea is to attack your opponent and intercept their attack before it ever lands."

I start to relax a little more as I identify with what he's saying. Why would anyone wait for someone to attack them if they could break in and do it first? Zander swears fulfilling his hunger through a well-planned route is much better than jumping at the first chance to kill, but I don't believe him. The thrill and rush of adrenaline I get every time my hunger erupts and tries to send me after someone are so completely intoxicating, there can't be anything better. I'm not sure whether it's a good thing or a bad thing that Noah and I have the same tastes in that regard. It could lead to some unfortunate situations very easily.

"So, I guess we should start with the basics. There are four different ranges in Jeet Kune Do, kicking, punching, trapping, and grappling. Kicking is usually the one people are most familiar with. Why don't we start there?"

"Okay. Just tell me what to do," I say.

"Start with your feet apart and your hands up in front of you in a loose fist." Noah pauses to see if I'm in the right position, frowns, and steps closer to me. His right foot taps against my left. "Open up a little further. You need a solid base or you'll fall over when you kick."

I reposition my foot and ask, "Like that?"

He nods. Settling into the same stance, Noah demonstrates the most basic kicks for me. I tried to talk my grandma into letting me learn cardio kickboxing once. She refused, of course, but I had spent a little time learning about it before asking, so the kicks Noah shows me are somewhat familiar. They remind me of something else as well. I mimic his movements perfectly. A low buzz of anticipation shoots through my veins.

"Great. You wanna try some harder ones?" he asks. I

nod my head eagerly. "Okay, this is called a heel hook kick. Watch me, and then give it a try."

I watch with rapt attention as his leg snaps out sideways to full extension, then half a second later his knee bends and he pulls his heel back to where I expect his imaginary opponent's face would be. I can picture a person's head cracking against the heel, see it whip around and leave them lying on the floor unconscious. My mouth splits into a grin. That's my kind of kick. Noah nods for me to give it a try, then blinks in surprise when I execute it with precision.

"Huh," he says, "are you sure you haven't tried this before?"

"It's not that different from ballet, actually, just faster."

He looks at me doubtfully. "Really?"

I nod. "Watch."

Starting in third position, I sweep my leg out to the side, extending it completely before pulling it behind me in attitude position and continuing the motion into a turn on pointe. My leg comes down lightly to rest back in third position. "See?" I say.

Noah grins. "That's cool. You're going to pick this up faster than I thought. Come on, let's keep going."

I'm more than happy to agree with him by this point. We work through the punching and trapping pretty quickly. Not grinning like an idiot while I hit the mitts Noah holds out for me is more challenging than figuring out any of the punches. I'm not actually hurting anyone, but there is something primal and fulfilling about slamming your fist into something. Maybe it's the knowledge that I *could* hurt someone, maybe it's the energy released every time I throw a punch. I don't know, but I absolutely love it! Even the trapping is fun. When we get up to the grappling range, Noah hesitates, frowning and running his hands through his hair.

"What's wrong?" I ask.

He blushes. "I've, uh, never practiced grappling with a girl before. They have their own division, for good reason. There's a lot of contact in this part."

"Oh."

That's all I can say, because the feel of my own cheeks turning red distracts me too much to say anything else. In my head, I'm saying, contact? What's wrong with that? I thought Noah was attractive the first time I saw him in class. Seeing him sweaty enough that his snug t-shirt is showing off his muscles in the nicest way possible, well, it definitely isn't discouraging. But in the deepest part of my heart, I balk at the idea. There's only one person I want to find myself with in that kind of situation.

Instantly, I shut down ideas like that. Situations like that can't happen with Ketchup, I remind myself.

Despite my shame, I can't completely put off thinking about grappling. Maybe it's just the endorphins running through my body after our workout, but I find that I'm not wholly opposed to the idea of Noah's hands on me. As my mind starts to run away with itself, I remember Noah is staring at me and my blush goes scarlet. I hope as hard as I can that Noah doesn't notice, but when he laughs and drops his hands to his sides, I know I'm out of luck.

"You know, it's not that big of a deal to skip it," Noah

says. "If you wanted to keep learning you'd want to know, but it's not like we're going to be getting that into it for our project anyway. There won't be any mats, and I'd like to avoid cracking my head against the tile if I can help it."

I breathe a sigh of relief. "Yeah, that'd probably be good. I'm pretty sure Mr. Littleton expects a blood free scene."

"No kidding." Composed again, Noah gestures at the mat between us. "Do you want to try and put what you learned into use? It probably doesn't seem like very many skills, but we could definitely spar with what you know."

"No," I say quickly. Noah looks surprised, but I shake my head fiercely. I had a blast training with him today. It was so much more fun than I expected, but I'm not stupid. My kind of fun turns into violent chaos way too easily. "I'm not ready for that. I need more time to practice before I actually try to spar with anyone. Way more practice."

Noah doesn't seem to agree, but his confusion about my reluctance quickly morphs into a smile. "So, does that mean you'll come back and practice with me again?"

"Yeah," I say out loud while my brain screams no.

Noah's grin widens. "Great. I was hoping you'd like Jeet Kune Do."

"I loved it. Thanks for teaching me, Noah."

"No problem," he says. "We can come back next weekend, if you want."

I'm about to accept his invitation when I remember that I already have plans. "I'll have to let you know about next weekend later."

"Oh, if you're busy, that's okay." He keeps his smile and

casual stance, but I can hear the disappointment in his voice. The silly, girly side of me smiles at the idea that Noah really is interested in seeing me again. The part of me that still has a functioning brain hurries to reassure him.

"Zander has a football game next Friday night, first game of the season. Saturday I have a dance competition. The weekend after that would be fine, though," I say. I pause and think for a moment. "Maybe we could get together before the game on Friday, and then you could come watch the game with me and Laney."

His expression brightens for a moment before turning cautious again. "I'm not much of a football fan."

Now it's my turn to be disappointed. "Oh, okay then. It was just an idea."

I turn away and sit down on the edge of the mat so I can put my tennis shoes back on. The fear returns that Noah is only here to get a good grade on this project. It shouldn't be a big deal. I'm used to people rejecting me in one way or another. This is by far the slightest, but I thought he'd want to come to hang out with me. Maybe I was wrong. The sudden tightness in my chest surprises me with its strength. Without warning, I'm struggling to hold back tears, telling myself I'm being an idiot at the same time.

Noah's hand on my shoulder startles me enough to put any tears on hold. "Hey," he says, "listen, it's not really about football as much as Zander. No offense, but he freaks me out. I don't know what was going on with him the other night, but he scared my little sister half to death. I've seen overprotective before, but Zander..."

"That had nothing to do with you, Noah," I try to explain. "He was reacting to Ivy, not you. I don't think he even saw you there."

"What does he have against Ivy?"

"Nothing! I mean…they've got issues. They're a mess, but it has nothing to do with you."

Noah shakes his head and sits down next to me, somehow managing it without taking his hand off my shoulder. It's the smoothest way I've ever seen a guy sneak his arm around a girl, but I find I don't mind as much as I should. I do, however, resist leaning into him. Well, until he tightens his grip on me and pulls me closer.

"Look, Van, I don't want to sound like a coward, but your brother is intense."

His head turns enough to catch my gaze. He asked if Zander was home when he called earlier, but I didn't think much of it. Would he have backed out of picking me up if he had been home? Is that cowardly? I know how dangerous Zander is, so it's hard to blame Noah. The concern that seems to be directed more at me, than himself makes it even harder.

"I want to keep hanging out with you," Noah says, "but if Zander has a problem with that, I'd rather not find out right away. You know what I mean?"

Defense for my brother springs to my lips. My mind works a little faster, and I pause. Zander didn't actually meet Noah at the studio. With Ivy there, it would have been impossible for him to notice anyone else. It would be just my luck to find out Zander's hunger has a Noah-sized craving. It's happened before. My heart aches thinking about it, but Noah's hand rubbing up and down my arm draws my attention back to him.

"Okay," I say quietly, "I get what you're saying."

It won't be like I'm lying to Zander about Noah. He already knows about him. I'll just avoid the two of them ever meeting until I can be sure Zander won't kill him.

"Zander always goes back to the locker room to clean up after the game before coming to find me. I understand if you don't want to be there when he comes out, but that doesn't mean you can't watch the game with me."

Noah sighs and takes his arm from around my shoulder so he can drop his head in his hands. "Maybe I shouldn't have even said anything. I feel stupid for bringing it up."

"No, it's okay," I say. "You're probably right. It might be better if you didn't meet Zander yet."

Taking his head out of his hands, Noah looks over at me. I saw the hint of worry for me in his eyes before. Now it's too blatant to miss. "Van, how bad is Zander's temper? Has he ever..."

"Noah, please. Zander would never hurt me. You're taking his reaction to Ivy completely out of context," I lie. "Ask anyone at school. Zander is the nicest guy you'll ever meet."

"Then why did you agree it would be best not to meet him yet?" Noah asks.

I scramble to come up with a believable reason, and surprise myself by finding the truth. "Zander and I, we're really all each other's got anymore. We live with our grandma, but the two of us have been through a lot together. We're pretty protective of each other. Zander especially."

"So, I do need to be careful of him," Noah says.

Yes, definitely, I think, but I say, "No, of course not. It's just that Zander will get in the way trying to make sure *you're* not going to hurt *me*. Zander's a great guy, but he has scared off some of my friends before."

"That's exactly what I'd like to avoid," Noah says. His arm comes back around my shoulder as he smiles.

I admit I like the feel of his arm around me—not nearly as much as someone else's—but I still wonder about one thing. "So, you're scared off pretty easily, are you?"

The sound of Noah's rich laugh instantly warms me and makes me feel a little silly for even asking. "Scared off? Not exactly. I'm just realistic. Your brother is huge. I have to tip toe to make five foot ten. If Zander doesn't want me around you, I have the feeling there won't be much I can do about it, no matter how much I might want to."

A feeling I haven't felt in a very long time creeps down every inch of my spine. Noah understands seeing me could be dangerous. Sure, he has no idea just how dangerous, but a pounding from my brother is still a pretty terrifying option. He knows there's a risk to being around me, but apparently he thinks I'm worth it. I haven't been worth the risk to a guy in… well, since what feels like forever ago.

Before I can get too excited about this possible relationship, something tugs at my heart, reminding me that isn't true. There's one person I've always been worth the risk to. Ketchup won't ever give up on me, no matter how hard or how often I push him away. Suddenly, Noah's arm around my shoulder makes me squirm.

"So, game next weekend then?" Noah asks.

Trying very hard to push away thoughts of Ketchup and what can never be, I say, "And Jeet Kune Do the weekend after."

"Sounds like a plan." Noah stands up and offers me his hand. I take it and let him pull me back to my feet. We're heading out of the gym, almost to his car, when I remember one more thing I need to warn him about.

"Hey, Noah," I say, stopping him from walking away after he opens my door, "could you do me a favor and not mention us practicing together to anyone. My grandma would kill me if she found out."

"Not a fan of martial arts, huh?"

"More like not a fan of anything even remotely violent," I correct.

Noah looks mildly surprised, but says, "No problem. My mom wasn't real excited about it either, although it's a great way to burn off extra aggression. Maybe if Zander gave it a try he'd have an easier time dealing with Ivy."

Walking to his door, Noah doesn't seem to expect me to respond to his comment, so I don't. I use the few seconds of alone time to wonder. All our lives we've been drilled to stay away from any semblance of combat, but what if Noah's right? I felt great practicing with him today. What if controlling our hunger can't be done by starving it? That certainly didn't work for Oscar. What if the only way to beat our hunger is to give it what it wants, but in a controlled, structured way?

Zander swears that's what he's doing when he plays football. I feel the same when I sneak off to the boxing gym. But those are both sports. I've never considered that punching a bag and knocking down other players could be taken a step further without backfiring. If it works with sports, why wouldn't it work with combat? Obviously, there's more potential for things to go badly, but it could work. I think. My thoughts turn even more contemplative as I think about how things might have turned out if our hunger had been handled differently from the beginning.

If Oscar had been given the chance to battle, would he have made the same choices? If Zander tries, will it keep him from killing Ivy? Will it help me survive turning sixteen? The possibilities give me hope, but it's tempered by fear. What if we try, and find out we can't stop once we start? What scares me the most is that after the taste of battle Noah gave me today, I don't care whether this is a path toward finally gaining control, or losing it completely. The experience was too delicious to give up. I'll be back to fight again, and all I can do is hope it won't end with Noah's blood on my hands.

11

QUICKLY LOSING

*M*y mountain bike falls against the side of the house with a clatter. I should probably lock it up, but I'm too tired to care. Covered in sweat and a shade darker from spending the day out in the sun has left me thirsty, exhausted, and hopeful. The hopeful part of me stays buried deep inside as I walk into the house. Books scattered all over the living room only seems unusual when I realize Van isn't here with them. I call out for her, and no one answers, not even my grandma. Curious, I cross the living room to the kitchen and find it empty as well. I'm about to check upstairs when I see a note on the counter.

Grandma,

Went to the gym with Noah, my new English partner. Be back in a couple hours. Call my cell if you need me.

Love ya,

Van

She went to the gym with Noah? And didn't even text me to let me know where she was going? What on earth does working out have to do with an English project, anyway? Maybe she suggested a work out before they got started on their project to keep her hunger at bay? That's why I spent the morning mountain biking. It makes sense, but Van assured me she didn't react to this Noah guy at all. Either she lied to me, or something else is going on. I don't particularly like either option.

I almost whip my phone out right then and call her. The fact that she's at the gym and probably doesn't have her phone on her while she's working out doesn't stop me as much as the fight I'm sure will break out when I confront her. We both have hunger issues, but Van also has a hot temper that has nothing to do with her hunger. If I attack her for sneaking off with Noah and possibly lying to me about him, she'll get angry, and whether her hunger wants Noah or not, her anger will feed it until it finds someone she wants and pushes her to act. Our argument will have to wait until the risk of Van hurting someone is at a minimum.

Staring at the phone in my hand does remind me of what I was planning on doing before I saw the note. I scan through my contacts and tap on Laney's dopey grin. The irony of the mental rant I just gave my sister doesn't escape me.

"Zander?" Laney asks when she answers her phone.

"Hey. Do you have Ivy's number?" It's blunt and not very polite, but I have no intention of getting dragged into a long, drawn out conversation with Laney. Of all Van's friends, I enjoy talking to Laney the least. Even the twins that dress like three-year-olds are better than Laney. She never shuts up.

"Ivy's number? Sure. What do you want it for?" she asks

coyly.

Just shoot me now. I roll my eyes. "She offered to help me with my math."

"And you're taking her up on her offer?"

"Obviously. What's her number?"

"Hmm, are you sure that's the only reason you want her number? You and Ivy seem to be running into each other quite a bit lately. I know you've sworn off girls since Lisa, but I'm beginning to wonder. Is there something secret going on between you two?"

I don't think Ivy had any idea how much she was asking of me when she didn't give me her number. I'm tempted, very tempted to hang up and forget the whole thing. Yeah, right. I have to see Ivy again. "Laney," I say patiently, "if there was something going on between me and Ivy, don't you think I'd already have her number?"

"This could all be an elaborate attempt to cover up what's really going on." Her conspiratorial tone annoys me. Not only is she partially right, which stings, but her mention of deception pulls my thoughts back to Van's note and my irritation doubles.

"Just give me her number, Laney."

Laney has never shown any fear around me at all—I don't think she's smart enough for that—but the edge to my voice spurs her to do as I say. "Fine, fine. You don't have to be a jerk about it."

I shake my head at her. Jerk? That was pretty mild, if you ask me. She's the one making this difficult. A few seconds later, I have Ivy's number, and all but hang up on Laney when she tries to ask me more about what Ivy and I are going to be studying.

I have everything I need now, her number, physical exhaustion to keep my hunger in check, and a good reason for calling her. Calling her should be easy. Instead of dialing her number, I set the phone down and head upstairs for a shower. I take my time washing and rinsing away the dirt and sweat from this morning. When the sheeting water does nothing to calm my anxiety, I finish up and move on to getting dressed. It doesn't take long enough. Too quickly, I'm back in the kitchen staring at my phone.

My fingers move independent of my brain and start dialing Ivy's number. I'm surprised when she picks up on the first ring.

"Well, that took you longer than I expected," she says.

"What?"

"I was expecting your call half an hour ago."

"You knew I was going to call?" I ask.

Ivy laughs, and I relish the sound despite my confusion. "Laney called the second after you hung up on her," she says.

"I didn't really hang up on her. I was just done talking."

"You hung up when she was in the middle of a sentence."

"When is Laney not in the middle of a sentence?" I grumble.

Ivy chuckles and says, "That's true. She does talk a lot."

"A lot is an understatement."

When Ivy laughs again, it strikes me that I'm not reacting to her at all. Hearing her voice certainly awakens something in me, but it isn't my hunger. For once, it's easy and fun to talk to Ivy. That realization makes me happier than I've been since meeting her.

"So," Ivy says, "I'm guessing you subjected yourself to calling Laney to get my number for a particular reason. Did you want help with your math, or was there something else?"

I can't answer right away. Trying to figure out whether she actually sounds hopeful that I'm not just calling about math homework takes all my mental power. Tired as I am, I can't figure it out.

"Yeah, I need help with my calc again."

"Oh." It's only one word, but this time I'm sure I can hear her disappointment. An eager to please side of me I haven't seen in a while suddenly rears to life.

"I was thinking that since it's kind of late in the afternoon we could get together to study, and then maybe after that we could get something to eat. As a thanks for helping me." I grimace at my last line. I wanted to make sure she knew I wasn't just calling for school, and then I ruined my invitation by making it sound like I was only offering to be polite. As I'm berating myself, I realize Ivy hasn't said anything.

"Uh, Ivy?" I ask.

She's silent for a few more seconds before speaking. "If I help you with your homework, I want something in return."

Her demand catches me off guard, but I manage to respond. "Dinner isn't good enough?"

"Dinner's good," Ivy says, "but I want one other thing. I want to ask you a question, one you have to answer."

Dread spreads through me like a disease. She has to have dozens of questions, none of which I can answer. She's been nothing but pleasant to me despite the way I've treated her. I should have seen this coming. Of course she was just biding her time to figure out what is behind my bizarre behavior. Ivy offered up the exchange lightly, but I know she means it. If I don't answer a question, she won't meet me today. She'll be safer if I refuse.

That thought makes me cringe. I'm putting her in so much danger just to satisfy my selfish desires. Ivy has yet to say she knows how dangerous I am, but I've given her enough evidence that it has to be a foregone conclusion by now. She knows she's taking a big risk and all she wants in return is one answer. That's a fair trade, isn't it?

"One question?" I finally ask.

Ivy hesitates. "Just one for now. One study date, one answer."

Date, I like the sound of that word no matter how much I shouldn't. I'm about to agree to her conditions when I stop to think about the possible ramifications. What if she asks me how I was able to bruise her arm just by grabbing it?

"There are some questions I can't answer, Ivy."

"Okay," she says after a moment, "I'll let you choose which of my questions you want to answer. How does that sound?"

Hoping at least one of her questions will be as harmless as what my favorite color is, I say, "Deal."

"Great," Ivy says happily. "When and where should we meet?"

I hadn't actually thought that far ahead. I scramble to come up with an option that is safe enough. "Do you know the park a couple blocks down from the high school?"

"Sure, I pass it on my way to school every day."

"Let's meet there. There won't be many nice days like this left soon." Plus, there will be a lot of people there with us. It's out in the open, which helps, and I can leave easily if I need to.

"The park sounds good. What time?"

"How soon can you get there?" I ask without thinking.

I expect her to laugh or tease me, but instead she says, "Fifteen minutes."

I breathe a sigh of relief. "See you in fifteen minutes, then."

"See you soon."

Ivy sounds pleased as she says goodbye. I stuff my cell phone back in my pocket, pleased as well. It's a feeling that fades quickly, though. On the phone, it was easy to talk to Ivy and agree to her strange demands. Face to face, it won't be like that. I'll be fighting myself every minute. It will be torture, and I just agreed to it willingly. Why couldn't I have just settled for talking to her on the phone?

Shaking my head, I gather up my books and head out to my truck. I know I'm about to walk into a potential disaster. Knowing doesn't stop me from being excited. The whole way to the park, I fight the kind of stupid grin I despise seeing on Laney every time she starts blathering on about one thing or another. I try to talk myself out of doing this. I remind myself what could happen over and over again, but every time I almost turn around, the sound of Ivy's voice filters back into my mind. Her laugh is worse than my hunger. I think I would do anything to hear it again.

When I reach the park, I scan the parking lot for Ivy's car. This isn't the only parking lot for the large park, but this is the one closest to her house. I don't see her car anywhere, so I get out and wait on a bench where I'll be able to see her pull in. I don't have to wait long. Less than five minutes later, I spot her green sedan pulling into the lot. I wait impatiently for her to park and make her way over to me. Equal parts bliss and agony sweep through me at the sight of her. Ivy smiles as she draws near, but pulls up short of actually reaching me.

"You must live close by," Ivy says, "I thought I was going to beat you here."

"I'm only about a mile away." I stand up and tighten my hand on my backpack strap when she takes a step toward me. This was such a bad idea.

"So, where do you want to sit?" Ivy asks.

I glance around the park, looking for somewhere with people, lots of people. Crowds always pose the danger of containing someone my hunger will want, but I feel confident that no one will be as big of a lure as Ivy. I spot a cluster of benches near the pavilion in the center of the park. I gesture toward it, making Ivy raise an eyebrow at me.

"Are you sure the noise won't bother you?" she asks, looking at the band performing in the pavilion.

"No, it'll be fine. I usually listen to music when I do homework anyway."

Ivy shrugs and turns toward the sultry salsa beat. She isn't actually dancing, but I swear her hips roll in time with the music. She's a good ten feet away from me when she turns back to find me staring at her. A smirk that hints she knows exactly what I was staring at lights her features. A blush threatens to spread over mine, but I force it away. Doing my best to ignore my embarrassment, I hurry to catch up with her. My hunger growls and roils inside of me, worsening with each step, but as I get closer to her I can smell her perfume and see the details of her face more clearly. Opposite desires slam into each other and keep them in a precarious balance.

The picnic tables appear in front of us just in time. I swerve to the opposite side and sit down. Ivy doesn't say anything about my choice of seating, sitting down across from me with a neutral expression. It isn't nearly far enough away, but I focus on my feelings for her and hope they prove stronger than my hunger. "Okay," she says, "what are you having trouble with?"

That's a pretty long list. Ivy only wants to know about the math, though. Opening my book and turning it so we can both see, I point at one of the problems I got stuck on last night. "I'm not sure what I did wrong here. I thought I followed all the steps, but I keep messing up."

Ivy's finger touches down next to the problem, and I yank my finger back quickly. I can see the muscles in her arm tense momentarily before relaxing. "Show me what you did, and I'll tell you where you went wrong."

"Alright." I grab my notebook out of my bag and hand it over to her. She spends a few minutes going over my work before spinning the notebook back around so I can see. Going through the problem, she shows me what I did, and what I should have done. I try really hard to pay attention to everything she says. If her finger wasn't so distracting, it would be a lot easier. Thoughts about math keep getting interrupted by thoughts of how easy it would be to crush the delicate bone in her pointer finger, or my mind wondering how it would feel to have that same finger run over my skin.

"This is why you're having such a hard time with math," Ivy says, her voice suddenly much too close to me.

My eyes flit up and widen when they come right up to hers, less than a foot away. She's leaning forward over the table with one hand raised as if she was trying to get my attention. "What?" I ask as I lean back from her.

"You're not paying any attention to what I'm saying. You're never going to figure it out if you don't listen." There is an odd mix of annoyance and amusement in her expression. It scrunches her nose and makes her look even more irresistible than usual. Only knowing that if I actually touched her it wouldn't be the soft caress I want it to be keeps me from reaching out to her.

"Sorry, I got distracted."

Her lips twist up into a teasing smile. "By what?"

"By..." I can't think of anything to say that won't embarrass me. Opting for a diversion, I say, "Maybe if you explain it again, I'll understand."

The way Ivy's eyes narrow slightly tells me she knows I'm dodging her question, but the smile still lingering on her lips softens the accusation. She shakes her head and looks back down at the book for a moment before looking back up at me. "Okay, I'll try again, but..."

Rather than finishing her sentence, she stands up

and walks around the table. Even though I want more than anything to be near her, I panic. Ivy stops a few feet away from me.

"Do you mind?" she asks. "I flunked reading upside down in grade school."

Yes, I mind. Go back to your own side! Whatever you do, don't sit down next to me. "Sure, go ahead," I hear myself say.

Ivy smiles and starts to sit down. It isn't until she is right next to me that I see how quickly she's breathing, how her fingers are shaking. No part of her is touching me, but the pure delicacy that she is spreads out around her and sinks into my pores. My hands ball into fists as I curse my disobedient mouth for telling her she could sit down. Without looking at me, Ivy starts explaining the problem again. I focus every spec of my mental power on her words. I'm so focused on figuring out the steps that there is very little room for anything else. Slowly, torturously, I tamp my hunger down enough that I can somewhat focus on the numbers in front of me.

"Now take the reciprocal, and…" Ivy says a long while later.

I look at the fraction and wait for the rest of her instruction. Several seconds of silence pass before I risk looking over at her. It makes me smile to see her head bobbing lightly and her fingers tapping a slow beat on the tabletop. Her lips are moving ever so slightly, mouthing the lyrics of the song playing in the background.

"Now who's the one getting distracted?"

Ivy jumps in surprise. When she looks over at me, she

laughs easily. "Sorry. I love this song."

I look over my shoulder at the trio on stage. Young, dressed in casual jeans and t-shirts, with instruments that look far from new, they belt out the lyrics with passion. "You know this group?"

"No, but I know the song. It's by one of my favorite bands."

Listening, I realize this song is nothing like the energetic music that was playing when we first got here. I'm not sure if this band has rather eclectic tastes, or I didn't notice the bands switching. The slow beat flows through the air, its mellow lyrics settling around me. I feel some of the tension from holding back my hunger dissipate from my shoulders. It's not much, but it helps.

"You like it?" Ivy asks.

I nod, too wrapped up in the song to really answer.

"Wanna take a break?" she asks.

I nod again and say, "A break sounds good."

Ivy stands up first and waits for me to join her. We leave the table and calculus behind and walk over to the pavilion. There isn't a huge crowd, but there are at least thirty people seated randomly around the grass in front of the band. As I edge closer, I keep my senses keen for anyone who will spike my hunger. There is a faint pull from one of the distant listeners, but they aren't close enough to be a real problem.

Needing the buffer of warm bodies around me, I wander into the center of the group and sit down. Ivy sits down next to me, closer than she was at the table. I want to stay near her, but I scurry to the side, needing relief from her presence more than anything else.

A few feet apart, her nearness is dulled enough by the others that it doesn't show in my body language, but not enough that I'm not still fighting off urges to see her writhing in pain. My fingers dig into the soft grass in an effort to keep them from doing something they shouldn't. I look over at Ivy to gauge her reaction to me moving away. She's already looking at me, smiling softly. Her gaze only stays for a few seconds before turning back to the band. The way her smile electrifies my skin lasts a lot longer.

We listen to song after song, not touching, not speaking. A few are more upbeat than the first, but most carry the soothing tempo that tone down my hunger. I quickly decide that I need very much to download this band's albums and have them with me as often as possible. I'm wondering if I can download it on my phone before I have to make good on my promise of dinner when I feel Ivy move.

It isn't just her body moving closer, but her energy. Like the taste of her on my tongue, I swear I can feel the energy of her life force when she gets near me. It is a strange experience, one I've never had before. Suddenly, her energy tilts toward me as Ivy's head touches lightly against my shoulder. It comes on too quickly for me to jump out of the way. It seeps into me, stealing my breath, and latching onto my hunger more intensely than ever before.

My hunger drinks her in and begs for more as my head is furiously screaming at me to get away from her. I can't respond to either for a moment. I am paralyzed by having so much of her at once. My fingers pull free of the grass, fully intent on finding her body and causing the most exquisite damage possible.

My hand brushes against her shoulder as it seeks out her neck. My vision dims as my hunger begins to take over. A few more inches, and her breath will be cut off. The decent into suffocation will inspire fear, fear that will escalate and spike as the pain begins. My breathing becomes fast and heavy in anticipation.

The sharp piercing bark of a loose dog breaks through my focus only a brief second before it barrels right across mine and Ivy's legs, its tail slapping me in the face as it passes. As if waking up from a nightmare, I suck in a panicked breath and scramble away from Ivy. My chest constricts at the thought of what I almost did. My whole body is quivering as I stare back at her.

The sadness and frustration in her eyes eats at me, but there is no way I can get that close to her again. Forcing myself to pretend my calm has returned, I settle back on the grass several feet away from her and turn my full attention back to the band. Seconds, minutes pass without a word spoken between us.

Slowly, my hunger fades back to a manageable level. I think my fear of hurting her is mainly responsible for that, because my desire to hurt her hasn't changed in the least. I don't know how long it takes before I feel in control enough to partially relax. That's when my promise to answer a question creeps back into my mind. As we sit on the grass and listen to a cover band play Ivy's favorite songs, fear settles into my mind. I have no idea what she will ask me. What I do know, though, is that I am quickly losing my will to resist giving her any answer she wants.

12

SECOND CLASS DREAM

"o, dinner?" I say as we approach our cars, several paces away from each other after learning my lesson earlier.

"Dinner sounds great. Where do you want to go?" Ivy leans against her car, and the slowly fading sunlight falls over her face and shoulders. The pink and orange of a desert sunset warms her skin tone, making her look flushed and happy despite her earlier frustration.

"How about the Artichoke Café?" It's a nice restaurant, and a busy one, thankfully. I don't do secluded booths that are dim and romantic. Actually, I don't usually do restaurants at all because it's too risky.

"Where is that?" Ivy asks. "I don't think I've ever heard of it before."

"It's in Downtown, on Central."

Ivy frowns and looks down at her keys. "Do you want to just ride over together? I'm not very familiar with Albuquerque yet and I get lost easily, especially Downtown with all the one-way streets."

If she sits next to me in the truck, there will be at least two or three feet between us. It's a big truck. I'll keep both hands on the wheel to make sure there's no chance I'll accidentally touch her. I'm getting even more tired as the day goes on, thanks to this morning. We'll be in an enclosed space together, but it's still warm enough that I can turn on the air conditioner to keep her scent from filling up the cab too much. The safer suggestion that she just follow me is on my lips, but her vulnerability puts me over the edge.

"Yeah, sure. We can ride together. I'll bring you back here to get your car after."

"Thanks," Ivy says with relief.

I open the door for her when we reach the truck, but resist helping her step up to the seat, and keep my distance. When I close the door on her, I take several long deep breaths as I walk around to my side. I have to hold my breath until I turn the truck on and cool air blasts out of the vents.

As we drive, I try to fill in the huge gaps of things I don't know about Ivy. Talking helps distract me a little. I ask her about living in California, moving to New Mexico, and even why they moved. For some reason Van had thought it very suspicious that Ivy's family moved in the middle of the semester rather than during summer. Turns out, Ivy's dad was slotted to take over the New Mexico office of the financial firm he works for. The guy he was replacing didn't retire until two weeks ago. I shake my head at Van's ridiculous obsession when I hear that.

We walk into the restaurant talking about what Ivy

misses about her old home. Pausing long enough to tell the hostess we want a table rather than a booth, Ivy tells me about how she was learning to surf before she moved as we walk through the restaurant.

We are led to a two person table in the center of the dining room. I smile at the hostess's choice. It's perfect. There's no chance of Ivy sitting next to me, and we're surrounded by hungry patrons, none of which immediately sets off my hunger. I take my seat, gauging the level of hunger being this close inspires. My shoulders relax when I realize it is manageable enough to bear for a while.

"So, how did Van's study date with Noah go?" Ivy asks.

Shaking my head, I say, "Wouldn't know. She didn't even tell me she was going out with him. There was a note on the kitchen table when I got home."

"A note? Who leaves notes anymore? Why didn't she just text you?"

"I don't think she wanted me to know. The note was for my grandma." Thinking about the note irritates me all over again. I can't keep it out of my voice when I speak again. "They weren't even studying. They went to the gym, for some reason."

"Oh," Ivy says, "they *were* studying. They had to go to the gym to get started on their project."

"Why? What was their topic?"

"They have to do a battle scene. Noah does some kind of martial arts. I can't remember which one, but he was going to teach some to Van so they could decide whether they wanted to use it in their scene." Ivy looks pleased to have been able to defend Van, until the heat of my emotions leaks into my expression. Her eyebrows rise in surprise. "Zander, what's wrong?"

"Van is doing martial arts with Noah?" I ask through my teeth.

Ivy shrinks back against her chair. "Um, yeah. Is that bad?"

"It..." I close my eyes and suppress my anger and fear as much as possible. "It could be."

What on earth was Van thinking? Not only are we both forbidden from trying any kind of combat training, but all it's going to do is make her hunger worse! One minute she's spouting off about Ivy being some kind of threat, the next she's running off and putting herself in the worst possible situation.

I push back my chair and storm away from the table, pulling out my cell phone as I go. I have no idea what time she left with Noah. All I know is that she was gone when I got home around three o'clock. Knowing this may get heated, I push through the doors of the restaurant and walk outside. The only hope I have as I dial Van is that if something bad had already happened, my grandma would have called me. The ringing of the phone cuts off sharply, followed by the sound of Van's guilty voice.

"Hey, Zander," she says slowly. "What's going on?"

"Tell me nothing happened to Noah! Tell me right now, Van, that you didn't just ruin everything for us!"

"What are you talking about?"

"Martial arts?" I snap. "Are you freaking kidding me?

You know how dangerous that is! What the hell were you thinking?"

"How do you know what I did today?" Van asks quietly.

I falter for a moment before continuing my tirade. "Who cares? What happened today? Is Noah okay? What exactly did you two do this afternoon?"

"Nothing happened!"

"Don't lie to me, Van!" I warn.

Her growl races through the phone and snaps at me viciously. "I'm not lying. Nothing happened!"

"I don't believe that. He was teaching you to fight and nothing happened? You really expect me to believe that?" How could she have been so stupid? That was way too big of a risk to take!

"You know, you don't know everything, Zander," Van argues. "You don't know what I'm capable of, either! You think your way is the only way. You laugh at me and think I'm an idiot for having friends and trying to live a normal life. You think I'll hurt them because I won't be able to control myself. You don't know anything about me if you think I'd ever hurt one of my friends!"

A sob breaks through her yelling. "I'm stronger than you think, Zander, and I'm not stupid. I didn't let things with Noah get out of hand. I paced myself. I was smart about what I let him teach me. Maybe you can't handle it, but I can have friends and this stupid curse at the same time. I've already given up one guy I love for you. Don't ask me to do it again."

She sniffs again, and I know she must be crying. "Please don't ask me to do that. I just want to be happy for once, Zander. Can't you understand that?"

I rub my hand over my face and sigh. Most of my anger fell away when I heard my baby sister sob the first time. Right now, all I feel is regret, regret for yelling at her, regret for stomping on her hopes and happiness so often.

"Yeah," I say softly, "I can understand that."

I do want Van to be happy. I've just always wanted her to be safe even more. Before today, I never saw the value of giving up safety for the warmth of friends and love. It was always a second-class dream. There's been so much more pain than anything else in my life lately. I guess I just forgot what it was like to care about someone and have them care in return. I wouldn't have traded my afternoon with Ivy for anything.

"Look, Van, I'm sorry I yelled at you. I knew you were hiding something when I saw the note in the kitchen. It's just that when I found out where you went today, I panicked."

"I…I wasn't really trying to lie about Noah, I was just afraid to tell you," Van admits.

The way my chest tightens really scares me. "Van, you can't be scared of me. You're the only one I can share any of this with. You can't be afraid of me like everyone else." I've lost so much already. I can't lose her, too.

"I won't do it again, okay? I'll tell you the next time I practice with Noah," Van offers.

"Do you really think it's a good idea to try it again? Even if things really went fine today, what if it gets more intense? What if you lose control at some point?"

"Zander, please trust me on this. I'm not going to hurt Noah. I'll stop before I ever get close. I promise," Van says.

Sighing, I lean against the building. "You can't promise that. There's not always a clear line, or a warning, especially this close to your birthday. Things could change for you at any moment and you might not be prepared."

"It was nothing like I thought it would be, Zander," Van says. "The fighting, I mean. It didn't make my hunger worse. It was like...like it fed it without me having to hurt anyone. It was great, actually. Maybe we could do it together sometime. At least we wouldn't be able to really hurt each other."

"I don't know, Van. It sounds risky. You know your hunger gets carried away. It would be safe enough with me, but you could never let go like that with anyone else."

"Sometimes you have to take risks, Zander," Van says quietly. "Just think about it, okay?"

"I'll..." A noise from behind me makes me turn. Ivy's concerned face is watching me from the corner of the building. I instantly feel like the biggest jerk in the world. I completely forgot about her. "Ivy, I'm sorry, I'll be right there."

"What?" Van screeches in my ear. "Did you just say Ivy? Where are you, Zander? Are you with her?"

Oh, crap. I really should have covered the speaker when I said that. I don't even bother saying anything. I just end the call and slip my phone back in my pocket. Half a second later, it's buzzing against my leg. I close my eyes, knowing exactly how much trouble I just got myself into. Here I was just yelling at my sister for being an idiot and putting herself at risk, and then she finds out I'm doing exactly the same thing, only worse.

"Zander, is everything okay?" Ivy asks. The softhearted

concern in her voice melts away the weight of the impending fight with Van. Being torn apart by my hot tempered little sister can wait.

"Yeah, everything's fine. Sorry for running out like that. I just needed to check on Van and make sure she was okay," I say.

Ivy frowns. "Why wouldn't she be? I mean, none of us really knows Noah very well, but I don't think he'd try to hurt her." Her heads tilts to the side as if she's trying very hard to find the answer in my expression.

"No, it wasn't that," I say honestly. "Van and I aren't allowed to do things like martial arts because of the violence. If my grandma finds out what Van was doing today, she'll kill her. And I would probably get into trouble, too, for letting her do it. We'd both be grounded for the rest of the year."

Disbelief settles on Ivy's face. "Seems a little harsh."

"Well, not if you knew my family. There are reasons my grandma is so strict."

"What reasons?" Ivy asks.

"Is that your one question?" I ask, hoping desperately it isn't.

"Will you answer it if it is?"

Without hesitation, I say, "No."

She looks equally disappointed and frustrated, but she merely shrugs. "Then that's not my question. Now, can we go back in and finish dinner?" she asks. She approaches me casually, her hand brushing lightly against my arm in an invitation to follow her.

I step back from her at the stab of hunger that rushes

through me. "Sure."

Ivy turns away quickly and saunters back to the front door of the restaurant, staying just out of reach as we walk back to our table. Our waitress gives us a strange look when we sit back down, but I barely notice her. My eyes are fastened on Ivy. She sits down like nothing happened and takes a bite of her risotto. At first I feel relieved that she's letting the matter drop. Our dinner continues quietly, though, and I begin to wonder if she's just biding her time until I drive her back to her car so she can bolt and get away from me. The idea of her wanting to run bothers me, a lot.

I try to get her talking again a few times, but her answers are always short and subdued. What Van said about needing to take a risk keeps running through my mind. She didn't know when she said it, but I did take a risk. I took a big risk calling Ivy. It was probably more stupid than anything Van did today. I'm scared to death that I'll regret ever meeting Ivy. That doesn't change the fact that I want to be with her. It's the first risk I've taken in a long time, and I can't stand the thought of walking away from her with nothing.

We pull into the parking lot where we left Ivy's car an hour later. I stop my truck right next to her car and turn to say something to Ivy. She hops out before I ever get the chance. Surprise at her quick exit keeps me from moving for a few precious seconds. I shake it off and jump out after her. She's already opened her door when I catch up.

"Ivy, wait," I say, grabbing her arm out of need to stop her. Even as tired as I am, my hunger flares to life and I yank my hand away as fast as I can. Ivy's eyes stare at my hand, turning glassy and bright in the moonlight. The hurt radiating off of her is painful. I want more than anything to wrap her in my arms and apologize for every stupid thing I've done to her, but I can't. I'll hurt her if I touch her.

"I need to get home, Zander. Thanks for dinner," she says quietly. Then she turns to get into her car. I panic and say the only thing I can think of to make her stay.

"You never asked me your question."

Ivy pauses. Her body turns slowly, but her eyes don't meet mine. My heart rate inches up every second she doesn't say anything. It feels like it's about to explode by the time she finally speaks. "I changed my mind about the rules. I get to ask one question and you have to answer it."

My shoulders sag in defeat. I fall against my truck and rub my hand over my face. I can't answer most of her questions. I can't let her go, either. It only takes me a moment to decide between Ivy and my secrets. "Okay, what's your question?"

Ivy's eyes come up and pierce mine. "Why are you doing this to me? Why are you toying with me, Zander? You pretend to be nice to me, but you clearly can't stand me. Why not leave me alone and stop all of this?"

The fact that her question isn't about the bruises or the fighting surprises me, but what really shocks me is what she said about me. I stare at her in disbelief and say, "You think I don't like you?"

Ivy looks at me like I'm crazy. "Uh, yeah. You act like you hate me practically every time you see me. The only time you were actually nice to me was when I offered to help you with your calculus. I never really expected you to call, and when you did, you made it pretty clear it was only so I could help you study. But then you're so nice to me out of nowhere, only to go right back to acting like I have some contagious disease. I don't know why you're doing this to either of us. Just leave me alone, okay?"

I can't seem to work out a response to her. My brain is still trying to catch up. Yes, I've been horrible to her, but that can't be all she sees when I look at her. My silence deepens Ivy's frown and she turns away from me. It only takes me half a step to reach her side. I hook my fingers on her shoulder and turn her gently so she is forced to look at me. My hand trembles from the brief contact.

"Ivy, I don't hate you. The reason I reacted to you like I did the first time we met…and the other times, was because I liked you too much and it scared me. It wasn't because I didn't want to be with you."

Ivy glares at me. "What? That doesn't even make sense."

"I know," I say. "It doesn't make sense, because you don't know me like everyone else around here knows me."

"What are you talking about?"

"I don't get close to people, ever. You've already heard rumors about how I don't date, and I'm basically a loner. Well, there are reasons for that, very good ones, and until I met you I had every intention of living up to my reputation," I say. "The second I saw you, I wanted you, and it scared me to death."

Ivy's expression goes from angry, to confused, to surprised and a little bit happy in a matter of seconds. "You…I thought…you really like me?"

"Yes," I say, sighing deeply.

"Then why do you pull away every time I get near you or touch you," she asks.

"Because I know that's what I should do," I say. Ivy frowns again, clearly not understanding. But who would? I do my best to make some kind of sense. "Ivy, I know I should stay away from you, because pulling you into my life will only get you hurt. I've lost too many people close to me to believe that won't happen. It's practically ingrained in me to push people away. Every time I touch you, I get scared that you'll be hurt, and I pull away."

Scrounging up every last spec of will power I have left, I lift my fingers and trail them down the curve of Ivy's face. My fingers quiver with the desire to do more. The hunger racing through me is unbearable. I pull my hand away before my willpower evaporates completely. "You have no idea how hard it is for me to touch you," I say honestly.

She thinks I mean that purely because of my past, and that's fine with me, but I know every second I'm in contact with Ivy brings her closer to her death. I take a big step back. Relief attempts to wash through me, but it vanishes when Ivy's hand presses lightly against my chest. I fall back against my truck, agony spreading out from her hand like wildfire.

"You're shaking," she says in surprise. She looks up at me with the shimmer of tears in her eyes as her hand drops away. "You really mean it, don't you?"

"Yes."

"You like me?"

There's so much more I feel for her than like, but I can't and won't admit to any more than that. "I like you very much, Ivy."

Suddenly, the only emotion left on Ivy's face is happiness. "I like you too, Zander."

I can't help it. I smile like every other stupid teenage boy in the world would. For a while, we just stand there smiling at each other like idiots and not caring in the least. Without meaning to, I'm the one to break it up when I yawn. My exhausting morning allowed me to spend time with Ivy, but it's starting to catch up with me now.

"I guess I should let you get home," Ivy says.

"I guess."

"Will I see you again?" Ivy asks.

I smile. "Definitely."

"When?" She grins shamelessly when I laugh at her directness.

"I'm not sure," I say. "I can't go out much during the week because of football..." And because as much as I want to be glued to her side, I know that would be suicide. "And I've got a game this Friday, and Saturdays are usually pretty busy with sports or chores."

"I'm not really allowed to go out on Sundays," Ivy says. "Family time, and all that."

"So, that pretty much leaves us with Friday night after the game?" Once a week, I can handle that. "We can always call each other, too. Plus, I really do need help with my math. If we can't get together, maybe you can as least walk me through it over the phone."

"Okay," Ivy says. "I'll plan on Friday night, and you could always meet me in my homeroom class if you need help, too."

"That's right, I'd almost forgotten about that. I'm sure I'll see you in there next week," I say, "but for now, I should get going before I fall asleep."

"You do look tired. I hope that isn't from being around me all night."

Actually.... "No, of course not. I went mountain biking this morning. That's all."

Ivy nods and says, "Oh, okay. Get some rest. Goodnight, Zander." She moves slowly, after what I said earlier, her hand reaching up to touch my cheek lightly. She gave me enough time to prepare myself, so I don't flinch away despite the torture she is causing me. She smiles up at me. "See you soon?"

"Very soon," I assure her.

I hold the door open as she gets into her car. Before I can close it, Ivy says, "You know, that wasn't the question I was planning on asking you."

"Next time," I say, refusing to let fear creep into my voice.

"Next time," she repeats. The firm edge to her voice assures me she won't forget.

Next time, I'm going to have to answer Ivy's most burning questions. I've lied to people my entire life. I should be able to lie to her too. I want to lie to her, but I know that once I'm faced with her curious, beautiful eyes, I won't be able to do anything but tell her the absolute truth about whatever she wants to know.

13

HONEST ANSWER

stomp away from Grandma's car, frustrated that Zander has managed to avoid me again. I stayed up as long as I could to wait for him Saturday night. When I nodded off around three in the morning, he still hadn't come home. I doubt he was with Ivy that late since her parents seem pretty strict. I have no idea where he went, though.

Sunday morning he disappeared again. When he came back, not only did he stick close to Grandma for the rest of the day, making it impossible for me to talk to him about Ivy without freaking Grandma out, but that taste was back. When I tried to confront him before school, I found his room empty, but that wasn't the scariest part. Hanging out of his laundry basket was the shirt he had on the day before.

I don't know what made me go over to look at it. I couldn't have seen the drops of blood on the sleeve from the doorway, but I certainly saw them when I picked up the shirt. Then this morning, Grandma announces that Zander had to be at school early so she would drive me. He won't be picking me up from school, either. I am just about ready to kill my brother.

Ketchup rushing over to me is a welcome relief to my horrible morning.

"You look pissed," he says. "What happened?"

The whole stream of insanity bouncing around inside of me almost spills out. Almost. I stop myself in time.

Ketchup looks at me expectantly. "Did something happen the other day? You never called, but…"

"No," I say quickly, not wanting to talk about Noah. "It's Zander, again. I need to figure out what he has in common with Vega."

"Did that weird taste thing happen again?"

I nod, my stomach churning as I remember the sickening taste. "There's got to be a reason for it."

"Have you tried asking Zander again, or your Grandma?"

The shake of my head makes Ketchup frown. "Why not?"

Reasons spiral through my mind. There are so many, but the one that is the most honest is what slips past my lips. "Because I'm afraid to."

Ketchup stops walking. Unwilling to be without him quite yet, I stop as well. My eyes stay down, but I don't need to look up to feel Ketchup move closer to me. His hand touches my cheek briefly, hesitates, then falls away.

"Van, I wish you would just talk to me. Tell me what this is really about." He sighs, knowing I can't tell him without me having to explain. He continues in my silence. "I don't know what they have in common. Vega is a gang member, something I seriously doubt straight-laced Zander would ever consider. There have been rumors about Vega and drugs, but again, Zander's not the type. Unless Zander is running around killing people, I can't imagine what they would have in common."

My entire body goes ice cold. I look up at Ketchup, my body trembling. "What did you just say?" I whisper.

"What? About the drugs?" Ketchup searches my expression as worry clouds his features. "You think Zander might be doping?"

"No, not that." My hands are shaking so badly and I can barely control them. "No, the last thing."

"You mean Zander killing people?" Ketchup says slowly. His arms wrap around me and pull me to his chest. I can feel his heart pounding. He sighs with so much regret it nearly suffocates me. "Van, I'm so sorry. I never should have said that. I didn't think."

I'm too scared to respond. Where has Zander been at night? What is he doing in those hours when the rest of the city is at home in their beds? Why was there blood on his shirt this morning? He's always been the one with the most control. I shake my head, unwilling to let myself believe that Zander could be doing something so terrible.

"Hey, hey," Ketchup says, his voice begging. He pushes my face up to meet his gaze. The agony in his eyes is nothing compared to what is racing through my veins right now.

"Van, please. I'm sorry."

I don't want to think about the possibility that Ketchup

is right, but in the darkest corners of my mind I know I can't brush this aside. If it's true, I have to know.

"Ketchup," I say haltingly, "I need to find more people that have killed someone."

For a moment, Ketchup just stares at me. It takes him a while to realize I'm not joking. When he does, his whole body tightens. "You really think…?" He rubs a hand across his face. "Okay, um, short of wandering around Westside and tasting people, how do we find people like that?"

"Prisons?" I offer.

Ketchup scowls at me. "I am not taking you to a prison." He's quiet for a moment before saying, "What about a senior center?"

"What?"

"Well, think about it. The center in my neighborhood where my grandpa used to hang out has a strong Veteran population. If they went to war, there's a good possibility that they were involved in the fighting. I mean, it's not the same as what Vega does, obviously, but maybe it could work." Ketchup shrugs. "And it's safer than a prison."

I don't know if it will work. What if the weird taste is only attached to violent crimes? I have no way of knowing. That may not even be what it means. It's a place to start, though. I don't know what else to try.

"Will you take me?" I ask quietly.

"Of course," Ketchup says. "I'll take you after school today."

I sit down at our usual lunch table, focused more on the impending trip to the senior center than anything else. Ketchup isn't here, yet, and I find myself missing him more than usual.

"Van!" Ivy pounces, startling me almost out of my chair. "Do you absolutely hate me? I'm so sorry I told Zander about training with Noah. I had no idea it was a big deal. I'm so sorry!"

Her wide-eyed, high speed apology slams into me. I stare at her in surprise. As I push my chair farther away from her in an effort to cool my hunger, a million thoughts run through my mind. I want to attack her for outing me, but I know that won't accomplish anything useful. It makes me want to scream, but I force myself to stuff my anger and hunger away as best I can.

"It's fine. Don't worry about it."

Ivy blinks at me in surprise. "Really? You're not mad? Zander looked furious when he stormed out of the restaurant."

Restaurant? I thought they were studying! I am seething at Zander, but I push it aside for now. It's a struggle to get my thoughts back on the conversation. "We talked and it's fine now."

"I felt awful when I heard him yelling at you."

The compassionate expression on Ivy's face seems somehow false. There's an edge of delight to her apology that freaks me out. I realize why when I think of the things Zander said to me that night.

"You heard him yelling at me?" I ask.

Ivy's eyes dart down to her feet once then back to me. "I didn't really hear what he said. I just heard his raised voice when I came out of the restaurant. He calmed down right after that."

I can't tell whether she's trying to make me feel better about overhearing us by saying she didn't catch our words, or deliberately hiding what she knows. Either way, she's lying. My irritation amps up my hunger and I have to move my chair further away from her.

She heard at least some of our argument. My brain calls up the fight, and I scramble to remember everything Zander said. He asked whether Noah was okay, not me, implying I was the dangerous one. Zander begged me not to be scared of him, and questioned whether I could really not lose control fighting with Noah. He also mentioned my birthday and how things might change for me. I'm sure she's smart enough to draw some damaging conclusions. I have a feeling math isn't the only thing Ivy's good at.

"I had no idea you'd get in trouble for training with Noah or I never would have mentioned it. I promise Van," Ivy says.

"I know. It's okay," I say tightly.

Ivy sighs and relaxes. "Zander said he was upset because of your grandma's rules, but he didn't explain why she's so strict. He just said there were reasons."

"Reasons," I sigh. My mind inevitably strays to that night.

There are the obvious hunger-related reasons my grandma doesn't want us fighting, but there are even deeper reasons as well. Losing someone you love changes you forever. It makes you go overboard, take things farther than you normally would.

"Yeah, there are definitely reasons. When your family experiences violence firsthand, you do everything you can to make sure you never see it again."

"Violence?" Ivy asks, quiet and intensely curious at the same time.

My mind snaps back to the present. Visions of blood and insanity vanish, leaving me staring at Ivy's eager eyes. I immediately shy away from her gaze. "Never mind," I say quickly.

"Wait, what happened? Why is your grandma so strict?"

"It's personal." I stab at my mushy mac and cheese and refuse to look up.

"I'm just trying to understand so I quit getting you in trouble," Ivy complains. "Just help me out, Van. Nobody else will."

Dropping my fork, my fingers clench the edges of my food tray. Cracks spread out from my fingertips. "What is that supposed to mean?" I say through my teeth.

"What?"

"What do you mean by nobody else will help you? Have you been snooping into my personal life?"

That last part came out a little loud. Heads turn in our direction, but look away as soon as they see me. Fine by me. The only person who doesn't react is Ivy. She faces me dead on with a patronizing expression.

"If you didn't act like everything about you was some

huge, monstrous secret, I wouldn't have to ask other people about you to figure out who I'm sitting next to at lunch," Ivy snaps.

We'll see how long she's sitting next to me after that! "If I want you to know something about me, I'll tell you. My other friends respect that. Why can't you?"

"Maybe it's because you haven't saved my life, yet," Ivy snaps. "The rest of them do whatever you say because of what you've done for them, but you can bet they all have the same questions I do."

"And what questions are those?" I ask. Let's get this all out in the open, if that's what she wants. What is she really after?

Ivy squares up her shoulders and juts her perfect little chin out at me. "Why is your brother in a psych ward?"

"He went crazy."

"Why can't you fight?"

"People we know died."

"I saw your hand get burned in Home Ec. How'd the burns disappear?"

"They didn't. I never got burned in the first place."

Ivy grits her teeth and fires again. "Why is Zander so strong?"

"He works out a lot."

"Why don't you like me?"

I lean toward Ivy, pushing my anger and hunger alike to their limit. "Because you have secrets, too."

Her eyes open wider in surprise, but I don't stay to bask in it. Without another word, she slides her tray down a few seats and stews in silence. Turning away from her, I search the cafeteria for my actual friends. Ketchup and the twins are thankfully on their way to the table, now.

I contemplate grabbing Ketchup and opting for sitting outside or in the halls, anywhere but here. Before I can gather up my tray, Noah slips into the chair across from me. I'm too surprised to say anything. I panic, knowing that Ketchup is on his way over. Hanging out with Noah is one thing, him sitting at our lunch table…with Ketchup, that's something else entirely. A hurried excuse that will get him out of here forms on my tongue, but not fast enough.

"Who are you?" a none-too-pleased voice says next to me. Unfortunately, it's not an unfamiliar voice. My stomach drops right along with my head. I am not going to make it through this day without losing my mind.

"I'm Noah." He extends his hand politely. Ketchup glares back at him.

"What are you doing at our table?"

"Uh, I needed to talk to Van. We're English partners."

"Does this look like English class?" Ketchup snarls.

"Ketchup, please," I beg.

Ketchup's eyes flare. "Please what?"

"He just wanted to talk for a minute."

The way his eyes pierce me is unnerving. "Talk? What happened? Why is he here? I would have thought you'd have told me if you saved…"

I cut him off before he can finish his sentence. "Nothing happened. Noah is my partner for the English project. He wanted to talk to me. That's it. Just let it go, okay?"

"That's it, huh? I don't believe you, Van. No one ever just…"

He stops himself this time, but the damage is already done. Abandoning Noah to the harsh absurdity of my table of friends, I stand up and make for the exit, racing to the outside before my tears can fall. I burst through the doors and round the corner. My body falls against the rough bricks of the building. Their prickly surface digs into my back and keeps me from sliding down.

I have maybe ten seconds of peace before I hear footsteps. Hope that it's Noah come to cheer me up is dashed when Ketchup comes around the corner. His tortured expression is a far cry from the hostility he was just shoving down Noah's throat. His mouth opens, but he can't seem to figure out what he wants to say.

"Nobody ever just wants to be my friend, right?" I ask. "That's what you were going to say, wasn't it?"

"Van, I didn't mean…"

"Yes you did, because it's true." I take a deep breath. My ragtag group of friends all owe me. Every one of them is my honest to goodness friend now, but they never would have had anything to do with me if I hadn't saved their lives. I give up and slide to the ground so I can wallow.

"I didn't mean to sound like such a jerk," Ketchup says. He sits down next to me. "I thought you were lying, that you didn't want to admit you had to rescue someone else, that he was only there because he felt like he had to be."

That familiar stab of rejection buries itself in my chest. "I wasn't lying," I manage to whisper.

"You didn't save him?"

I shake my head. "He saved me, actually," I say without thinking.

"What?" Ketchup demands.

I try to backtrack, but Ketchup will not let this one go. Finally, I give in and tell him about what happened in the alley. Well, I tell him as much as I can. Ketchup is stunned at the tale of me getting mixed up with a trio of chollos. He doesn't bat an eye about me fighting, and he doesn't look for evidence of bruises or cuts. He doesn't seem to know whether to be angry or grateful when I mentioned Noah breaking up the fight. In the end, the only emotion that sticks around in Ketchup's eyes is sadness.

"Why didn't you tell me?"

Shame makes me look away. "It was stupid to walk home. I was embarrassed, and I was fine anyway."

"But…"

I hold up a hand, not willing to discuss it anymore. Ketchup grunts in annoyance, but doesn't press the issue. Instead, he goes back to the original topic. The skepticism is clear in his voice when he says, "And now he's your English partner? Isn't that kind of weird?"

"I know. I was worried at first, too, but he hasn't pulled anything. I even offered to let him off the hook and do it alone, but he said no."

"Van, I don't know Noah very well, but he's been here a few years. He's heard the rumors and stories. He knows about your…interesting past. How can you be sure of his motivations?"

I shrug. Admitting Noah's biggest motivator for ignoring the vicious stories constantly circulating about me is because he likes me is not something I want to discuss with Ketchup.

"Are you sure he isn't after something?" Ketchup asks. "Van, I don't want you to get hurt."

"Is it really so hard to believe someone might just like me?"

"By someone, you mean a guy," Ketchup says, jealousy sneaking back into his voice. When I don't answer, Ketchup knows the answer is yes. He sighs and leans his head against the wall. "Noah likes you?"

"I think so. Is it that surprising?" I ask.

Ketchup is quiet. His hand moves slowly to take mine, and for once I let him. "Is it surprising that a guy thinks you're beautiful and amazing?" he asks softly. His hand tightens around mine. "No, it's not surprising. Everyone should be able to see that about you. Everyone should see you like I do."

Tears that have nothing to do with anger build in my eyes. They scare me because I know their source, and I know I won't be able to hold them back. "Ketchup, please," I whisper.

"It's not true," he says as if he didn't hear me.

He doesn't continue. I'm forced to ask, "What isn't true?"

"What I said about nobody wanting to be around you unless you save them. I wanted to be with you long before you saved me." He smiles and leans closer to me. "In fact, the only reason you had to save me was because I was already hanging around you when that car lost control."

I try to block out his words, but they've already sunken deep into my mind. I lie to myself every day, trying to convince myself that Ketchup is only here for the protection I provide and the loyalty my rescues require. I'm so convincing, everyone else believes it. The only one I can't fool is myself. No, I'm not the only one who can't be tricked. Ketchup will never give in to my make believe, no matter how hard I try.

"Why Noah?" Ketchup asks. His anguished voice breaks my heart.

"Because he likes me without needing a reason," I say simply, honestly.

"Do you like him back?"

I shrug unconvincingly. "I don't know. Maybe."

Ketchup seems to take my answer as a sure sign of my feelings for Noah. His voice cracks when he asks, "More than me?"

"I..." My throat seizes up, and I can't speak. I turn my head into his shoulder and hide from him. Ketchup's hand sweeps up my back and tangles in my hair. He presses me closer to his chest. My body trembles as I take in a deep breath. "Ketchup, I can't be with you. You know that," I whisper.

As he shakes his head, I expect his usual argument, the same one he's thrown at me a million times before. He surprises me this time. "I know you think that, but it doesn't matter right now. I just need to know."

He pauses, and I can see his free hand clench into a fist. "Do you like him more than you like me?"

"No." It's an honest answer, but the sudden hope that fills Ketchup's eyes scares me and I rush to clarify. "But maybe

I should give him a chance. If I can't be with you, maybe it's time…"

"No," Ketchup says angrily.

My face crumbles. "Ketchup, it's not fair of me to keep doing this to you. I can't be with you. You shouldn't waste your time waiting for me."

"You'll keep seeing him, then?" Ketchup demands before I can convince him.

"Yes." Tears slide down my cheeks when Ketchup shudders. "We have our project to do…" I say, not convincing in the least.

"But that's not the only reason. You *want* to see him again."

"Part of me does," I admit.

The tension in his body tells me exactly how he feels about my answer. He is bursting, dying to ask me, tell me, demand that I don't do this. He wants to stop me from ever seeing Noah again. I can feel it pouring off of him, but he doesn't ask. Never. He would never ask me to do that.

Instead of what he really wants to say, he says, "I'll wait."

I can't stop my tears from falling in earnest. They cascade down my face. "Don't," I beg him. "I don't want you to wait."

"I'll always wait, Van. I love you."

It must kill him to walk away, then, but he does it. He leaves me to cry, not out of vengeance, but again, because he knows that's what I want. Ketchup always gives me what I want in the end. I only wish I could do the same for him. What I can give is so paltry in comparison. I wait until the click of the door hits my ears before whispering, "I love you, too."

Then I drop my head to my knees and sob.

14

CARTE BLANCHE

*E*verything after lunch is a blur. I don't speak to Ivy or Noah. I know I won't get the chance to confront Zander until I get home from work tonight, so I force myself to focus on going to the senior center with Ketchup after school. A quick text message to Grandma explaining my plans to "volunteer" are met with happy approval. I, on the other hand, am sick just thinking about it. What if Ketchup is right?

It is with trepidation that I cross the parking lot to Ketchup's car after school. When I finally make it to him, his subdued demeanor lowers my eyes.

"Ready?" he asks.

I nod and slip into his SUV. The drive is quiet at first. After about ten minutes, I can't stand it anymore. "Ketchup, I'm sorry about earlier."

When he looks over at me, his smile is faint, but genuine. "You don't have to be sorry about anything. I had no right to act the way I did. Forgive me?"

"I don't need to. I'm the one…"

"Van," he interrupts, "I know this situation sucks. I don't understand it, at all, but I want you to know I'm here for you, no matter what. Nothing else needs to be said right now."

I have the feeling what he means by that last line is that he doesn't want to talk about me hanging out with Noah anymore. There are still plenty of things that need to be said— mainly me apologizing for being such a horrible friend to him. But I don't say anything else. I should make myself pull away from him, quit torturing him. It's the right thing to do, but I can't. Deep down, I cannot get rid of the hope that one day things will change and I can live the life I want, with the person I want. Ketchup must feel the same. The sense of relief that settles around me may be false, but I hold it close until we pull up to the senior center.

We walk in together, with Ketchup greeting friends of his late grandfather and me following along behind, not sure whether or not this is going to work. Ketchup leads me deeper into the center. He pauses at a plain wooden door. Even with it closed, I can hear voices, several men arguing.

"This is the unofficial 'Vets Room,'" Ketchup says. "I've known these guys a long time. I've heard their stories dozens of times. All three of them served in the front lines in Vietnam. They've never talked much about the actual killing they did, but they've talked about what it was like over there. If you're right about what the weird taste means, these guys should cause the same effect."

"But what if it doesn't? Even around Zander it doesn't happen all the time."

Ketchup puts his arms around my shoulder and reaches for the door knob. "Then we'll come back again, just to make sure. We'll come back as many times as it takes, okay?"

"Okay," I say quietly.

Ketchup opens the door and I brace myself. I even find myself holding my breath until I can't stand it anymore and breathe. When I do, the air smells faintly of tobacco and arthritis cream, but that's it. I'm pulled out of my contemplation when I am poked with a cane. I jump back at the hard nudge and glance over at the source.

"Who's this pretty little thing?" a wrinkled old man asks.

Ketchup grins at his elderly friend. "This is my friend, Van."

"Van?" one of the others hollers. "What kind of name is Van?"

"It's short for Vanessa," I offer. The old man scowls at me. I try not to laugh.

Not wanting to be the center of attention, I tug Ketchup toward a couch. He follows with a smile, asking the three gentlemen how they're doing. That inspires a whole round of complaining from each of them. Ketchup takes it all in gracefully. When they are done complaining about aches and the complicated nature of Medicare, their interest turns back to me.

"Why'd you bring a girl here, anyway?" the guy whose name turns out to be Gus asks. He's also the one who poked me. "This is a gentlemen's club."

The other two mutter similar complaints, but Ketchup fends them off. "Hold on now. I bring someone new you all can tell your stories to, and you're complaining? Every week you three complain that no one new ever comes to visit you."

When the three look sufficiently chastised, I ask to hear a story. Apparently they instantly forget their qualms from a few seconds ago, because suddenly all three are tripping over each other to be the first to tell a story of *way back when*. Their fighting in the war never comes up, but I actually find myself enjoying their tales. The two hours I had to spare before heading off to work go by much more quickly than I expected. Before I know it, Ketchup and I are saying our goodbyes.

Ketchup is saying goodbye with his hand on the door when it hits me. I can barely even stand when the taste slams into me. My hand clutches at Ketchup's arm. His eyes snap over to me, and his goodbyes wrap up half a second later. The door is pulled shut as I double over. Before I can collapse, Ketchup has his arms around me.

"Van, are you okay?"

My hand flies up to my nose and mouth in an effort to keep the taste away, but it's already seeped into me. All I can do is breathe and wait for it to pass. Ketchup holds me until I start breathing normally again. My head falls back against his chest in relief. Alone in the hallway, nobody notices the two of us sitting on the floor. I'm grateful for that. I need a few minutes before I'll be able to stand up.

"It happened again," Ketchup says, a statement, not a question. "I was really hoping it wouldn't."

So was I.

"It means you were right," I say quietly. The grief that inspires is a heavy weight to bear.

"Maybe not. It could mean something else." The hope in his voice is faint, and we both know he is wrong. Ketchup's head rests against mine as his arms tighten around me. His voice is small when he asks, "Who?"

"Who did Zander kill?" Tears well in my eyes. "I don't know, but there have been nights lately when he hasn't come home until really late. I don't know where he's going, or what he's doing, but I found blood on one of his shirts this morning. What if…what if he ends up locked up like Oscar?"

That can't happen. Not only can I not bear the idea of losing another brother, there are more complicated reasons I can't have Zander taken away from me.

There was a time when I was little, six or seven, that Mom and Dad sent the boys to summer camp for two weeks. It was the first time they had been away from home for that long and they were so excited to go. I was excited to have Mom and Dad's attention to myself for two weeks. They were only gone two days when I started to get sick. At first Mom thought I had eaten something bad when my stomach started hurting. Two days later, she thought it must have been a nasty flu. Then the fever started. The doctors prescribed antibiotics, but they didn't help. My brothers had been gone a week when Mom called Grandma in a panic.

The next thing I knew, Zander and Oscar were home and I felt a million times better. Nobody bothered to explain anything to me, but I heard Grandma tell Mom and Dad that they couldn't separate us for so long. She claimed she didn't know why we had to stay in contact with each other to keep the sickness away, but she made my parents promise they would never keep us separated like that again.

She said it would get better with age, but the most we could ever go without being near each other was a week before our bodies would start shutting down. The staff at Peak View can't understand why Oscar always feels so much better physically after we visit him. Once a week is the most often we're allowed to see him, and as hard as it is to sit in that room with him sometimes, it kills us both to know he spends most of his days sick and begging for contact.

What will happen if Zander is locked up and I can't get to him often enough? What will happen to me?

Going to work and forcing myself to make it through two classes is torture. I am exhausted when the last dancer finally leaves. I trudge through the front door and scan the parking lot for Grandma's Volvo. The sight of Zander's truck sends a whole wash of emotions through me. Anger tops the list, but fear and disgust are there in pretty large concentration as well. It takes me a few minutes to collect myself and climb into the truck.

Before I can say a word, Zander says, "I know you're pissed at me, but this needs to wait until we get home. It's not safe while I'm driving."

The fact that he is right makes me nod. Not knowing how to even start keeps me from saying anything. As we drive, I struggle to figure out what to say to him. What happened today is eating away at me, but how do I accuse Zander of killing someone? There is still some lingering hope that I'm wrong. If I break open something like that, it can never be taken back. Reluctantly, I hold onto the topic of murder and focus on my anger at Zander over Ivy instead. It builds quickly as I relive our conversation from that night. By the time we make it home to an empty house, I am ready to let him have it.

Zander stops and faces me when we get to the living room. "Okay, go ahead."

"That's it?" I fume. "Go ahead? No explanation?"

"Just say what you want to say, and then I'll explain. You'll never let me get through it without yelling at me anyway," Zander says.

His calm frustrates me more than I can even say. "Fine. If that's the way you want to do this, then fine." I take a deep breath and unleash every ounce of the frustration and anger that has been building over the last two days.

"What in the hell were you doing with Ivy Saturday night? Are you crazy? I told you I wouldn't stop hanging out with Laney because of Ivy and you acted like I was insane! You got *mad* at me for not bailing on my best friend! I've spent the last week trying to find ways to vent my hunger so I don't kill her, and you're taking her out to dinner? She *is* dinner for you! You want to kill her! Why on earth are you putting yourself in that kind of situation? That's not getting used to her, that's suicide!

"One slip and you'll be wiping her blood off your hands! Don't you understand that? I can't lose you too! I love you. You're all I have left. How can you do this to me? What if you get sent to prison and I can't visit you? What if you get sick? What if you die? You laugh at me because I think there's something wrong with her, but I'm trying to protect you! I don't want to see you locked up like Oscar, or worse. I'm doing everything I can to make sure she doesn't hurt you, and you're playing right into her hands! Why, Zander? Why are you doing this?"

I have to suck in a huge breath of air after my tirade. It lodges in my chest, held in anticipation of Zander's answer. Given what I found out today, I am more scared than ever that Zander will kill Ivy. I can't let that happen. Silence slithers through the air between us. It tightens around my throat and chokes me until I start to fear I'll pass out. Zander stares at his feet, not answering.

"Why?" I ask again. "Why would you put your life, our lives, at risk like this?"

His lips finally part, but I'm not prepared for his answer. "Because I'm in love with her."

"What?" I shriek. My left eye starts twitching. It's never done that before, and for a moment it's all I can focus on. It's all I will let myself focus on. I must have misheard him. He can't have really just said what I think he said. As if he knows I'm doubting my own ears, he repeats it.

"I'm in love with her, Van."

"No," I say. My head starts shaking back and forth. "No, no you're not. You can't be in love with her. You've only known her for a week. She's not…you can't…it's just your hunger that wants her. You're not thinking straight, Zander."

My brother stands up and walks over to me. His hands on my shoulders fail to calm my mounting hysteria. "Van, it's not my hunger. It's me. *I* want her."

"But…you want to kill her, too."

"Yes," he says through clenched teeth, "but I can handle it."

"I don't understand. How did this happen?"

Zander shakes his head wearily. "I don't know. When I ran into her in the parking lot that first day, I stood there wanting to crush her windpipe, and suddenly I couldn't stop staring at her lips. I realized how beautiful she was, and I wanted to protect her."

I shove his hands away from me and fix him with my glare. "You're the one you'd be protecting her from. Do you even realize that?"

"Of course I do!"

"No, this is stupid, Zander! You're going to hurt her. You have to stay away from her." It's the advice he's given me dozens of time, now coming out of my mouth. It's a strange feeling, a flip-flopped kind of déjà vu I don't like in the least. Even more disturbing is my usual retort spilling over Zander's lips.

"I won't do it. I can't stay away from her, Van."

Sudden, consuming fury blossoms in my heart and rips through my veins. When I manage to speak, the words have to squeeze through my teeth and are laden with venom. "So, when you tell me to stay away, I have to do it, but when I tell you to do the same thing, you tell me no? How is that fair, Zander? Explain to me how that's fair!"

"It's not fair, but that's how it is," Zander has the gall to say to me.

"That's how it is?" I seethe. Thinking of Noah sitting down across from me, only to be attacked by Ketchup, replays in my mind over and over again. Me running, Ketchup following, his promise and my secret reply, they all scream the injustice back at me. It's too much.

My fist explodes right on Zander's jaw. I can see the surprise on his face as he stumbles over the coffee table and lands on the floor. I don't give him a chance to react. Pinning him down with my knees on his chest and my fist cocked back for another punch, I grab his shirt with my other hand and yank his face up to mine.

"How dare you," I growl at him. "How dare you refuse to stop seeing her when you made me give up Ketchup! He was my friend since kindergarten and you never said a word about him. Not until I started developing feelings for him did you demand I stop seeing him!"

"I'd never met him before then," Zander says, blood dribbling from the corner of his mouth. "His parents never let him come to our house. I had no idea I was going to react to him."

"I don't care!" In the back of my mind I know he's right. I still don't care. "I tried to make it work. I could have kept him away from the house."

Anger flashes in Zander's eyes for the first time. "He wouldn't stay away! That idiot kept coming around, looking for you, stalking you. He was so determined to spend every freaking second with you that there was no way I'd ever be able to control myself when he was always here! I couldn't be around you when he was there. It was a choice between me and him, your brother or some kid from down the street."

"If you just would have let me explain to him..."

"Explain that we're a couple of murderous freaks who lose our minds and kill people when we get hungry? You want to know what would have happened after you told him that?" He pauses to see if I'll answer. When I don't, he continues in a dark, frightening voice. "He would have left you, Van. He would have run and never looked back. At least this way, you still get to keep him as a friend."

The hand I had been holding ready to slam into my brother's face tightens, begging me to connect. "That's not true," I argue. "Ketchup is the only person who has ever wanted me for me. He wouldn't have run. We would have dealt with it."

"No he wouldn't have."

"Shut up!" I lower my fist. My head shakes back and forth quickly in an effort to clear my mind and get back to the main point of this argument. "This isn't about Ketchup. It's about you and Ivy. I won't stand by and let you kill her, Zander. I refuse to lose another brother."

"I won't stop seeing her. I *can't* stop seeing her."

"If I can do it, so can you." I didn't get a pass with Ketchup, and neither will Zander.

My brother's head falls back against the floor. His eyes close, and I swear I can see moisture hovering on the edges of his eyelids. "You don't get it," he says quietly. "You were able to walk away from Ketchup because you're so strong, Van. You can do the hard things. Even the stuff I rail on you about, like having friends instead of keeping everyone at a distance like

I do, you do it because you're strong enough to keep control. You do what I can't. I refuse to let people in because I know I'll hurt them. I'm not as strong as you are, little sister. I never have been, and I probably never will be."

"That's not true, Zander. You're the strongest person I know. You always make the right decision. I'm the one with the history, the mistakes, the dozens of close calls. I'm hotheaded and wild. You're smart and calm. You can do this. Please, you have to walk away from her," I beg. "You have to stay safe...for me. Please, Zander, I'm begging you."

"You see yourself in completely the wrong way, Van. How many lives have you saved? How many have I?" His expression breaks and crumbles with some hurt I don't fully understand. "Yeah, you have a temper, but you're also the most passionate person I know. I wish I had even a portion of your ferocity. I hide. That's all I do."

My fists bang down on his chest. "You're not hiding now! You're taking Ivy out to dinner and planning study dates with her!"

"I want to stay away from her, Van, but I can't. You don't understand what it feels like when I'm around her."

"Then tell me!" I explode.

Zander scrunches his face, and says, "Every time I see her, I want to hurt her. My hunger craves her more than with anyone else I've ever met. I lied to you when I said it wasn't any different."

My hands cinch tighter around Zander's shirt. He hurries on.

"What is different with Ivy is that I love her more than

I want to kill her. Sometimes my hunger flares and it tries to overpower how I feel about her, but she laughs and it pulls me back. As much as I want to sometimes, I could never hurt her. I love her, Van."

The honesty and ache in his voice finally breaks through my manic day. He means every word of it. My brother loves the girl I am positive is only here to destroy us. There is no chance I'm ever going to convince him to walk away from her either. I breathe out a sigh of absolute defeat.

"Does she know?"

"No. I can't tell her, yet."

"Don't."

"Why?" Zander demands.

"Because…just don't, okay? I know you don't believe me, but Ivy is more than you think."

"Leave her alone, Van," he demands.

Resentment shoves my hands against his chest, hard. "If you don't have to leave her alone, neither do I. I won't let her hurt you."

Zander doesn't argue. He glares at me fiercely, silently.

"What is going on in here?" Grandma demands.

Both of us glance over at her in surprise. I didn't even hear her come in. She looks just as startled as I feel. Her eyes sweep over the scene of me kneeling on Zander's chest, my hands keeping him pinned to the ground, Zander trying to push me off of him, and both of us looking like we're ready to kill each other.

"What are you two doing?"

I can see her shock quickly turning to fear, so I push

off my brother and stand up. "I was just giving Zander some dating advice."

"Dating ad..." My grandma's face momentarily brightens before going completely white. "Dating? Zander, she doesn't mean that Ivy girl, does she?"

"I most certainly do," I say, glancing at my brother with a brutal scowl.

"Grandma, it's okay. Don't worry about it," Zander says.

My grandma doesn't take orders well. Her cherub features, still holding onto their youth, flash scarlet. "Young man, do not tell me what to worry about. I have seen more, felt more, and lived through more than you can even imagine. I know exactly what I should and should not worry about. You will meet me in the kitchen as soon as I hang up my purse and sweater."

She doesn't wait for him to agree. His affirmative "Yes, ma'am" is a foregone conclusion. I screamed at him, hit him, and his only response was anger or frustration. A few short sentences from Grandma and his head drops doggedly. Fear of the little old woman who used to be a pastry chef drags him slowly toward the kitchen.

For an hour, I listen to them argue. It is an eerie sort of fight, one where neither of them actually raises their voice. I can barely hear their argument, but it is fierce and heated all the same. She asks, demands, and threatens my brother. The dangers of letting him see Ivy again are clearer to her than anyone else.

Zander, Oscar, and I aren't the first in our family to have to battle our hunger. It's a curse our family has held for endless generations. When it will strike comes randomly, passing my dad and my grandma, but not her father. She was three years old, her mother long gone, when she lost her father. Her last memory of him was watching him gut a young girl he had picked up somewhere on his way home, and seeing the police gun him down in their living room a few minutes later.

Grandma knows the risks, horrors, and pain of what we are, but when she walks out of the kitchen shaking her head and drying tears from her eyes, I know she has failed. Zander won't give up this one duplicitous girl for anyone or anything. He has chosen the path sure to lead to her death and most likely his as well.

Long minutes later, Zander comes out of the kitchen, stopping when our eyes meet. I stand up and walk over to him. I can't summon up any sympathy for him, not with thoughts of Ketchup filling my mind.

"I'll play nice with Ivy, not because I think you're making the right choice, but because I believe you that you love her, and because you're my brother and I don't want to hurt you. Don't think this is over, though, big brother. At some point, I'm going to ask you to do something hard for me, and you're going to do it. No matter what it is, you'll do it, carte blanche, no questions asked. Got it?"

Zander swallows hard, the only sign he's ever given me that he might be afraid of something. For a moment, I wonder if he's thinking the same thing I am, and I'm afraid he's going to deny me. Slowly, his head nods. "No questions asked," he agrees, the dread of my unspoken request already hanging over him.

15

INDESTRUCTIBLE

My unconditional promise to answer Ivy's questions has weighed on me all week, even more than my promise to Van. Not because I fear what Van will ask me to do any more than I fear answering Ivy's questions, but because I know Van won't call hers in any time soon. She's too fixated on Ivy right now. Shocked as Ivy was when Van apologized to her for blowing up in her face, I expected it. When Van gives her word on something, she means it. It's not always a good quality. Like with her investigating Ivy.

Van must make a pretty good sleuth, because Ivy hasn't mentioned anything unusual happening with her lately. My sneaky little sister has been nice as can be to her all week. It's killing her hunger to do it, too. Maybe I should have some sympathy for her struggle, but I don't. She could always just leave Ivy alone and give up on the ridiculous belief that she's hiding something. We've met in her homeroom twice and talked on the phone several times. She even met me after practice yesterday, and not once have I seen, heard, or felt anything suspicious from her. Unless you count her love of pistachio ice cream. That's definitely suspicious.

A hand slaps against my shoulder pads, knocking away thoughts of Ivy. "You ready for this?" Samuel asks.

"Yeah, I guess. Los Lunas doesn't have a very strong offense."

Samuel shakes his head at me. "How do you stay so calm before a game? I feel like my skin is about to jump off my body. I can't remember any of the plays, and I feel like I'm going to hurl."

"You'll be fine," I say.

"Seriously, how do you do it?"

I shrug. He scowls at me as he bounces nervously on his toes.

"The pressure just doesn't bother me," I say. It's true, but not in the way Samuel thinks. Pressure definitely bothers me when I sit down for a test. When I get out on the field, though, what do I have to worry about? No one is going to hurt me. No one is going to get past me. I have complete control over my portion of the field. Even knowing the college scouts are going to be watching tonight, I know I'll impress them.

"I wish it didn't bother me," Samuel says. "You may not care what girls think about you, but I do. If I suck out there tonight, my chances of getting Kaleigh Adams to go out with me shrink to nil."

The sudden desire to tell Samuel that I do care about what at least one girl thinks of me burns under my skin. Maybe I let what Van said get to me more than I thought.

Instead, all I say is, "Kaleigh will go out with you either way, Samuel. Just ask her."

"You think?"

I nod, but anything else I might have said is cut off by the coach calling us to the huddle. He isn't one for speeches or sappy motivational encouragement, so he keeps it short with a promise that if we don't play our best he'll make us run laps until we're all puking next practice. It doesn't sound like it would get a bunch of teenage football players excited, but everyone piles out of the locker room on a serious adrenaline high. I jog along behind them, wondering whether or not I'll be able to see Ivy from the field.

I don't see her anywhere in the throng of hyped up spectators, but I know she's out there somewhere with Van. What I do see are two men dressed in slacks and polos carrying clipboards in one hand and cell phones in the other. Their eyes scan the line of players exiting the locker room hungrily. Finally, my pace picks up and excitement starts to creep into my veins when they see me. My mouth splits into a grin. It's going to be a race to see who can reach me after the game first, Van and Ivy, or the scouts.

When I reach the huddle, all thoughts of girls and scouts are forgotten. It's time to find the pain. My hunger leaps up to the forefront of my mind, nearly taking control. With the way I've been teasing my hunger around Ivy this week, it's desperate for some nourishment. Not even my nightly forays into the desert to hunt have been enough. It sounds crazy even to me, but I swear my reaction to her gets worse every time I'm near here. That's not the way it's supposed to work.

Usually my hunger for someone lessens each time I am around them and don't succumb, like I'm desensitizing myself. It's hardly a fast process, given how in the almost three years since meeting Ketchup, my hunger has only gone from an all-consuming need to an intense desire to see him suffer. I don't know how long it will take before I can be around him for more than five minutes, but for Van's sake, I'm trying.

As Coach finishes up his last minute instructions, we break away from the huddle and flow onto the field. I'm all focus until I see the runningback across the line. His hands are already shaking, but when he catches sight of me, he flinches. I don't do it to intimidate him. I simply can't help grinning, my smile widening when all the blood drains from his face.

Somewhere to my left I hear the center hike the ball. Chaos ensues around me, but not within me. Inside, I am the perfect calm, taking in everything going on around me, and watching the ball get shoved into the trembling runningback's arms. He blows past the first few defenders, but hesitates before darting to the side. I can almost hear his heart thudding against his chest as he puts everything he has into attempting to get around me. I almost give him some ground, make him feel like he has a chance, but then I remember the scouts.

His eyes widen to the size of golf balls as I barrel toward him. He shoots forward one more time, one saved burst of speed held back for just this moment. It isn't enough. It never is. One arm clamps around his body, while my free hand swipes across his middle and dislodges the ball. I don't know where the ball goes. I don't care. My hunger wants to hurt him, begs me to crush the life out of him. We slam into the ground and skid to a stop. My hunger scrabbles around inside of me, soaking up the pain of the impact, the forming bruises, the struggle to breathe.

My chest is heaving as my hunger continues to rage. I roll away from the runningback and will my body to move farther from him. Not going back to finish what I started is torture. I breathe in, slowly. My eyes close as I focus on not giving in. Remembering my little sister in the stands, remembering what will happen to her if I am taken away, forces a precarious calm over me.

The crowd is screaming and jumping up and down on the bleachers when I stand back up. Someone from Los Lunas must have picked up the fumble. Secretly, I'm glad for their recovery. I'm not that interested in scoring, just in staying on the field. The kid I just knocked the breath out of looks at me in disbelief when I extend my hand to help him up, but he accepts. I haul him back to his feet, holding onto him for a few extra seconds to make sure he won't topple over again, but also to soak up the remaining bits of pain clinging to him. The ache in his shoulder is the last to fade.

"You alright?" I ask.

"Yeah, I guess," he says, rolling his shoulder.

"Good. Don't hesitate next time, okay?"

He looks at me like I'm crazy, blanching at the thought of there being a next time. But there will be. I run back to my position and get right back into the game. The receiver who burned our corner and caught the ball doesn't get past me. He makes the mistake of trying to break his fall and dislocates his shoulder. Who cares about the points scored, that was the highlight for me. The part of my mind I can actually control felt bad for him, helped get him over to his bench, but the hunger-controlled side ran amuck in celebration of the agony pouring off of him. Stepping away from him nearly broke my will. I was grateful when he was removed from the field.

Every Los Lunas player that touches the ball anywhere near me gets a taste of my power, and my hunger gets a taste of them. I try to take it easy on the quarterback when he attempts to sneak past the line. He probably isn't used to getting hit. It takes him a few minutes to get back up, but he is fine in the end. The only person I feel any guilt about hitting is the runningback from the beginning of the game. He looks terrified every time he knows the ball is coming to him, but he doesn't hesitate. Not once out of the eleven times I face him. That almost puts a dent in my hunger. Almost.

I honestly don't even look at the score board until the game is over. I stare at it as I attempt to rein in my hunger and come down off the high so much pain has given me. I guess it shouldn't surprise me that we won, but even I am shocked to see 42-10 displayed. I had no idea we scored that many times. Even though I'm pretty sure I scored most of the touchdowns, it just isn't what I focus on during a game. What surprises me even more is when the Los Lunas runningback jogs over to me at the end and shakes my hand.

"Good game, Zander. I'm gonna be feeling it for a week, but that's the game, right?"

"Sure is," I agree. "You played pretty well yourself. Not many players are willing to come at me like you did. You've got guts."

He laughs. "Well, at least next week's game won't seem so bad after this."

I'm sure. I don't flaunt it, but I know I'm the best player in the state. If he can face me down over and over again and not balk once, he'll be perfectly fine against anybody else. "What's your name?" I ask.

"Grady Johnson."

"Are you a senior this year?" I ask. Out of everyone I tackled today, this kid impressed me the most.

"Yeah, why?"

"Come with me," I say as I jog to the side of the field. I don't give him any explanation, but he still follows. He catches up with me a few seconds before the scouts burst through the crowd, headed straight for me. Grady slows. He looks over at me with a questioning look, but I motion for him to keep coming. The scouts look ravenous as they race each other to reach me first. Neither of them even notices Grady at first. They blurt out congratulations and praise as soon as they reach me. I let their eagerness calm down a little before really paying attention to what they're saying.

"Zander, Alabama has had their eye on you for quite some time now. We could use someone with your ability on our team," one scout says.

"LSU is very eager to sit down with you, Zander. Coach Feldstein already has a jersey with your name on it ready to present to you as soon as you sign a letter of intent with us."

The first scout scowls at the second. "Alabama has a full ride football scholarship available," he throws out haughtily, "and you are our top choice, Zander. We'd love to have you come down and tour the campus, see the dorms where you'll be living, meet the coaching staff. We can arrange a visit any time."

Before the second guy can try to one up the first one, I interject. "Sorry, I don't think I caught either of your names." They stumble over each other to give me names and cards. "I haven't committed to any school yet, but I'd definitely be interested in seeing both the LSU and Alabama campuses before I make a decision."

Their eyes gleam eagerly.

"I've still got another year of high school, though," I remind them. "But if you need someone for next year, I think I can help you out. If you happen to need a runningback, that is."

Grady, who had been standing there soaking up the fanfare, looking a little unsure of himself, suddenly perks up. His head snaps over to me, clearly shocked.

"Gentlemen," I say, "this is Grady Johnson, and if you were watching me on defense at all, you should have seen that he was the closest one to getting past me all night. He very nearly got around me a couple of times. Against anybody else, he's going to get you major yards every time."

Both scouts stare at me for a split second in surprise before turning their attention to Grady. Stumbling through their first few questions, Grady gets a hold of himself after several minutes and starts talking about his stats, grades, and plans for the future. I stick around long enough to make sure he's not going to panic if I leave, but after that I turn away with a promise to set up visits with both schools within the next couple weeks. I get detoured a couple more times by my coaches or one of the fans milling around before ducking into the locker room. I think I've found a moment of peace despite the celebration raging inside until Samuel plops down on the bench next to me.

"What was the deal with handing the scouts off to that Los Lunas player?"

"He's a good player. I thought he deserved a little notice," I say. When Samuel looks at me skeptically, I follow my answer up with another good reason for dumping the scouts. "Plus, I hate talking to those guys. I know they want me to play for them, but I don't like feeling like a cow they're haggling over."

Samuel shakes his head. "You're nuts, man, but if you were going to shove someone else in their face, I'm shocked it wasn't me."

"Hey," I say, "if you really want to get tackled by college guys twice your size, I'd be more than happy to give you a boost."

He flinches dramatically. "I've still got bruises from practice on Wednesday. No thanks. Football gets me my athletic credits and extracurricular activities for my college applications. That's all I'm after. I'd get killed the first game for sure."

"More like the first practice," I joke.

My humor catches Samuel off guard. It may very well be the first time I've ever joked with him. I don't know what's wrong with me today. Laughing more than the paltry joke merits, Samuel punches me in the shoulder. "Thanks a lot,

Zander. I'll remember that next time you need me to chase off a girl."

With that, he dives back through the party and heads for the showers. After getting all my gear stored, I do the same. I finish first, thanks to Samuel's general prissiness when it comes to grooming. I rub a towel over my head and smooth my hair down with my hands while he pulls out some kind of foaming goop and a hair dryer. Regardless, I find myself waiting for him to finish. Maybe I'm starting to understand Van's insistence on having friends, or maybe I'm just nervous to be put face to face with Ivy. The game took a lot out of me, but my hunger for her isn't getting any better.

Samuel and I walk out of the locker room straight into the blaring music of the traditional party raging around the field. I try to spot Van or Ivy through the throng, but end up finding someone else instead. The curly redhead isn't someone I'd normally take any time to notice, but after talking to Samuel before the game, I elbow him and point in the girl's direction. When he sees her, he licks his lips nervously.

"Go talk to her."

"No, man, she's with her friends. I don't want all her friends to hear her turn me down. I want to talk to her when she's alone," he says.

"Samuel, she's a girl. When are they ever alone?" He grimaces, but doesn't make a move toward her. "Besides, she's less likely to say no with her friends standing there. She wouldn't want to embarrass you or look like a jerk in front of them."

He shakes his head. "I don't know, Zander."

Before I can do any more convincing, Van bursts through a group of teens, arms waving at me. She runs forward and throws herself at me. "Zander, that was awesome! You plastered those guys! I loved it!" Her enthusiasm is hard to ignore this time. I grin back at her.

"You enjoyed the game, then?" I ask, knowing she's still riding the high of feeding her hunger. That's another perk to playing football. Van gets something out of it, too. I'm hard on her, but I'll do anything I can to help keep her safe and sane.

"Did I enjoy it? Are you kidding me? Football is so much better than basketball. I wish they played it year round. When you tackled the quarterback...that was awesome. Quarterbacks are such pansies. You should try to smash more of them," Van says seriously. She doesn't add, because they feel the pain more than anyone else on the field since they're usually so protected. She doesn't need to add that. I felt the richness of the QB's pain even better than she did.

The rest of Van's crowd finally catches up to her. Stopping well out of my reach, Laney and Ketchup halt. Ketchup has no idea why I can't stand him, but regardless of the fact that he still refuses to stay away from Van, he does have enough brains to always keep his distance from me. My hunger knows he's there. I'm in control enough to ignore it for now. It's impossible to ignore Laney, though. She's jabbering away to Ketchup, who looks like he has a headache. Laney can give anyone a headache, but I know that's not the only reason for his glum attitude.

Van told me Noah was going to watch the game with her.

I look around, but I don't spot him anywhere. Ivy, however, is trailing Ketchup. She glances up at me and smiles. Hunger simmers under my skin, but it's thankfully dulled somewhat by the crowd of people and my physical exhaustion. I smile back, and she moves around Ketchup toward me. I brace myself for her impact on my hunger.

When she reaches me, I want to grab her. My hand moves to take her. As my hunger spikes, I realize it isn't my emotions trying to swallow her up, and redirect my hand to flick Van on the shoulder as I take a few steps away. She looks over at me, and says, "What was that for?"

"Where's this Noah kid? Did he bail on you?" I can't help notice Ketchup's expression darkening even more. Guilt drills at me. He wouldn't be so unhappy if it weren't for me. Maybe someday it won't be this way, but for now it's best he stays back.

"Noah had to take off," Van says vaguely.

I frown at her. "I wanted to meet him."

"Not yet," she says, her eyes drifting to Ketchup before dropping down.

Ah, she's afraid my hunger will want him. "You have to find out sooner or later."

Her eyes snap up to mine. The fierceness of her glare stabs at me. "Well, if I get a choice, it will be later, okay?"

"Later for what?" Ivy asks, suddenly next to me.

"Nothing," I say as I quickly move away from her. I focus on the press of bodies around me and on how tired I am. Even still, it takes a lot of effort to keep my hands at my side and speak in a normal voice. "Did you enjoy the game?"

The corner of her mouth curls up uncertainly. "Yes?"

"Is that a question or an answer?" I ask. "You must not have enjoyed it."

Van snorts at Ivy's reaction, making her blush. "I did enjoy it. You were great. It was just a lot more violent than I expected. I never went to the games at my old school. Are you okay? It looked pretty brutal out there."

"Brutal for the other team," Samuel pipes in. "Zander never even gets a bruise. The guy's indestructible."

Curiosity flares in Ivy's eyes as she gazes at me. Unfortunately, I'm not the only one who notices. I can picture Van writing down her reaction in some secret *Harriet the Spy* type notebook. Eager to get the topic off me and onto something else, I turn back to Samuel, and say, "Kaliegh's still standing over there. Go ask her out before she leaves."

"I'll talk to her at school," he says, brushing me off.

"Quit being a wuss, Samuel."

He looks like he's about to give me another excuse, so I turn just enough so that he can see my hand as it takes Ivy's. Instantly my hunger cinches around my neck, strangling me with the desire to hurt her. I fight it down desperately, and realize everyone around me has frozen. Even Laney stops talking for the first time since I've known her. Ketchup's and Van's eyes are both smoldering, though I'm sure for very different reasons. The only person's reaction I really care about is Ivy's. I look down at her, half afraid to see her expression.

Despite the shock that has left her eyes wide and lips slightly parted, pleasure gleams in her expression. Timidly, she squeezes my hand. It's a huge effort, but I manage to smile at her. She smiles back, but she's the only one.

16

TO HELL

want nothing more than to pull Ivy away from everyone. I want to be alone with her, without staring eyes filled with anger and shock. My hunger is doing more of my thinking than anything else, though, so I resist the urge and make myself endure the scrutiny of everyone around me. At least Samuel decides to take my advice and head toward Kaleigh. After seeing me take a chance with a girl, the guy who asks his teammates to scare away girls for him, I guess he figured he could try too. Good for him. I watch him approach her, slip into her group of friends effortlessly, and join the conversation. Kaleigh laughs at something he says and I see Samuel relax.

Confident that he's at least on his way to asking her out, I scavenge for a good reason to get away from everyone else and get some space from Ivy without anyone asking questions. "You want something to drink?" I ask.

"Sure."

I start pulling her away, hopeful that I can get even

deeper in the mass of students and let go of her hand before I lose it. Van's voice, trying and failing to sound natural, cuts through the music and stops me. "Get me a slushy, will ya?"

Our eyes meet and my hand tightens around Ivy's. Van doesn't care about the slushy. She wants to make sure I come back to the group. She doesn't want me to be alone with Ivy. The irritation her drink request inspires builds under my skin. It shouldn't, because I know she's right. I know I shouldn't be alone with Ivy, either. Realizing that she's only trying to protect me, I soften my grip and tone of voice.

"Ketchup, do you want anything?"

He looks up, surprised I spoke to him. It takes him a minute to realize I am serious. "Uh, sure. Diet Coke."

I nod and turn away with Ivy. I hope she doesn't notice how stiffly I'm holding her hand. I want to be able to hold her tightly, pull her close to me, but even doing this much is enough to make me explode with desire and hunger. Without anyone else glaring at me as a distraction, it gets harder to resist. My hand starts tightening on hers. I know any second it's going to start hurting. I can't stop my hand from squeezing hers. I want her knuckles to grind together, crack and crumble. I want to hear her cries of anguish.

An image of her cradling her broken hand, crying eyes filled with hurt and betrayal, flashes in my mind. My hand springs away from hers immediately. I push away from her until at least three feet are separating us. It's the most I can manage with the entire high school population crowded under the bleachers.

"Are you okay?" Ivy asks. I look away, ashamed at my

lack of control.

Ivy stops and looks up at me. "Hey," she says, "what's wrong?"

"I'm sorry, Ivy. I told you that isn't easy for me."

"I know. It's okay." She doesn't push me about it. She walks beside me, not too close and not too far away. "So, Van said there were some scouts at the game watching you tonight. Were those the guys talking to you after the game?"

"Yeah, they both wanted me to go to their campuses and visit so they can try to convince me to sign with them. I've still got another year of high school, though, so I'm not sure why they're already pushing me to make a decision," I say, glad for the change in topic.

"Why do you have another year left? You're already eighteen, aren't you? You should be a senior."

Dodging a real answer, I say, "You've seen how good I am at math. Isn't that enough of an answer?"

"You're not bad at math. You just need to focus more." Ivy looks over at me, her eyes narrowed slightly, concentrating. "What's the real reason, Zander?"

I don't answer right away. We reach the snaking line to the concession stand and secure a spot. I look over the heads of the people in front of me in an effort to see the beginning of the line. We're going to be here a while. When Ivy's hand touches my arm lightly, the current that runs through me jerks me back around to face her.

"You don't have to tell me if you don't want to," she says. "I didn't mean to pry. I was just curious. I feel like I don't know very much about you yet."

"Does that bother you?"

She shrugs, looking down. "Not enough to make me stay away."

"But you still want to know?"

Ivy's eyes trail up my body to meet mine. The intensity of her gaze makes me forget everything else. I watch as one finger comes up and taps on my chest. The sparks of hunger her touch evokes is equaled by the desire to capture her.

"You are a very mysterious guy, Zander. I want to know everything about you. But if you don't want to tell me about this, that's okay. I understand if it's too personal."

Van may doubt her, but I can see the honesty in her eyes. "The last few years were tough for my family. A lot of really bad things happened to us, to me. I was really sick for a while, then I got behind at school my sophomore year. I barely made it through the year. It just kept getting worse. More bad stuff happened the next year. It was too hard to deal with everything. I got sick again because of the stress and everything, and missed the last half of the year. Rather than let me fail every class, the school said I could just start the year over. It meant another year of high school, but it saved my GPA and my eligibility to play sports."

"Can I ask what happened?" Her voice is quiet, but the slightest bit insistent.

"My..." It isn't because of trust that I hesitate, it's because I can't make my mouth form the words. Ivy briefly touches my arm, and for once it calms me more than enrages my hunger to know she's there. There isn't much I can tell her because it would require me to explain about turning sixteen and being too dangerous to be sent to school, or any of what happened because of that, but there is one thing I can tell her.

"My parent's died. I was the one who found them."

Ivy's arms tighten around her body. "Zander, I'm so sorry. How did they die?"

Pulling into the driveway, I notice both my parents' cars are here. That's odd. Dad doesn't usually get home from work until after six, and Mom is supposed to be at her book club today. What are they both doing home already? There could be a dozen logical reasons for them to be home, but as my feet plod toward the house, the quiet seeping out of it chills me. Our house is never quiet. Even with me and Van gone, Mom loves music. She played cello all through high school and college. I can hardly think of a time when classical music wasn't filling every nook and cranny of our home.

The smell hits me when I reach the front door. I don't even have to open it. It seeps through the tiny spaces around doors and windows and crawls under my skin, seeking out my hunger like nothing else can.

Blood.

My hand is frozen on the handle as my hunger claws at me, screaming in a psychotic frenzy to be let loose and feed. It's so much blood. Even the smallest amount will usually set me off, but this time is different. My hunger can't sink its teeth into me this time, not knowing that on the other side of the door is where I'll find my parents. Fear of opening the door outweighs everything else.

I have no idea how long I stand there. Time vanished the moment I caught that horrible scent. I don't even make a conscious decision to turn the handle and push forward. My body moves as my head shakes back and forth, begging it to stop. But it doesn't.

The metallic tang of blood douses me from head to toe. It's so much, I never would have been able to control my hunger if I hadn't seen Mom at the same time. Her beautiful blond hair is fanned out around her head. Each lock slowly turns red as it soaks up the blood seeping from her body. There are a dozen different wounds, but most disturbing are the tears not yet dried on her cheeks, the pleading expression in her eyes.

Maybe I should hold her, though I know she's already dead. Maybe I should close her eyes. My eyes turn away as they blur with my own tears. I force myself to continue through the house. Everywhere I step there is more blood. My shoes stick to the floor with every step, and the small effort it takes to peel the soles away from the wood drains me of energy. I'm stumbling when I turn into the living room. Dad lying face down on the blood soaked rug drops me to my knees. I can feel the wetness dampening my jeans, but it's all I can feel. The rest of me shuts down. My senses have abandoned me and made room for sickening shock. Feeling anything ever again seems impossible until a noise draws my eyes to the couch.

"They were murdered at our house. I was at football

practice and Van was at dance class. I finished practice and went home to get something to eat before I went to pick up Van. That's when I found them," I say, the words tumbling out of their own accord now. Aside from Van and the police, I haven't talked about that day to anyone. I haven't even been back to the house.

I don't look at Ivy. I know that all I'll see in her face is pity, so I keep my eyes down. If I could close my ears to her voice as well, I would. For so long after it happened, it was all anyone could talk about when they saw me. Not all of the words were ones of condolences. Those other kinds of comments are the ones I fear will come from Ivy. When she does speak, her question surprises me.

"Zander, would you consider this a date?"

Looking up at her, I see only seriousness on her face. "What?"

"I know we didn't come together, but we planned on hanging out after the game. Does this count as a date?" she asks again.

Not sure whether she's trying to distract me, or if this is somehow related to what I told her, I shrug helplessly. "Uh, I guess so. I've been thinking of it as a date all week."

"If this is a date…then I get a question, right?"

My stomach drops, my body tightens, and dread fills me from the tips of my hair to my toenails. Whatever she asks, I promised I would answer. The single word slips from my mouth unwillingly. "Right."

Ivy hesitates. Her eyes dart around before settling on me. She looks nervous, but her curiosity and concern are too much for her. "Why is Oscar in a mental hospital?"

Van told me Ivy knew about Oscar, but not why he was being held. After what I just told her, I guess she doesn't need to be told anymore. Closing my eyes to the inevitability of her reaction, I force myself to give her an honest answer.

"Oscar was very unstable at the end. He didn't know what he was doing."

"He's the one who killed them?" Ivy asks quietly.

I nod, but can't utter the actual words.

When everyone in school heard what had happened, it was unbearable to walk down the halls. Van handled it her way, and I handled it mine. Van's way landed her in the principal's office more times than I can remember. Mine pushed everyone away. Almost everyone. Lisa wouldn't let me push her away, and she paid for it.

My eyes close when Ivy doesn't respond. What else could I have expected? Of course she's smart enough to realize I'm just as dangerous as Oscar. My body turns away from her in a futile attempt to spare myself from her reaction.

There is a moment where I can't feel Ivy anywhere near me. So when her fingers rest against my cheek, it startles me enough to make me look up, hungry and frightened.

"I'm not afraid of you, Zander," Ivy says quietly.

I stumble back. "Maybe you should be."

Ivy takes a step back, but makes no move to get any farther away from me. She drops her arms to her sides and looks at me without moving. Ten, fifteen seconds go by before I give up and ask, "Ivy, what are you doing?"

"I'm looking at you."

"Why?"

"I'm trying to see this scary person you think is inside you, but I can't find him. All I see is you, Zander. You're not your brother. You aren't going to turn into him," she says.

"You don't know that for sure. I don't know that," I argue.

Ivy steps toward me, closing the distance between us to mere inches and setting my hunger on fire. "You've had plenty of opportunities to hurt me, but you haven't."

"Yes I have," I say as my fingers hover over her arm where the bruises I gave her have finally faded.

"You didn't mean to do that. It was an accident."

That word sends a jolt through me. An accident. It was an accident. Her lifeless eyes stare up at me, her mouth open in a silent plea. I can't stop seeing her. I close my eyes against the sight, but she follows me inside my head, silent and accusing. I can never get rid of her. The heels of my hands press into my eye sockets. It was an accident. I didn't mean to do it.

"Zander? Zander, are you okay?"

Ivy's voice pricks my bubble of torment and sends it skittering away on the sound wave. It doesn't go far, though, only back into the recesses of my memory that will never be deep enough to keep it buried.

"Zander, what's wrong?" Ivy begs.

"Nothing." A shiver runs through my body as the last hint of her image fades away.

"Did I say something that upset you? I'm sorry I brought up your family. I didn't mean to hurt you," Ivy says.

I shake my head and struggle to regain control. "No, it

wasn't my family. It was nothing. Just forget it, okay?"

"It wasn't your family?" Ivy's pleading expression is hard to resist, but I don't answer her. She looks at me, a mixture of compassion and need to know filling her expression. "What else happened to you?"

My arms cross over my chest. A single step back drops an invisible wall between us. I try to keep my voice normal when I speak, but I fail. "No more questions, Ivy."

The hard edge to my words makes her chin fall. I can't puzzle out her expression well enough to know whether it is in disappointment, hurt, or something else. It kills me to refuse Ivy anything, but I can't talk about that night. Not now, not ever. That is one secret I plan on taking with me to Hell.

17

TRAITOROUS MOUTH

ander hands me the drinks with barely a word and walks away. Not far, but far enough that I can't hear anything he's saying. It doesn't stop me from seeing the odd expression on his face. Troubled would be an understatement. He's trying to hide it, but I know my brother too well. No doubt Ivy is the source of his strangled mood.

"Are you going to give me one of those, or what?" Ketchup says.

I jump at the sound of his voice. I hadn't noticed that he'd come up behind me. Without taking my eyes off Zander and Ivy, I hold his soda out to him. He takes it with a grumble, which I ignore. My attention is focused on my brother. He held her hand half an hour ago, but now he is back to keeping his distance. An impenetrable buffer of at least three feet separates them at all times.

"Your slushy is melting."

Annoyed, I turn and glare at Ketchup.

"What? It is," he says. "What's your deal with Ivy

anyway? One minute you're ready to punch her teeth out, the next you're chatting with her at lunch."

I look around the area, and ask, "Where is Laney?"

"She got mad that I wasn't listening to her and went to get some nachos." Ketchup shrugs, showing how little Laney's whereabouts mean to him. That's one thing he and Zander have in common. Neither one of them can stand talking to Laney for more than five minutes.

"Maybe I should go find her," I say. I turn toward the concession line, but before I can get a good look, Ketchup hooks his arm around my shoulder and jerks me to his side. I look up at him, startled. "Ketchup, what was that for?"

Just then, a few of Zander's teammates plow through the crowd like a pack of wildebeests. Not a one of them are paying attention to what's in front of them. They knock a few others down as they charge forward. When I look back at Ketchup, he smirks at me. "You're welcome."

Throwing his arm off my shoulder, I wrinkle my nose at him and stalk over to a suddenly vacant bench to sit down. Ketchup follows, of course. He plops down on the bench and leans against the fence as he takes a drink. I do the same. The lightly carbonated slushy tickles my throat as it slides down. Usually it can make me smile, but not now. Not with Zander and Ivy chatting it up like everything is normal.

"I've seen you do some cool stuff, Van, but I seriously doubt Ivy is going to spontaneously burst into flames just because you keep glaring at her," Ketchup says.

That thought brings a smile to my face. Ketchup laughs and elbows me in the side playfully. "Really, what do you have against Ivy?"

I'm about to burst with the need to talk to someone about Ivy. I've tried handling it all on my own, keeping the details and possibilities straight. There's just too much going on to keep everything separate and orderly. When Noah and I were talking between classes, I tried telling him some of my concerns about Ivy, but he thought I was just being overprotective. I can't keep this all to myself anymore. Ketchup stuck by me when I started talking about strange, phantom tastes. I cross my fingers that he won't bail on me after this.

"I think Ivy is hiding something, and I think Zander is going to get hurt because of it."

Ketchup's eyebrows rise as he takes another long draw from his soda. His lips slide off the straw thoughtfully, drawing my attention. I turn away from him quickly. "You think she's playing Zander?" he asks.

"I think she's doing worse than that. I think she came here just to hurt him." It's a big accusation to make, one I couldn't bring myself to mention to Noah. I wait for Ketchup to laugh or elbow me again.

Instead, he leans closer to me until our shoulders are touching. "What makes you think Ivy's going to hurt him?"

The fact that he's at least willing to hear me out is encouraging. In a hushed tone, I spill out all her odd comments, sneaking questions behind my back, insistence on being near my brother, and strange reactions to Zander's bad treatment. As I'm telling him everything, it sounds a little crazy even to me. A small part of me orders my mouth to stop making noise. Deep down, I know I'm right. I watch Ketchup's eyes narrow in thought, his mouth twist into something between believing and passing off everything I've said. I decide to take a big risk and tell Ketchup more than I should.

"He hurt her, Ketchup. She showed up after practice and he grabbed her arm hard enough that she was still favoring it a couple days later. Despite that, she kept making an effort to be around him. And…" My voice trails off. Maybe I can't tell him as much as I thought I could. The words stick in my throat. My fight with Zander earlier this week starts replaying in my head. *He would have left if you'd told him the truth.* I argued that he was wrong, but my confidence isn't nearly so great sitting next to Ketchup with the words frozen on my lips.

"And what?" Ketchup asks. When I don't answer, he sets his drink down and curls his hand around mine. "You can tell me, Van."

Can I really? I stare at our hands intertwined. This isn't just the guy futilely trying to get me to date him. This is also my lifelong friend. He's backed me up plenty of times when I really needed someone on my side. And it's cost him to do that. Ketchup is incredibly good looking. He's fit and athletic, has strong features that could easily belong on film, thick jet black hair that reminds me of Superman, and the best smile I've ever seen. I know I'm not the only one who thinks this about him either. In any other reality, girls would be falling all over him, but because he's friends with me, no one at school will even think of asking him out. He and I are a pair, even if not in the way he wants.

"You know the way Zander feels about you?" I ask him.

His brow crinkles, but he says, "Yeah. What does that have to do with Ivy?"

"He feels the same way about Ivy, and so do I."

"What?" He stuck through the rest of my explanation with barely a comment, but this obviously doesn't make any sense to him. "I don't get it. I can believe you hate Ivy, but if Zander hated her, too, why would he be holding her hand and inviting her to football games?"

"Zander doesn't hate Ivy. I don't hate Ivy either."

"But, you said it was the same way Zander felt about me."

I sigh, knowing that explaining this without actually explaining everything isn't working very well. "Ketchup, Zander doesn't hate you." Ketchup stares at me, not convinced. I try to give him a little more. "Zander may think you're a little annoying and pushy, but he doesn't hate you."

"Annoying and pushy aren't strong enough emotions to force his sister to dump me, Van. There has to be something more to it than that," he says.

"There is," I say, "but it's not something I can explain to you right now."

Frowning, his thumb starts wandering back and forth across my hand. The sensation pushes me to close my eyes and memorize the feeling. I don't want him to stop. Ketchup's voice seeps through my focus and pulls me back. "It has something to do with Oscar, doesn't it?"

"Yeah," I say.

He nods slowly. "I still don't understand what's going on with Ivy."

"There are certain people Zander and I shouldn't be around. Ivy's one of them. For Zander, you're one of them."

"I'm not one of those people for you, though?" he asks, hope visible in his eyes.

"No, not for me," I admit, even though lying would probably make things considerably easier between us. His hand tightens around mine, and for a moment, I feel my fingers mimicking his.

"So why is Zander with Ivy?"

I shake my head wearily. "He thinks he's in love with her. He knows he should stay away, but he can't, or won't. But that's not really the strangest part. What's really weird about Ivy is that she's the only person Zander and I have both needed to stay away from. That's never happened before. Along with everything else, I know there's something wrong with her. She didn't end up in Albuquerque with me and Zander by accident, and she isn't interested in my brother because he's tall, dark, and handsome. I just can't figure out what she is after."

I wait for Ketchup to say something, my eyes travelling to his mouth in anticipation. My thoughts get a little jumbled as I stare. The way his lips press together as he thinks makes me wonder how they would feel against mine. I almost got to taste him once. Seconds before Ketchup actually got up the nerve to kiss me, Zander had come home and nearly devoured him. Ketchup thought Zander flew at him because he saw him trying to make out with his little sister. I didn't know what else to say at the time, so I let him believe it. Now, even with Zander standing only a few feet away, I'm desperate

231

to pick up where we left off.

Ketchup's head drops, stealing my focus, and reminding me of the impossibility of my secret desires. If my only problem was that Zander wanted to kill Ketchup, I know I could make it work. The sickness is a bigger problem. With how fast it progresses, I would have to see Zander every few days. We can never live very far apart. Zander will always be a very important part of my life.

At one time, I thought I could get around this by relying on Oscar. It would have worked perfectly since Oscar not only didn't want to maim Ketchup, he actually liked him. But that's hardly a possibility now. Maybe someday I will figure something out that will allow me to stay in my brother's life and have the one person in this world I want most, but for now I have to stay focused on keeping us alive.

I make myself refocus on my discussion with Ketchup, and hold my breath for his reaction. Expecting either agreement or disbelief, when Ketchup doesn't do either it throws me for a loop.

"So, it isn't just your brother being ridiculously overprotective that's stopping you from letting me do more than this?" he asks, lifting our joined hands just enough to make sure I know what he's talking about.

It *so* wasn't what I was expecting him to say that all I can do is stare at our hands. I know I should pull mine away. Until I can offer Ketchup a real future with me, I'm only hurting him. I know this is true, but my hand stays where it's at as I say, "No, it's more than that. Zander can't be around you."

"He's around Ivy, and you said it's the same thing."

"It's killing him to be so close to her. The only thing stopping him from hurting her is that he loves her enough to hold back, and no offense, but even if Zander doesn't hate you, he doesn't love you either." I smile, hoping it will soften the harshness of my words. The corner of Ketchup's mouth turns up, but not far, and not for long. "Ketchup, it's really, really dangerous for Zander to be spending so much time with Ivy. I'm terrified he's going to screw up and end up locked up or dead. They shouldn't be around each other. Ivy knows that, but she still hangs around. I don't get it."

"I do," he says softly.

When I look back over at him, I find his eyes already focused on me. The ache reflected there tears at my soul. "What do you mean?" I ask, startled that my voice is suddenly so shaky.

"Look, Van, I won't pretend to understand any of what you've told me tonight. I don't get why Zander can't be around me or Ivy, but I trust you enough to accept it. What I do know is that you are more than you're willing to tell me. You're just as dangerous as your brother, but just like Ivy, I'm not leaving." His hand slips out of mine. I instantly miss his touch, but to keep myself from grabbing for him, I curl my fingers into a fist. I can't give him false hope. That would just be cruel. He deserves better than that.

That's when his arm drapes across my shoulder and pulls me in. So much for the high road. I sit beside him stiffly, but I don't pull away. I want more than anything in this moment to let my body sink against his. Lulled by Ketchup's touch, what he just said doesn't make it to my brain immediately. When it does, the falseness of his comparison of himself and Ivy clangs like a raucous cow bell in my ears.

"Ketchup, Ivy isn't in love with Zander."

"It's a pretty good reason to overlook certain things," he says. "Believe me, I know."

I have to close my eyes and pretend I didn't hear that. "That's not why she's still with him."

Ketchup sighs at my refusal to acknowledge his feelings for me, but is good enough to lend some of his concentration back to our conversation. His brow crinkles as he thinks. I try to ignore the way his fingers tap on my shoulder, too, but it's awfully hard. Not only does it remind me that his arm is around my shoulders when it shouldn't be, it's really irritating. I reach up to grab his fingers and make him stop tapping. Either he saw the move coming, or he planned it this way, but his hand curls around mine right as I reach for him, and he refuses to let go. Then he distracts me with an answer.

"If Ivy knows Zander is dangerous, but isn't in love with him, then she must be trying to bait him into hurting her."

"Why would she do that?" I ask. It's not a new idea, kids have done that to me before—usually succeeding—but I don't see what Ivy would get in exchange for the huge risk she's taking.

"Maybe she's trying to expose him for what he is," Ketchup says, "and I don't mean like when Tommy Ned threw that baseball at your face just to watch the welt it gave you disappear within seconds. He did that to be a jerk and make you look like a freak."

"Which he did."

"You're not a freak, Van," Ketchup says sharply. I roll my eyes at him and urge him to spit out the rest of his explanation. I am too a freak.

"For Ivy to put herself next to Zander, she's got to have a bigger reason than that. She must want to show a bunch of people, or a certain person, how dangerous he is."

"Who would care that much?" I ask. "If Zander actually hurt Ivy, the police would get involved, but they would just think he was insane like Oscar. They'd lock him up and forget about him. Maybe it would be on the news for a while, but she wouldn't have really accomplished anything."

Ketchup leans back, pulling me along with him. Before I know it, my head is resting on his shoulder comfortably. This time, I am in control enough to start to sit back up, but his arm tightening around me makes me pause. I look at him, ready to tell him that we shouldn't. The pure puppy dog longing in his eyes begs me to give him just this one moment. I can't resist. I realize I don't want to. My head lies back down on his shoulder as a sense of warmth spreads through my body.

"Maybe we can find out who, if anyone, is behind Ivy's interest in Zander," Ketchup says.

"What do you mean?"

"When Laney asked you both to go to her house Sunday, Ivy said she couldn't because she wasn't allowed to go places on Sunday."

My "*and...*" is implied in my expression.

"I thought that was kinda weird when she said it. Unless her family is super religious, and Ivy is extremely obedient and pious—which doesn't really fit with her pink striped hair and attraction to Zander—she is lying. She's hiding the real reason she can't hang out on Sundays," Ketchup says. "And if we try hard enough, I'm sure we can figure out what she's really doing."

"Are you suggesting we spy on Ivy this Sunday?"

"Yep."

"You really think we can do it without being caught?"

"Yeah, no problem."

He says it with such confidence that I wonder whether or not he has reason to be so sure of his abilities. Has he spied on me before? That leaves me with both an icky feeling, and an excited hum running over my skin. I'm not sure which one is more powerful, but I'm definitely going to make sure my curtains are closed tonight.

Hoping my thoughts aren't blatant in my expression, I turn to look at Ketchup. With my head on his shoulder, it puts our faces rather close together when he turns toward me as well. His eyes are suddenly all I can think about. I used to tease him that his eyes were the color of mud. It made him furious every time I said it. They're still a strange mixture of grey and brown, but they don't remind me of mud anymore. Instead, the colors look to be slowly blending together, a potter's clay not yet molded into what it is meant to become. They hold immeasurable possibilities, and I think they are the most beautiful things I have ever seen.

"You really want to help me?" I ask him quietly. In the midst of thumping bass and melodramatic voices blaring through the party, I'm not sure how he even hears me, but he nods with conviction. "Everything I've told you tonight sounds like a bunch of crap, but you're willing to go along with it. Why?"

"Because I trust you," he says simply. The other reason is left unsaid, but it's echoed in the way he holds me. Because he loves me, too.

"We may get into trouble doing this," I warn him.

He grins. "That's nothing new."

"I'm serious, Ketchup. This may lead to serious consequences for you."

"I said I'll help, so I will."

Several minutes pass where neither one of us speaks. It isn't uncomfortable. I have no desire to look away from the intensity of his gaze. I want to be swallowed by it.

"You could have told me why you really broke up with me, Van."

"I still haven't told you, not really," I admit.

"Tell me."

I shake my head. "I can't."

"Yes you can. Nothing you can say will make me leave, Van."

"This will."

"No, it won't. Whatever this thing with you and Zander really is, we could find a way to make it work."

My chin drops down. "If I choose you, I'd have to give up Zander. He's my brother, Ketchup. I can't do that to him."

Ketchup's fingers glide across my cheek, tricking me into looking back up. His mouth hovers just above mine. "I'm not going anywhere, Van."

"I don't want you to," my traitorous mouth whispers.

The desire in his eyes staggers me. When he leans in, I don't move. I don't even want to. I want to recapture the moment I lost two years ago.

Incredibly loud slurping right next to my ear diverts my eyes to find Laney staring at me. I jump away from Ketchup and scramble to my feet. Laney turns on her heel to follow my frenzied movements. Looking annoyed as anything, Ketchup tries to follow me. He darts around Laney in an attempt to reach me. She's no help at all, turning out of his way and watching with a fascinated grin while trying not to drop her nachos.

"Van, wait," Ketchup says when I elude him.

I grab Laney's arm and start dragging her toward the parking lot. "I'm going home, Ketchup."

"Home?" Laney squeaks. "I just got back. Things are getting interesting. I don't want to leave, yet."

"I'll drive you," Ketchup says as he catches up to me and tries to grab my arm.

"I...no. No. Come on, Laney."

As I pass by Zander, he looks over at me questioningly, a hint of concern in his eyes. I shouldn't leave him there with Ivy, but I turn away and keep walking. He isn't the only one with problems. He'll be safe enough with so many other people around. I push through the gate without looking back. I spot Laney's car and make a beeline for it.

"Van, wait!" Ketchup grabs my hand and yanks me to a stop. I spin around to face him, unsure of what to say. Luckily, he talks before I have to figure it out. "What time should I pick you up on Sunday?"

There's so much more hiding behind those words, but I force myself to ignore all of it. "Um, I don't know. Early? What time do you think we should start?"

Before he can answer, Laney pipes up, and for once I know how Zander and Ketchup feel. "I thought you were going out with Noah on Sunday. Aren't you going to start writing your scene or something?"

Jealousy tightens Ketchup's grip on me. "Not until later," I say through my teeth.

"Eight o'clock then?" Ketchup asks.

"Sure." I slide myself out of his hold and shove Laney toward the new car she just got for her birthday. She has sense enough to shut up until we're inside and pulling away.

"So, you wanna talk about what just happened...or what almost happened?"

Glaring at her, I say, "No."

She shrugs and lets me be for now. If only my own heart and mind would do the same. All the way home, the only thing I can think about is the favor Zander owes me and how I know exactly what I want to ask for.

18

THE THREE G'S

When Noah pulls up in front of my house, I jump up and fly out of the front door with barely even a goodbye to Grandma. I have to get away. Zander has been a moody mess since Friday night. Grandma isn't any better, but they are the easiest thing I've had to deal with today. Spending the morning with Ketchup was torture. Not only was it awkward and weird between us, the only thing we saw Ivy do all morning was go into the converted garage in her backyard and come back out hours later.

What was the garage converted into? Now *that* we couldn't figure out without getting caught. Too many eyes to attempt a look in broad daylight. When we finally had to give up so I could make it back in time to meet Noah, the tension between us got even worse. I was about to choke on it by the time we got back to my house.

Climbing into Noah's car, I buckle myself in with a nervous smile.

"Hey, so how was the party after the game Friday night?" he asks.

My insides twist into a million shapes they shouldn't. "Uh, fine."

"Did you stay very long?"

"Not really. I was pretty tired. It was a long day." It's been a long couple of weeks, actually.

"Well, are you ready to do some writing?" he asks.

"I guess, though I'm not sure how much writing we're actually going to need to do. I don't think there's a lot of talking in a battle scene. Not unless you count yelling."

Noah laughs. "True. I'm sure we'll come up with something."

As we drive over to his house, I will myself to relax. At one point, the idea of Noah actually developing feelings for me was exciting. I let myself wonder what it would be like to have a normal relationship with someone. Ordinary sounded so wonderful at the time. Now, every moment I spend with Noah just inspires more guilt.

Thankfully, Noah lives on the opposite end of the school district, so I have plenty of time to try and collect myself. I push everything but our project out of my mind. Surprisingly, Zander and Ivy are the easiest to ditch. Ketchup is the hardest. He lasts until we reach Noah's house.

When we park in Noah's driveway, I stare up at the split level home in awe. Not because it's huge or lavish. It's pretty average sized, actually. The lawn is well cared for, but not perfect, and the mailbox looks like it's been backed into several times. I smile, wondering if that was due to Noah learning to drive. What I really love about his house is the tricycle left on the grass, the giant-sized scribble drawing done in chalk on the driveway, and the blaring sounds of pop music spilling out of an upstairs window. His house is happy and alive.

The impression doubles when we walk through the door. His little sister Amelia is running through the house with a fairy wand in her hand and a cape tied around her neck. A slightly taller, equally energetic boy chases after her with a Nerf dart gun spraying foam bullets in every direction. In the kitchen his mom and older sister are cooking dinner together and arguing about how the recipe should be prepared. Noah's mom is waving a spatula covered in something yellow and creamy at her daughter when she notices us.

"Noah," she says, smiling and dropping the spatula back into the bowl. She wipes her hands on a towel and holds one out to me. "And you must be Van. It's nice to meet you. I'm Elsa, and this is Kennedy, Noah's older sister."

Kennedy swoops past her mom and ruffles her brother's hair. "Nice to meet you, Van. We've heard *lots* about you from Noah here."

"Shut up, Kennedy," Noah quips. She laughs at him and saunters back to the stove.

"Mom, we're going downstairs to the den. Can you keep the little ones out while we're working?"

"I'll try," she says with a smile. After seeing them tear through the house a minute ago, trying might be the most anyone can expect. "Van, you haven't eaten yet, have you? We'd love for you stay for dinner tonight."

Caught off guard by her invitation, it takes me a minute to respond. "Uh, no I haven't eaten yet, but you really don't have to feed me. I'll just eat when I get home."

"You'll eat with us." End of discussion, apparently. She turns back to the stove to argue with Kennedy some more and gets another plate out of the cupboard to add to the stack already on the counter. I'm sure she's forgotten about us completely until we start to head downstairs and she throws one more comment over her shoulder. "Stay in the den, Noah. No girls in your bedroom, okay?"

"Okay, Mom," Noah drawls, rolling his eyes.

He leads me downstairs to a toy covered den. His growl of frustration amuses me. "Sorry this place is such a mess. My little brother and sister are walking disasters. It's impossible to get them to clean up after themselves."

"It's okay, Noah," I say. "It's actually kind of nice. I like the mess."

He looks at me with one eyebrow cocked. "I didn't picture you as a messy kind of person, despite the sponges and spilled cookies."

"I'm not, but this is different."

"How?"

I shrug, not sure what I mean myself. "It isn't dirty clothes or forgotten sandwiches. It's the mess of playing and being happy. They're too busy running around playing cowboys and some kind of fairy princess superhero game to worry about picking up. It's nice. It's a sign that your house is happy."

"You'll have to tell my mom that. It will make her day to

243

hear toys on the floor equals happiness. It'll mean our house is about the happiest place on earth," Noah says.

I laugh and start helping him clean up. When we have some free space on the floor, we sit down on a couple of bean bag chairs with a notebook and absolutely zero ideas. Fifteen minutes later, we still don't have anything useable. Throwing my pencil down, I sink into my bean bag.

"I have no idea where to start with this."

"Where to start..." Noah sits up. "Well, why do most battles and wars start?"

"The three G's," I say automatically.

"What?"

"God, gold, and glory. Didn't you have Ms. Ames for world history?" I ask.

Noah shakes his head. "I had Dunne."

"Oh, well that was always Ms. Ames' answer for wars. Some kind of religious proclamation of superiority, wealth being at stake, or the need to be the biggest and most powerful. Pick any war in history and she could give you one of those three reasons as the cause of it," I say.

"Hmm," Noah says, "I think Paris and Helen of Troy might disagree with Ms. Ames. Love can spark wars just as quickly as the other three."

"Paris and Helen aren't real people, Noah. They don't count."

Slouching into his bean bag, Noah looks at me thoughtfully. "You think they're the only ones that ever started a fight because they weren't supposed to be together? *West Side Story* is a classic movie, one everybody's seen. It's the same thing."

"It's *Romeo and Juliet*, another fictional story." I pick the notebook and pencil back up off the floor. I hold the pencil ready to write something, anything. This isn't really a topic I want to discuss right now. "Besides, we can't use love as a reason for our fight. There's only two of us, and if we were in love with each other, why would we be fighting?"

"We'd have to have a love triangle, I suppose, but you're right that we'd need three people for that," Noah says. He taps his chin. "Too bad Ketchup isn't in our class. I bet Mr. Littleton would let us add him in if we asked."

My head snaps up, and we lock eyes. His are calm, but his body is held taut. Mine is immoveable. Although, the feeling of insects crawling around under my skin is on the verge of making me jump up and bolt. "What?" I manage to ask.

The corner of Noah's mouth twitches at the sharpness in my tone. "Van, I'm not blind. Ketchup sat behind me the whole game. I could feel him glaring at me every second, and if I even got close to touching you, he *accidently* kneed me in the back or kicked me. It's obvious that Ketchup has a thing for you."

"Look, Ketchup is…my best friend," I finish lamely.

Noah frowns. "Best friend? Or something more?"

"We're not dating."

"Look, I know it may be none of my business," Noah says, "but I like you. I want to keep seeing you, and not just to do homework. If you're not interested, well, you can just say so and I'll back off."

I look down at the notebook, tapping the pencil against it to keep my thoughts focused. I love Ketchup. I always will. But I would be lying if I said Noah and his normal life wasn't at least a little appealing. Maybe it's the right thing to do. If I distanced myself from Ketchup, he might find someone else and be happier. If I were a stronger person I would do it. In the end, I answer Noah's question as honestly as I can.

"I don't know what I want," I say. "I do like you. You're really sweet, and you actually want to hang out with me, which is a big plus. It's just that there's a lot going on in my life right now."

I look up at him, hoping he can understand. Noah nods thoughtfully. "Does Ketchup know that?" he asks, a bit of annoyance creeping into his voice.

"What is that supposed to mean?"

Noah sighs. "Ketchup doesn't seem to care that you've put limits on your relationship with him. He still looks at you like you're his. And you don't stop him from acting like that."

"How am I supposed to stop him?" I snap.

"By putting some distance between the two of you, for one."

Meeting Noah's eyes, I don't know what to say but the truth. "Noah, I'm sorry Ketchup wasn't very nice to you at the game, but nothing I say to him will change that. He really is a good guy, but yes, it bothers him to see you with me. Maybe I should walk away from him, do the right thing, but I can't. There's too much history, too long of a friendship for me to do that. I'm sorry, but if you want to hang around with me, you have to accept the fact that Ketchup will be there too."

"Ketchup isn't going to run me off." Noah suddenly grins. "I just hope he's ready for some competition."

I shake my head, knowing Ketchup is more than up to the challenge. "Good luck," I say with a smile. "We've been friends since kindergarten. We've been through a lot together. It won't be easy to get him to back off"

"Then why aren't you dating?" Noah shakes his head. "Sorry, none of my business."

Shaking my head, I appreciate him trying not to be nosy, but I feel I owe him some kind of explanation, even if it's not much. "I know it sounds cliché, but it's complicated. Family stuff mostly. I can't really go into it, but Ketchup and I are only friends."

More questions burn in Noah's eyes, but he is nice enough not to ask. He seems glad for now to know that there is a chance for a relationship to develop between us. To be honest, so am I.

A few silent minutes later, Noah's mom calls us up for dinner. Well, she calls everyone, and everyone comes pouring out of both levels to converge on the kitchen in a rush. Dodging them is tricky. I end up flattening myself against the wall as I watch them fall into their seats. The three siblings I met earlier are joined by two more, a boy who looks to be about ten and a girl who can't be much older than thirteen. His parents sit at either end of the table, and two chairs have been squashed in at one end to make room for me and Noah.

"Are there anymore?" I whisper to Noah.

He chuckles, and says, "Nope, that's everyone. Hungry?"

I nod, but more than just the large family staring at

me holds me back. Zander, Oscar, and I once tried to figure out how many people in the world our hunger might want. We tallied up everyone we had ever come in contact with that spiked our hunger at school and compared it to how many people were in our school. It was hardly scientific, and probably not terribly accurate, but the numbers we got were a bit discouraging. On average, one in twenty or so people appeal to our hunger. Any time I get around a group of new people, I get nervous, and there are still four members of Noah's family that I have yet to really meet.

Before I can work up the courage to approach his family of my own free will, Noah slips his hand into mine and tugs me forward. He didn't do it just to get me started, either. He makes no move to let go of me as we cross the kitchen to the dining room. Maybe because he's partially dragging me.

I breathe a sigh of relief when Noah finally lets go of me to pull my chair out. Hoping I can melt into the general mayhem around me and stay at a safe distance until I can be sure, I fold my hands in my lap and don't say anything. Not more than two seconds pass before Noah's mom is introducing me to everyone at the table, telling me their names and letting everyone in on the details of the project Noah and I are working on.

That gets the ball of chatter and chaos rolling. As everyone talks and passes food, nothing at all rouses my hunger. After a while, I begin to relax and enjoy the banter. The whole rest of the meal, I have a hard time finding a second to take a bite with all the questions everyone keeps firing at me. Even little Amelia gives it a go, asking me about my dancing and if I'm Noah's girlfriend. That one hushes the entire table, including me. I glance over at Noah in a panic, but he handles it smoothly.

"Pickle, quit bugging Van and eat your potatoes."

Her whole face wrinkles in annoyance, but her miniature sized fork dips into the pile of mashed potatoes on her plate anyway. I do the same, not even noticing Noah's hand reaching under the table until he pats my leg and squeezes me reassuringly. He pulls it back casually and asks one of his sisters that I can't remember the name of how her volleyball game went the night before. The conversation flows away from me and on to what everyone else in the family has been doing. I soak it all in, amazed that so many people can function together and not end up with blood all over the walls.

When dinner finishes, I offer to help clean up, but both his mom and Kennedy wave me off. Noah and I try to work on our project a little more, but after an hour of getting nowhere, it's time for him to take me home. Leaving is an experience as well. I get a hug from everyone in the family, thanks for coming over, and an open invitation to come back anytime. When Noah finally manages to pull me out of the house, I stare at him in disbelief.

"Your family is…"

"Nuts?" he finishes. "Yeah, I used to try to warn people, but they never believed me, so I gave up. Sorry they kind of attacked you in there."

"No, it was great, Noah. Your family is awesome."

"Really, 'cause you looked pretty scared most of the time," he teases.

I smile and shrug. "A little, maybe, but it was nice. It was nothing like my family. It was happy and exciting. Thanks for inviting me over."

Noah steps closer, close enough to make me anxious. "Thanks for coming."

Nervous energy flutters through my veins. I can barely find my voice, but I say, "We didn't get much done on our project."

"That's okay. We have plenty of time." His head tilts to the side very slightly, as if he is considering something. He takes another step closer. There can't be more than an inch or two between our bodies now.

For a moment, I panic. I don't know what to do. Noah must see it in my eyes. His body tightens, but doesn't move. "Van, I really like you. I know that may freak you out a little, but I really hope you'll give me a chance."

Before I know what is happening, Noah's lips brush against mine. When he pulls back, I smile, amazed at the warmth of his affection. Noah's smile widens as he presses his palm against my cheek. "Do you know what the best part of tonight was, besides kissing you just now?" he asks.

I shake my head, unable to speak.

"Seeing you smile so much during dinner." He grins at me. "You have the most beautiful smile, but you hardly ever let anyone see it. I'd like to see you smile more often, and I think maybe I can make that happen if you let me try."

I nod slowly and say, "I think I would like that."

"I better get you home," he says with a smile. His hand grasps mine briefly to get me moving, but he doesn't push me any more tonight. He lets go once I begin to follow him.

The drive back to my house is quiet, but not uncomfortable. I make it up to my room before the fact that I just had my first kiss really hits me. I have imagined my first kiss hundreds of times, and that wasn't it. It's not that Noah's kiss wasn't sweet and wonderful; it's that it was with Noah. That's not how it was supposed to be. Every fantasy I ever dreamed up was of Ketchup. A sickening sense of betrayal lodges itself in my heart.

19

SATISFYING

*S*omething is going on with Van. I watch Ketchup drive away from our house with a frown. That's three Sundays in a row now that he's picked her up before breakfast and not dropped her off until right before Noah shows up either to take her back to his house to work on their project or go workout. The only thing that keeps me from thinking Van is two timing both guys is that she's my sister and I know her too well. Not only would she not get involved with Ketchup in that way without telling me, she wouldn't betray a friend for any reason.

I don't really know how to classify Noah and Van's relationship. She seems happy when she's around Noah, but guilty, too. I can certainly understand the appeal of Noah's life. It's everything Van has ever wanted, especially since our parents died. I worry that she is setting herself up for more hurt than she expects.

What also bothers me is that she still hasn't let me meet him. At first, I understood. She didn't know how it would even go with Noah. Now, with all the time she's spending with him, I need to know.

When my grandma isn't around, Van can't stop talking about how much training with Noah is helping her, about how nice he is, and how he seems to accept her even though he's heard all the stories. The problem with that last one is that Noah obviously doesn't believe what he's heard. If he did, things would be different. Not that I would ever say this out loud, but I have a suspicion that the praise for Noah isn't about how great this guy is. I saw everything that happened the night of the first football game.

She was so close to giving in to Ketchup. The brazen desire in her eyes was almost enough to convince me she should. To me, it seems like Noah is a distraction, and her talking about him so much is pure desperation. Whether I'm right or not, she seems determined to keep hanging out with Noah.

This has gone on for long enough.

In reality, I don't think she feels anything more for Noah than curiosity, but if I let this go on much longer it may turn into another Ketchup situation. If I burn Van twice, she'll never forgive me. So, I rush to change into something more comfortable and hurry downstairs. I make it down before Van even finishes fixing her hair into a ponytail. Noah isn't due to show up for another half hour, giving me enough time to slip into the kitchen where my grandma is working. Two rectangles of puff pastry are thawing on the counter. I look from the pastry to my grandma. She notices my staring and grimaces.

"Premade puff pastry? Is the world coming to an end?"

She shoos me away from the counter. "Do you have any idea how long it takes to make puff pastry from scratch? Too long. I have to be at Martha's house in two hours. I don't have time to layer dough and butter and run it through rollers a couple dozen times. These won't be nearly as good as mine, but they'll have to do."

"I'm sure they'll be great," I say, patting her shoulder. She looks over at me, with a curious expression.

"You're in a good mood."

Not that I blame her for noticing, but I'd rather avoid the topic of Ivy with her. I've seen Ivy the last couple of weekends, and she's kept her questions to less personal topics since the first game, but everyone was walking on eggshells around me for about a week after Ivy asked me about my parents and what else I was hiding. Having to talk about the day they died brought up too many unpleasant memories. For days, all I could see when I closed my eyes was the image of Oscar sitting on the couch staring at the blood on his hands, rocking back and forth and mumbling.

It took a week of Ivy asking me the most trivial string of questions every time we saw each other to finally relax. Well, about the memories, anyway. My hunger is still continuing to get worse. I don't understand why. I keep trying to figure it out with no luck. The increasing hunger and the knowledge that harder questions are going to come back up with Ivy at some point have kept me from enjoying the reprieve too much.

The time I've spent around Ivy the last few weeks has been bittersweet, though, and not wholly because of the hunger. The image of Van about to kiss Ketchup, that look of complete happiness, has haunted me. It is because of me that she holds back, and I don't know if I can ever fix that. I know she holds out hope that the situation will change. I do too, but the only changes that seem to happen are the kind that makes things worse.

When I first realized my hunger wanted Ketchup, I was on the verge of turning sixteen. My ability to control myself was becoming more fragile by the day. She *had* to keep him away from me. I thought after my hunger evened out things could be different. But that was when Oscar was there. He could be there to keep Van healthy if I couldn't.

When Oscar started disappearing for days at a time, frustrated and angry at Mom and Dad and pretty much everything, I was the only option. Oscar coming back didn't help anyone. Van and I needed each other then. There was no room for anyone else. With Van's birthday coming up, it's even more important that we're together. I want to believe I'll get used to Ketchup and the right situation will finally present itself, but I honestly don't know if that will ever come. Regardless of my disbelief, I will keep trying to give my baby sister what she wants more than anything.

Coming back to the conversation with my grandma, I say, "It's been a good week."

My grandma's smile is tight, no doubt thinking about my time spent with Ivy. I know she's dying to make a comment, but she doesn't.

"Hey, you don't need me for anything this afternoon, do you?" I ask.

"No, why?"

"I think I'm going to tag along with Van and Noah this afternoon."

"To the gym?" she asks. "Don't you get enough of a workout with football?"

I shrug. "It's not really the workout. I think it's time I get to know Noah a little better."

"Now that I can agree with. I don't like how he never comes in. It seems sneaky." Her eyes narrow just thinking about it.

"He's not being sneaky. He's being smart. Or Van is. She isn't sure how I'll react to him."

"Oh," she says, nodding. Her eyes drift to the kitchen window. It has a clear view of the driveway. "I'll be right here if you need me."

I smile my thanks and head back to the living room to wait. It seems to take forever, but eventually, I hear the rumble of Noah's car pulling up. Two seconds later, Van comes bounding down the stairs. Her happy mood falters when she sees me standing at the door. Noah knocks. Her head shakes briskly in fear. I turn the knob and pull it open anyway, bracing myself for any hint of my hunger.

When I open my door, the only reaction I have to Noah's overzealous grin is a desire to smack him. My hunger stays neatly tucked away. I'm the only one who knows that, though. No sounds come from the kitchen at all. Van isn't even breathing, and Noah's stupid smile is slowly sliding off his face. Just because I can, I wait a moment longer, screwing my face into an expression of deep scrutiny. I expect Noah to cringe, stutter something incomprehensible, run maybe.

He doesn't do any of those things. He stands stock still, but holds his composure, and extends his hand to me. "Hey, Zander, I'm Noah Harbach. Nice to finally meet you."

When I pause a moment longer, I finally catch sight of some evidence of fear from him. His hand shakes very slightly. I haven't passed judgment on him yet, but I do decide to give him a break. I take his hand firmly and shake it. "Nice to meet you, Noah."

He sighs with relief. "Is Van here?"

"Yeah."

I turn so he can see Van behind me. She isn't looking at him, though. Her eyes are targeted at me. Her question is clear. A quick shake of my head turns her fearful expression into a sigh of relief. My grandma pops into the hall then, smiling and introducing herself. After a quick round of getting to know you, she excuses herself and leaves the three of us staring at each other again.

"So, Noah," I say after my grandma is out of earshot, "Van's been telling me about your workouts, how much she's enjoying them. She mentioned that I might like to try for myself, and I was wondering if you'd mind if I came along today and gave it a try."

Noah's eyes widen, but he says, "Uh, sure. If that's okay with Van." He looks over at her. My sister glances over at me, searching me for any sign of deceit. When she doesn't find any, she nods her consent. Noah turns back to me. "Okay then. You want to ride with us, or follow in your truck."

"Follow," I say. I wanted to meet this guy and make sure

Van is handling the martial arts okay. I really don't need any more guilt about this situation than I already have. Plus, I have plans later. I can't meet with Ivy today, but that doesn't mean I won't see her.

With the driving arrangements taken care of, we all head out. Instead of driving to the gym Van has mentioned several times, I follow Noah to a park deep in an upper class neighborhood. Despite its impeccable appearance, it's deserted. I guess rich people don't spend much time at parks. When I get out of my truck, I watch as Van helps Noah lug a big black bag out of his trunk. She pretends to struggle with it, and he shoulders the bulky bag easily.

"So what happened to the gym?" I ask as I fall in beside them.

"Oh, well the gym is only open from noon to five on Saturdays, and since Van's been busy the last couple weekends, we haven't been able to make the session. So we found this quiet park instead. Nobody ever comes here, so it's the perfect place to practice." Noah drops the bag and starts pulling out punching mitts and blocking pads. He works to set out the equipment, but instead of helping him, Van walks over to me.

"Are you going to be okay with this?" she asks, her voice low.

"I'll be fine, Van. It's the same basic idea behind us playing sports. Football can be just as violent as any martial arts." I look at her pointedly. "It's not me I'm worried about."

"I've been doing this for a while now. I'll be fine. Just watch. You and Grandma always think I can't handle things, but I can."

She turns away to face Noah. He already has mitts strapped to his hands with his feet slightly apart to give him a strong base. I watch silently as he runs Van through a series of drills, explaining each movement to me as she does them. For the most part, Van keeps her punches and kicks at minimal force. She focuses on every movement she makes, but a smile slowly creeps onto her face as she progresses. When she finishes the last kick, she's grinning. She bounces lightly on her toes as she turns to face me.

"Wanna try?"

There's a half-second pause before Noah says, "Yeah, give it a try, Zander. I'll tell you what to do." He claps his mitts together in preparation, but Van grabs his wrist.

"I'll partner with Zander." She says it with such authority that Noah doesn't question her. He shrugs at the request, but hands the mitts over. My little sister beckons me to her, eager to pull me into this forbidden sport.

Van looks a bit nervous as I step up to her. I'm not sure of the source. Van and I may be able to heal quickly, but we can still get hurt. I don't think that's the reason behind her anxiety, though. I think she's actually worried I won't be able to control myself. It creates an odd feeling in me to know that.

Noah takes his place to the side of us, looking equally unnerved about Van facing me. It doesn't stop him from calling out his first set of instructions. Just a series of simple punches, I move slowly at first. I test Van's strength against mine. She holds up beautifully. I take it up a notch with the next set. That's when she starts to feel it.

Pain radiates down Van's wrists each time I hit the

mitts. It's small, at first, but it grows the longer I keep it up. When it really starts to affect us both is after Van switches to the larger blocking pad and Noah starts in with a variety of kicks. Van has to put a lot more force into blocking me, increasing the pain in her arms and burn in her thighs from holding her stance. My hunger starts taking notice. It gnaws at me and whispers to me, wanting me to push harder and faster. Against Van, it's easy to resist. Against someone else... it could definitely be a problem.

I can see why my grandma doesn't want us to have anything to do with this, but just like with football, it provides a controlled environment to cause pain. I suspected as much, but I never thought Van would be able to control her hunger even with so much structure. I'm impressed that she's handled it so well.

We continue to practice, Van and I both soaking up the pain we are causing each other in small bursts then wrapping it up immediately after. She actually seems to be enjoying the exercise. That is a surprise given how much she usually craves chaos. She's learned a lot in the past month. It gives me hope that her birthday won't be as bad as I've worried it will be.

When we are finally ready to wrap up the session, Van stares at me over the blocking pad with a hopeful expression. "What did you think?" she asks.

"I liked it. It was...satisfying. You did really well, Van."

Van grins, but all Noah can manage is to say, "Uh, good. I think."

"So you wanna keep doing it?" Van asks. Noah looks a less than thrilled about me crashing more of their "study sessions." I don't think Van notices his reaction, but she says, "We could practice together in the evening or on the weekends."

"Yeah, I think that's a good idea," I say. Not only will this help Van learn more control, it will be fun, too. Facing Van without anyone else watching will be more than satisfying. Neither one of us will have to hold back. It will be a steady stream of hunger nourishing exercise like she's never known. Football provides me with a good deal of relief, but I can already tell this will be so much better. For the first time, I wonder if my grandma knew this and still refused to let us learn.

As that thought bounces around in my head, her knowing eyes seem to follow its trail. For a moment, I doubt myself. She's told us so much, but she always has that look in her eyes that says she knows even more. Is there a real reason behind her forbidding us from fighting? Her dad was cursed with hunger, but he died when she was so young. She can't possibly know for sure.

20

FRAGMENTS OF AGONY

*G*iven that I get to see Ivy more often now, sneaking into her room at night shouldn't be something I still do. Since meeting her, I find myself doing all kinds of things I shouldn't. A quiet step over the window sill brings me into her room. She's sound asleep. My mouth turns up as I see that she's facing me this time. It's better if she's not, but I love seeing her beautiful face too much to really care. Slipping into the chair next to her bed brings me within a few feet of her. I take in the scent of her body, soap, sweat, and lotion. The blend is something I would recognize anywhere.

I don't come to her house every night. If I see her during the day, I force myself to be happy with that. When I don't see her, it's impossible for me to resist. Sundays are the hardest because she never calls me to talk, doesn't text me, and can't hang out. After a week of getting tastes of her, it feels like coming off an addiction so intense I know I'll never make it if I don't get another fix.

I saw her every day this week at least for a few minutes,

so this is the first time I've been to her room since last Sunday. Being with her at school and after my games is an equally enslaving mixture of torture and desire. It kills me to be with her, but I want the pain more than anything.

I know I'm seriously messed up, heading down the path that led Oscar to his current living arrangements, but sitting beside her at night helps me keep things balanced. On nights like this, I can be near her without rousing my hunger too much. It gives me the only semi-peaceful time I ever have with her, and it's something I can carry in the back of my mind to keep myself stable when we're face to face, clearly alive and awake.

Ivy's late night hours make not falling asleep here difficult, though. It was one-thirty before I could risk climbing through her window. Sparring with Van this afternoon isn't helping me stay awake. Soundlessly, I move the chair closer to her bed. My hand reaches out to hover over her for a brief moment. I want to touch her, but I would feel the warmth of her body, and tricking my hunger into thinking she is dead will become so much harder. Her eyes flutter—making my heart stop—then close again. I let out a breath and retract my hand.

I think I am safe now, but the sudden blaring of a car alarm snaps Ivy's eyes open. I'm fast, but I'm not that fast. Her bleary eyes seem to catch sight of something, widening and activating a warning siren in her mind, though devoid of recognition just yet. My mind is frozen. I watch, immovable, as her hand whips under her pillow. She pulls her hand back out and her body follows the path, ending in a kneeling position with the knife glinting in the moonlight. Her eyes finally see me.

"Zander?"

Speaking and thinking are not likely functions for me, at the moment. She has a knife at my neck, but there are only two thoughts completely unrelated to the blade running through my mind right now. The first one is that her tight fitting tank top and petite pajama shorts show off her toned body perfectly. The muscles of her abdomen are tight and quivering under her skin. I want to run my fingers over them.

The second coherent thought stops me from doing just that. Pain doesn't always accompany fear, but the precursor tastes like a gourmet appetizer to my hunger. Fear makes the pain more delectable the higher it climbs. Her racing heart, rapid breathing, and warm body have set my hunger ablaze. Like a twig snapping, it takes over completely. My refusal to listen to its desire is shoved away, and I watch in horror as my hands spring forward to grab her.

Ivy scrambles off the bed, knocking over a lamp in her panicked hurry. It crashes to the floor. The stained glass shade shatters. The movement and sound pauses me for a precious moment, but then the tang of blood hits me. I don't run or lurch forward. I'm not Van. Ivy's eyes widen as my legs carry me forward in a stalking, unstoppable gait. Each step is quicker than the last, more determined to bring me close enough to shatter her into fragments of agony.

Her eyes close, her arms drop to her side with the blade dangling uselessly from her fingers. She knows there's no point in trying to stop me. The pain of my heart ripping apart doesn't keep me from wrapping my fingers around her neck. I can hear the blade clatter to the ground, feel her hands grasping mine in an effort to tear them away. None of it matters.

"Ivy," someone calls through the door. "Ivy, are you okay?"

Not even fear of discovery overpowers my hunger. My fingers cinch even more tightly around her throat. I can hear her gasping breaths, see the blue tinge to her skin. Only the shock of a sharp bite from small canine teeth into my calf is capable of forcing my hands away from Ivy. She gasps in a painful breath and reaches for the door knob.

Panic overwhelms me. I have half a second to hide. No chance of making it out the window, so I roll to the side and flatten myself against the wall just before Ivy yanks her door open wide enough to poke her head out. I can see that the tip of the knife is sticking out under the door. The little Yorkie Ivy and her family just rescued earlier this week is yapping at my feet.

Its diminutive size could never physically hold me back, but its glowering eyes and incessant noise work to distract me and give me a few moments to regain control. Ivy told me about the new dog several times, but I never even considered it might be sleeping in her room tonight. Silently, I thank the noisy little thing for stopping me. My eyes close. My fingers dig into the wall to steady myself. A worried male voice pins me to the wall even more.

"Ivy, honey, what is going on in here? It sounded like a herd of elephants just ran through your room."

"Sorry, Dad. A car alarm went off outside and it scared me. I knocked my lamp off the nightstand and tripped over it when I got out of bed to shut the window."

I listen to every word in stunned silence. Why isn't she telling her father that the guy she's seeing just snuck into her room and tried to kill her? She's lying, and I have no idea why.

"Well, are you all right? Did you hurt yourself?" her dad asks.

"No, no, Dad, I'm fine, just a little startled. Go back to bed. Sorry I woke you up."

"If you're sure you're okay…" I see Ivy's head bob up and down. "Alright, honey, get a good night's sleep."

"You too," she echoes.

A second later, she closes the door quietly. Her hands linger on the white paneled wood door for a second. Then she drops down, retrieves the blade, and flicks it against my throat faster than I would have thought possible for her. My hunger surges again, but the memory of her bulging eyes and blue lips hold me back. I don't move. I don't speak, because there is nothing I can say to defend myself. I am a hunger-bound maniac with incredible strength and abilities, and I am at her mercy.

The blade pinches against my skin. About to break through, Ivy holds and stares at me. Nothing is said. My heart and hunger wage war against each other, while Ivy stares at me wide-eyed. Behind her, I can see curtains stir in the breeze, giving the only hint that this room isn't a work of art frozen in time for future generations to muse and wonder at. Close up, with the moonlight hitting her from behind, I can see the cut on her arm where a piece of the broken lampshade must have nicked her. A thin trail of blood dribbles down her biceps. It's such a small amount, but my hunger licks its lips eagerly.

"What are you doing here?" Ivy hisses.

"I..." My mind trips over itself trying to find an explanation that will work. It quickly realizes what an impossible trick that is. I just tried to kill her. There's no explanation for that but the truth, and I'm not about to offer that up.

The tip of the blade digs into my neck deeper. My hunger surges, almost forcing me back over the edge of my control. "Why are you in my room in the middle of the night?"

I don't even try to answer.

"Tell me, Zander, or so help me I'll scream and my dad will call the police. I'll tell them you were here and...and that you...I'll tell them you broke into my house." Her hand is firm against my neck, but her bottom lip is trembling slightly. Even still, I believe her. I have to give her something. I have to talk and distract myself before I tear her apart.

"I wanted to see you...and it's easier this way."

"Easier? What is that supposed to mean?" she demands.

"When you're asleep, it's easier for me to be around you."

"Why?"

I balk at answering her and she digs the blade in further. I can feel a bead of blood start making its way down my neck. The scent of it makes me whimper.

"Why?" she asks again.

My eyes close, and I know I am about to invite my own

death in for tea. My hunger balks at the thought of dying and begs me to reconsider. "Because when you're asleep, I can trick myself into thinking you're dead."

"What?" she squeaks. "Why would you want to think I was dead?"

"What you said about me and my brother. It wasn't true. I am exactly like Oscar."

She blinks. Once. Twice. Three times. "You want to kill me?" she whispers.

"Yes. I mean no." My frustrated growl makes her jump back. "Part of me wants to hurt you very badly, Ivy, but the rest of me wants to protect you."

"I...don't understand. Why do you want to hurt me?"

"I don't know," I say, cradling my head as I slide down the wall. My hands can't keep the battle raging inside my mind and body from spilling out. It tumbles out in a feral, mournful growl. "I don't know what makes me want to hurt people. I'm sorry, Ivy. I'm so sorry."

The shuffle of her feet on the carpet is almost soundless. The screaming inside my head quiets at the sound of her footsteps. "Stop moving," I snap. The sound vanishes.

"Can I talk?"

"Yes, just don't let me hear you move, Ivy. I can barely stop myself from coming after you right now. Distract me, but don't move a muscle. And cover up your cut."

"How can I distract you?" she asks quietly.

"Tell me what you're thinking."

"I...don't think you want to hear it."

She's right. I don't want to hear it. "Then tell me why

you keep a knife under your pillow."

"Um, okay," she says quietly, a whisper that betrays her nerves. "Back in California, we lived in an apartment. It was nice, but during the summer before we moved, our neighbors were renovating their apartment. They moved out while the work was being done, but the construction crew had keys to get into the building. My parents were out one night, and I had gone to bed, when one of the crew came back. He broke into our apartment with a screwdriver and started in the living room with the electronics. I heard him when he dropped one of his tools on the glass coffee table."

"What did you do?" I ask.

"I grabbed a lacrosse stick and crept out of my room."

"Ivy, that wasn't very smart."

Her huff of irritation makes me smile. Hearing her voice with all my other senses shut down begins to ease me back toward control.

"Anyway," Ivy continues, "I wasn't trying to attack him. I'm not stupid. I had left my cell phone charging on the kitchen counter. I thought I could grab it, run back to my room, and call the police."

"I'm guessing your plan didn't work very well."

She doesn't answer right away. "He heard me, freaked out, and pulled a gun. I don't think he meant to shoot it. He was as scared as I was, but the bullet almost hit me. He ran away and I called the police and my parents. They caught him, but I couldn't sleep after that. Every noise I heard made me think someone was in the apartment. My mom didn't want a gun in the house, but eventually she let me have the knife."

With her story ended, Ivy falls quiet. My yearning for blood and love slowly begins to ebb.

"Go lay down. Get under the blankets and lie very still."

I struggle to keep my tenuous calm as I hear her move to the bed. She does it as quietly as possible, but the squeak of springs and rustle of blankets are still enough to tense every muscle in my body. I stay curled up at the base of the wall until the battle raging inside me calms back down. Only when I'm confident of my ability to control myself again do I move. My feet tread carefully over to the round black trashcan with lime green flowers on it, and I pull it over to the side of Ivy's bed.

"What are you doing?" Ivy whispers.

"Cleaning up the broken lampshade. I don't want you to get cut again. The smell…it isn't good for me, and I don't like for you to be hurt."

She doesn't speak again, and the only sound in the room is the subdued plink of glass falling into the plastic bin. Luckily, most of it only broke into separate pieces rather than shattering. I get the mess cleaned up, though I take my time doing it. By the time I finish, Ivy is so quiet that I'm almost sure she's asleep. I set the trashcan back in its place. A sound proves me wrong about Ivy being asleep.

"Zander, are you okay?"

I hang my head and sigh. "You're the one that got attacked. Why are you asking me how I am?"

"Because I'm worried about you," she says quietly.

"Why didn't you tell your dad I was here?" I ask as I walk to the end of her bed and sit down on the floor with my back to her.

Ivy doesn't answer right away. I debate slipping back through her window and telling Van what I just did. She'd be more than happy to give me the thrashing I deserve for my stupidity. She wouldn't hold back, either. I think she's been chomping at the bit to finish what she started the day she punched me and tackled me to the floor.

"I didn't tell my dad because I know you're not what you think you are. You aren't a bad person, Zander. You've got some problems, but you're not alone in that. We've all got problems."

"Yeah, but how many other people's problems involve killing people?"

"You'd probably be surprised," Ivy says, almost too quiet for me to hear. Her comment pricks my curiosity, but she continues before I can ask her about it. "Zander, I've tried to put aside your issues because I don't want you to run away from me, but I think after tonight I need some real answers."

Every cell in my body howls in agony. Not because they are trying to convince me not to tell her anything, but because they know I've already made my choice.

21

TASTING DEATH

etchup grins at me when I crawl into his car. I'm barely even awake enough to smack him in the arm. That only makes him laugh. I'd like to hit him again, but I slouch down in my seat instead. Ignoring him is all the reaction I have strength for right now. Maybe it's the fact that Zander isn't here, or it might be my sour attitude, but Ketchup doesn't lurch away from my house like he usually does when he picks me up. He looks over at me seriously, his posture soft and inviting. Then again, it might be the fact that when Zander told me last night after he picked me up from work that he wouldn't be able to take me to school today, I called Ketchup instead of asking Grandma for a ride.

I didn't call Ketchup because anything has changed. The more time I spend with Noah and his family, the more my desire to have a normal life grows. I called Ketchup because Zander has been acting really weird since Sunday night. Well, Monday morning, I should say. I don't know where he was all night, but he didn't get home until after three in the morning

272

again. All yesterday he acted nervous, but at the same time relieved. It was a weird combination I couldn't explain. Then he tells me he can't take me to school because he's picking Ivy up so they can go out after practice. He didn't want to tell me what they were doing, but I wouldn't let him go until he admitted they were going to a movie.

Maybe to anyone else that would seem harmless enough, but I know better. Hunger mixed with him and Ivy sitting up close and personal in the dark is the fast track to disaster. I freaked out and yelled at him, just barely holding back another punch in the face, but he wouldn't relent. He kept saying it was fine. He had everything taken care of. I have no idea what that meant, but when he slipped and said Ivy was going to help him, I knew something was wrong. He clammed up and refused to even speak to me after that. There's no way Ivy can help him unless she knew what the problem is.

He told her something.

"Hey," Ketchup says, "are you okay? You aren't usually this crabby in the morning."

"Couldn't sleep last night."

Ketchup startles me by slipping his hand over mine. "Van, what's wrong?"

Shaking my head, I look over at him. "Something's up with Zander...something's wrong. I'm afraid something bad is going to happen."

"What do you mean?"

"I think he told Ivy something he shouldn't have, and now they're planning on going out tonight. Alone. He's acting

273

weird…taking risks, keeping secrets, acting moody and edgy."

"Isn't that how it started with Oscar?" Ketchup asks without looking at me.

My eyes pinch shut, and I have to force the lump in my throat back down. "Yeah."

My bottom lips starts trembling. Ketchup's arm wraps around my shoulders and pulls me against his chest. I bury my face against his shirt and take slow deep breaths. I don't want to cry, not in front of Ketchup. He's stubborn and pigheaded, but he can't stand to see girls cry. If I start blubbering in front of him, I'll never get him to focus. A few minutes later, I pull away from him slowly. His eyes meet mine, and I can see the concern building by the second.

"We'll figure something out, okay, Van? Whatever it takes, we won't let Zander end up like Oscar. Just tell me what to do." He's absolutely serious, and I love him for it. He doesn't understand even half of what's going on, but he'll do anything I ask of him. He let go of my hand when he moved to hold me, but I take his now and squeeze it.

"Thanks, Ketchup."

He smiles and doesn't say anything. The flick of the kitchen curtain draws my attention. Grandma stares down at us with one eyebrow raised. A clear *what are you two doing out there* is reflected in that one look. Before she decides to investigate, I say, "Let's get going, okay?"

Nodding, Ketchup lets go of my hand reluctantly and shifts into drive. He presses down on the gas, but lurches to a stop a second later. "Van, you forgot your backpack. Do you want me to run inside and get it for you?"

"Uh, no," I say, "just go."

"But, Van…"

My voice takes on a demanding edge. "Go, Ketchup."

He shakes his head and presses on the accelerator. I wait until we're out of my neighborhood and nearing the school to speak again. "How would you feel about ditching school today?"

The way his eyes light up and one corner of his mouth twitches into a half smile almost makes me regret asking. "Sure. Where do you want to go?"

"I want to go see Oscar."

Clearly not the answer he was expecting, his eyebrows rise in shock. "What?"

"Please, Ketchup? I need to talk to him about Zander. He's the only one who can tell me what's going on with him… whether or not it's the same thing that happened to him."

"Van, are you sure? I've never been to see him before. What if it freaks him out?'

"It won't," I say.

He looks at me doubtfully.

"Unlike Zander, Oscar always liked you. He'll probably be happy to see you. Nobody outside the family ever visits him."

Stopped at a four way stop with no one else around, he reaches down and takes my hand. This time his grip is firm, but nervous. "You said the last few times you've gone to see him, he hasn't been very coherent. What makes you think he'll be any different today? I don't want to risk taking you to see him if there's no point. I know how much his outbursts upset you."

"I need to go. Besides, I don't think he'll act that way if Zander isn't around," I say.

If what Ketchup and I found out about the strange taste is actually true, things will go much better with just the two of us. Lately, when Oscar sees Zander, he keeps saying weird things, like how close Zander is to joining him, how he knows. It scares me to death to think of what Zander may have already done, but I have to know for sure.

"Please, Ketchup."

He sighs and rolls through the intersection. "Fine. How do I get there?"

The route is ingrained in my memory, so we make it to the hospital without a problem. My usual fear of stepping through the doors is missing today. We stalk right up to the front desk. I grab the visitor log and start signing us in. A familiar face stares down at me.

"Van?" Rita asks. "What are you doing here? This isn't your assigned visiting day."

"I know, but I really need to talk to Oscar. Zander is sick. I was hoping you'd let me slip in for a few minutes to talk to him."

Rita looks doubtful. "I don't know. Knowing Zander is sick may only upset him."

"But, if Zander doesn't get better..." I leave it hanging, letting her imagine what it would be like to tell Oscar his brother is dead without any time to prepare himself.

Now Rita honestly looks worried. "I know all three of you have some kind of genetic disorder..."

Ketchup looks over at me with a question in his eyes, but I can't stop to answer him.

"...but I thought you and Zander were doing well." Rita presses her hand to her heart.

I feel bad lying to her, but to be honest, if I don't stop Zander from ruining everyone's lives in time, we may all be in danger of dying. "Please?" I beg.

"Al right, but I can only give you fifteen minutes today. Oscar has therapy soon and he can't miss that."

"Thank you so much, Rita! You have no idea how important this is."

Rita's eyes tear up. "Your poor family has been through so much, I'd hate to cause any more distress. Tell Zander I hope he feels better soon."

She completes the sign-in process and asks us to wait in the lobby for an orderly to collect my brother. The wait seems to take forever, but the ugly plastic clock on the wall says it's only been ten minutes when Rita waves us over. She buzzes us through, and guides us to the room with the metal table and chains. I hate this room, but I force myself to open the door and step inside. Ketchup's hand, which pretty much hasn't budged since he took it in the car, tightens around mine. If I weren't who I am, it would hurt. Instead, it only reassures me. There's no way I could have asked Noah to come with me.

Ketchup and I stand in the middle of the room. As usual, it takes Oscar a few minutes to realize we're here. When his head starts to come up, I brace myself for his reaction. Last time, he started ranting at Zander the moment he saw him. We didn't stay long. This time, he shocks me by smiling.

The expression seems so foreign on him now. Even more surprising is the laugh that bursts out of him.

"Well, if it isn't my favorite condiment," Oscar says. "You know, there was I time I almost started calling Van mustard, you two were together so much. I don't know how many times I walked her over to your house, Ketchup."

He sits back in his chair. The leather cuffs holding his wrists securely to the table are digging into his flesh, but he doesn't seem to notice. "Looks like things haven't changed much, have they? I was wondering how long it would take Van to ignore Zander and get back together with you. It's nice. You two look good together."

"Actually…" I start. Ketchup's fingers cinch around mine. I decide to let it go, for now. Oscar seems to notice our exchange, which is surprising, but doesn't comment on it.

"Sit down," he says amiably. Neither of us moves. "Come on, I won't bite. Can't even reach you if I wanted to."

We look at each other and start forward at the same time. We slip into the chairs across from him, but keep our distance.

"You seem to be doing really good today," I say.

"It comes and goes," he says with a shrug. "It helps that Zander isn't here, and it helps that Ketchup is. We should do this more often."

"Why does it help that Zander isn't here?" Ketchup asks.

Oscar's eyes darken. "Because Zander is a liar. I hate liars. I hate, *hate* liars. Liars, liars, liars. All they do is ruin lives. Liars, liars, liars."

My body tenses. Fear that this will become another

ranting litany that sends him back to insanity forces me to interrupt him. I came here for answers, and Zander's lies are chief on the list. "What is Zander lying about?"

"About what he did."

"What he did?"

"To Lisa. To Lisa. Zander lied about Lisa. I know, but he won't admit it. He can't hide it from me. I can see through Zander's lies," Oscar mumbles.

I should go on, keep him talking while he's lucid, but I can't. I am too shocked. Thinking Zander had killed someone was hard enough, but Lisa?

I remember that night. Two months after Zander turned sixteen, just after he had come out of seclusion, I was sitting with Grandma in our living room. Mom and Dad were out and she and I were making tiramisu. Zander had gone out four wheeling with Lisa that night. Nobody called like you might think. I suppose they probably called Lisa's family, but no one called us. Zander simply burst through the door and stumbled into the room. He fell to his knees before he ever made it to the couch. I'd never seen him like that. He always held everything inside. When Grandma reached him, he started bawling like a child. I was so scared, I dialed my parents right away. They raced home in a panic.

It took an hour to get him calmed down enough to tell us about how the four wheeler had slipped and rolled off the trail. Zander came through it okay. He thought he'd broken a few bones, but they were already healed. Lisa wasn't so lucky. Zander said he tried to protect her, get her out of the way of the bulky machine, but it came down on her before he could do anything. Her neck was broken, her life ended.

At least, that's what he told us had happened.

My hands start shaking. "What do you know about Lisa?"

"Pretty little Lisa, she couldn't be scared away. She saw what Zander was, but she let herself believe. She closed her eyes and played pretend that he would love her 'til the end," Oscar says in his creepy sing-song voice. His eyes snap up to mine, the anger in them flattening me against the back of my chair. "He did. Zander did love her *'til the end*. Right up until he killed her."

"What? No, man, what are you talking about?" Ketchup asks.

I shush him and force myself to meet Oscar's gaze. "How could you possibly know that?"

"I could taste it on him."

Ketchup goes very still. He looks over at me with fear and sadness in his eyes. He knows as well as I do that we were right. Even still, it is so hard to accept what Oscar is saying that I badger him for more proof.

"What do you mean you could taste it? What did it taste like?"

Oscar's face screws up, as if he's tasting death right now. "Every time he comes near me, I can taste it. It doesn't taste like pain. Pain tastes like truffles to me. Not the chocolate kind, the prized fungus only the most refined restaurants use. The earthy, meaty exquisiteness of them are exactly how pain tastes to me, the most beautiful sensation. Death tastes different, stale and bitter. And it never seems to leave. It clings to Zander still. I hate the taste of death. I hate that he brings it here."

I want to argue with him. I want to believe that if Zander did kill someone, it was someone bad, and for a good reason. I don't want to believe it was Lisa. Lisa was such a sweet girl. She cared about Zander, and he cared about her. At the time, the guilt that poured out with his tears seemed too much for the enjoyment I know his hunger must have gotten out of her death. I'd wondered that night if something was wrong. The look on my grandma's face said the same, but I never let myself question him. Zander was my brother. I didn't want to believe something like that about him.

I know Oscar is telling the truth. I don't know what to do with that knowledge, though. So, I do what I did last time. I stuff it down deep, and ask the next question I don't really want the answer to.

"Why…why can't I taste it on him all the time like you can?"

Oscar's interest perks up. "All the time? Does that mean you taste it some of the time?"

"It's really random," I admit quietly. Oscar nods slowly.

"You're too young to taste it all the time. Van, Nessa, Nessie, Vanessa, you're still too small, just a baby hunter with chaotic, crazy hunger. But you'll mature. You'll turn sixteen and you'll be able to taste the real pleasures and evils of this world." His hands tighten into fists and pull at the shackles that won't let him go. "Just wait until you turn sixteen, and then you'll taste Zander's secrets all the time too."

My head drops down. I was already worried enough

about my birthday. Ketchup shifts in his chair, reminding me of his presence. I glance over at him with hooded eyes. His hand is still in mine, but his body is rigid. Everything Oscar just said rings in my ears. Tasting, pain, death, even me turning sixteen and changing, I can't imagine how that must have sounded to him.

He let me slide on the bare minimum before, but I think he just got a lot more in the way of answers than he wanted. Seeing the familiar indicators, I relax my fingers and attempt sliding them out of his grip. I get about half way before he grabs me back and holds me tighter than before. He doesn't look at me, though.

There's nothing to do but let Ketchup make his decision and get on with what I came here for.

"Oscar, I need you to tell me what it was like before you came here. What changed? Did Mom and Dad say anything to you about how you were acting?"

Oscar's face screws up in disgust. "I don't want to talk about that. Why do you want know?"

"Zander's been acting strange," I say after a moment's pause. "I think he's going to get in trouble."

"I told him. Told him. Told him. I would see him here soon."

"Oscar," I snap. His mouth stops blabbering and he looks up at me. "I need to know if Zander's in trouble."

"Trouble," Oscar says. He nods deeply. "Tell me everything."

So I do.

I force myself not to look over at Ketchup once during

my explanation. I hadn't been planning on letting him in on the secrets of our family right now, or any time, to be perfectly honest, but what else was I going to do. There was no chance I was going to ask him to step out. Not only would that be incredibly unfair after I forced him to bring me here, but also, as much as I love Oscar, I do not want to be left alone with him. My mouth spills out the details of Ivy and Zander's bizarre relationship as I pretend Ketchup isn't listening to a word of it. I tell him about our hunger reactions, my suspicions, Zander's love, his likely confession, and his slip that Ivy was somehow going to help him.

At that last part, Oscar's entire body goes rigid. His eyes latch onto me like a barbed dart, painful and difficult to be free of. "She thinks she can help him?" Oscar says. "She won't. She won't help him. She doesn't really want to. Ivy, Ivy. Ivy is lying. Ivy Guerra. I don't like her name. Vines and War, that's what her name means. She will wrap herself around Zander and strangle the life out of him, start a war that none of us can win. Ivy Guerra can't be trusted."

"I…what? Her name means war? What are you talking about?"

Oscar tsks at me, one finger of his bound hand bobbing up and down. "I told you to keep up with your Spanish, Van. It's always useful to know languages. Shows you things that others miss. Guerra means war. Ivy is here to start a war."

"How could you possibly know that?" Not that I disagree with him, but he's actually crazy. I suspect Ivy is trouble because of what I've seen. I want to stop her, but I'm not going to launch a full out campaign against her on the word of my murdering, psychotic brother.

The dull thud of Oscar's head hitting the metal table startles me. I look down at him. Panic creeps under my skin. Is this the end of his lucidity? It can't be. I have more questions still. "Oscar. Oscar! How do you know Ivy is here to start a war? You have to tell me or Zander might get hurt."

"Oh, Zander will get hurt." The muffled slur of his words makes them even more ominous. "That girl is no good. If you want to save Zander, you have to stop her, but he'll still get hurt. Save him and hurt him, don't save him and hurt him. Pain, either way. Delicious pain. Hunger will be the only one that wins. Hunger always wins."

My fingernails are digging into Ketchup's skin. Pain ripples around his wrist, but I pay it no mind. All my focus is on Oscar. "How do you know about any of this, Oscar?"

"They didn't want me to know, but I found out. Someone tried to help me, and I didn't believe them. I searched and asked and demanded and screamed until someone told me. They didn't want me to know, but I found out. I found out, and it made me angry. So, so angry. Furious. Irate. I wanted blood and pain and death when I found out. Nothing could feed my hunger enough, not after being starved for so long. I found out, and they paid for it. I made them pay."

"Oscar," I whisper, his words making more sense to me than I wish they would. He made them pay. They didn't want him to know. He made them pay. My shaking rattles the uneven legs of my chair against the floor, a skittering noise that fries the last of my barriers. I ask my last, most frightening question. "Oscar, why did you kill Mom and Dad?"

"Because," he hisses, "because, because they lied to us. They knew. All along they knew who we were, what we were, but they tried to pretend, change us, turn us into something we aren't, starve us, deny us, make us suffer for years and years and years! They said they loved us, but they lied! They lied! They lied! THEY LIED!"

22

SICARIUS

'm almost running as I drag Ketchup down the concrete stairs of Peak View Hospital. The orderlies dragging Oscar out of the room and down the hall when he wouldn't stop screaming topped off an already disturbing experience. I wanted to ask him more, find out what my parents lied about, but there was no more talking to Oscar at that point. Admitting it hurts, but part of me was glad they drug him away. Do I really want to know what lies I've been told since birth?

When I reach Ketchup's car, I finally find the strength to drop his hand. He doesn't move, but I sag against the back of his car and hang my head. The silence of the parking lot is soothing after Oscar's outburst. At least for a few minutes it is. Then my floundering brain nudges me, reminds me that Ketchup is still standing next to me, not speaking a word. I know I need to say something.

"Ketchup, I…" That's as far as I get.

I work to find something, anything, but before I can,

Ketchup's hands are suddenly on my face, pulling me toward him. His lips press against mine fiercely, crushing me, and sending a rush every bit as strong as my hunger coursing through my body. The last hour evaporates from my mind. The last two years are forgotten entirely, and I'm suddenly back on my porch with Ketchup, a silly girl with unrealistic dreams. Except my dreams don't seem so far away now. My hands slide around his neck and pull him closer. He deepens the kiss hungrily. I want more. I want nothing else in this world.

Ketchup shoves me away from him without warning. The angry glare on his face knocks me back. "You should have told me!" he snaps. "The hunger, the urges, the fact that your brother wants to kill me! You should have told me, Van. You shouldn't have run away from me. You should have given me the chance to understand and help you. I wouldn't have run. I wouldn't have left you."

"Will you now?" I ask, barely managing to make myself heard.

His anger holds for a few more seconds. In that brief moment, I fear my heart will explode. Then his shoulders slump and he pulls me against his chest. As his arms wrap around me, I know I will never feel safer than I do in his arms. He leans down next to my ear and says, "I'm not going anywhere, Van."

For the first time in two years, I give in to him completely. I cinch my arms around him and bury my face in his chest. "Ketchup, I'm so sorry."

"I know," he says. "It's okay."

There's so much more I want to say to him right now. I want to tell him how much I love him, how I've loved him this whole time. I want to tell him to kiss me again, but this time, in the way I always imagined our first kiss would be. My heart is begging me to tell him it will be like this forever.

Reality keeps my mouth shut tight. There's still Zander. If he gets too close to Ketchup, there won't be any forever. There will only be death. As he holds me, I can't bear to say anything of the kind. So I don't let myself speak at all. The wishes and the truth both stay buried until I can figure things out.

Ketchup is the first to break the silence. "Did you understand any of what Oscar told you today, because I didn't. I'm not even sure we should believe him."

"We should definitely believe him." I may not have understood half of what he said, but this is one thing I'm sure of. Ketchup isn't.

"Why? Just because Ivy's last name is Guerra doesn't mean she's here to start a war. It sounded crazy, Van."

Pulling away from Ketchup enough to look him in the eye, I say, "I know Oscar is nuts, but he isn't a liar. You saw how upset he got when he talked about my parents lying to us. That's always been a huge deal for him. He's never once told a lie to anybody."

"Still…"

"Ketchup, please. I know what I'm talking about."

He shakes his head. "Fine, what are we going to do about Ivy?"

"We're going to find out what's in Ivy's garage and why

she spends her Sundays locked up in there," I say.

"When?"

I take a deep breath, knowing this might be a huge mistake. "Now. Let's go."

Climbing over Ivy's wooden fence proves easy enough. Making sure nobody was home before we could hop over the fence was the trickier part. When we first arrived, there weren't any cars in the driveway, but neither of us knew for sure whether or not her mom worked during the day. We had to watch the house for a long time, eating lunch as we did, and wait for some sign that anyone was inside. Eventually, we decided it was safe enough to get started and made our move.

Ketchup and I stand at the door to the converted garage, my hand on the locked doorknob. I jiggle it again just for good measure. Not discouraged yet, I look around for other options. There aren't any windows, which seems a little odd. I slip around each side. Nothing. My hope for a backdoor that isn't locked is foiled too. There isn't even a door. I head back to the front of the garage, but Ketchup stops me halfway. He points up. My eyes follow, and I groan.

"Seriously?"

He nods, "Sorry, but it looks like that's our only way in."

The skylight on the roof is one of several. "They look like they're screwed down. How are we going to get them open? I don't want to break anything or she'll know someone was here."

"How about we get up there, and then try using these," Ketchup says, holding up a pair of screwdrivers.

"Where did those come from?" I ask.

He shrugs. "My car. I have a tool set in the trunk that my uncle gave me."

Hmm. The longer I watch him, the guiltier he looks. Ketchup sucks at fixing cars. His uncle wouldn't even think of letting him try to tighten a screw for fear of the whole car exploding. We'll come back to this later.

"So, are you going to boost me up, or what?"

A few seconds later, we're both on top of the roof twisting out screws as fast as we can. We're much more exposed up here. Even still, as I'm unscrewing the second to last screw on my side, I look over at Ketchup and ask, "You've done this before, haven't you?"

"Breaking into a garage? Can't say that I have." He pauses. "Well, I did have to break into our garage once when the garage door opener jammed."

"Ketchup..."

"What?" He pretends for a moment longer, but then he sighs. "Okay, breaking into things isn't exactly a new thing for me," he admits, "but it's not like I steal stuff. I just practice. It's a useful skill to have."

"Where do you practice?"

He shrugs. "Houses in my neighborhood mostly. Cars too."

"Have you ever come to my house at night?"

The squeaky noise of his screw fighting to get loose is suddenly the only sound. I don't push him, but I wait. Finally, he gets the screw loose and looks up at me. "It's not what you're thinking."

"What am I thinking?"

"That I peek at you through your windows, or something," he says. "I just get really worried sometimes, Van. After what Oscar did…well, sometimes I can't sleep knowing you're there with only Zander and your grandma. What's your grandma gonna do? And Zander, with the way he's looked at me since that day on the porch, I'm not always sure he's going to protect you either."

He looks back down at the remaining screws. I want to reach across the half-loosened skylight and kiss him. I don't. I wonder if he's trying not to do the same thing, because he doesn't look at me when he speaks again. "I've never broken into your house, though."

"Then why?"

"Just in case I ever need to."

I know Zander would never hurt me. Regardless, a little dash of reassurance that Ketchup will be there if I ever need him lightens my mood. We finish our work quickly after that, and Ketchup lowers me down. I land badly because of the strangely uneven floor and stumble. Ketchup lands right behind me, and steadies me. My eyes linger on the warmth of his smile for just a moment before turning away and staring wide-eyed at the room around me.

Crimson drapes coat the walls in an alternating pattern of thick velvet fabric and bare, black walls. The floor is black, too, all but a thick band of white running down the center of the room that leads to the low platform I fell on. Inside the white band are symbols and words that have no meaning to me. I step back as I realize they continue up onto the raised platform. I still have no idea what they say, but my eyes follow the pattern to an even more incredible sight. There's an…altar at the back of the platform. An ornately carved table of the blackest wood I've ever seen stands sentinel on the very center of the back wall. Here the drapes are farther apart, leaving a wide expanse of black wall. This wall isn't bare. It's filled with weapons.

And I'm not talking about guns. Swords, knives, things I'm not even sure what they are, all hold places of honor on the wall. They look old, too. Really old. The detailing on the handles is incredible, and some of them even have designs on the actual blades. They're gorgeous, but very, very creepy. The book on the altar is freaking me out, too. It's just a book, but the picture painted on the front makes both of us cringe.

A person—I can't tell whether it's supposed to be a man or woman, or something else entirely—is standing in a pool of blood. The creature's mouth is open, caught mid-scream with a look of pure agony on its face. At first, it looks like the blood is pouring out of the creature. When I look closer, I see that the blood droplets are running up the person's body toward its mouth. Like it's eating it.

My own blood seems to run and hide in my core, my fingers and toes going icy cold. The similarity certainly isn't lost on me. Kneeling in front of the blood-eater is a young woman. She's the most disturbing of the pair. Dark, wavy hair frames a peaceful face. Her quiet smile in the face of what is standing behind her doesn't make sense. The knife she's holding to her own throat makes even less sense.

"What is this place?" Ketchup asks.

"I don't know, but it's beyond freaky."

He nods. "If I had any doubts before, I don't anymore. Something is definitely wrong with Ivy. I mean, what does she do in here? Swords, weird writing all over the floor, some bloody guy on a book. What is she messed up in?"

"What is Zander messed up in?" I ask.

We're here in her dojo from Hell, and I still have no idea what's going on. Reluctantly, my fingers stretch toward the book. I know the blood eater must be someone like me, someone who feeds on pain and anguish, but what could this book possibly say? Does it hold whatever answers Oscar found? Is the reason behind his murder of our parents hidden within its pages? My hand shakes as I flip open the cover.

Sei stato scelto. Solo coloro che hanno dimostrato...

"I have no idea what any of this means, do you?" I ask.

Ketchup scans the passage at the front of the book and shakes his head. "I'm sure we can find out, though. Give me a minute."

He pulls his phone out of his pocket and has a translation app open a few seconds later. "Why do you have that on your phone?" I ask despite the serendipitous usefulness of it.

"I suck at Spanish."

"You cheat on your Spanish homework?" I'm actually kind of shocked. Ketchup has the scoundrel act down pat because of the way everyone treats him, but I know he's a pretty straight laced guy.

"Not all the time. The instructions on our homework

are always written in Spanish. How am I supposed to do it if I don't even know what I'm supposed to do?"

I roll my eyes. "I don't think this is Spanish."

"No problem. This translator can do a bunch of languages. It'll even identify the language if you type in a few words." His thumbs start tapping away like mad. He gets the first sentence down and the app immediately comes back with an answer of Italian. Kind of surprising, since with a last name like Guerra, I didn't figure Ivy for having Italian ancestors. As Ketchup starts typing in the passage, I wonder whether Guerra is her real last name.

"Okay, I got it," Ketchup says. "Here, take a look."

You have been chosen. Only those who have shown courage and strength are chosen for our most sacred of missions. The trials of your choosing have proven your worth, but you must endure one last tribulation. You must sacrifice for your beliefs one final time. The rewards for your sacrifice will be the highest possible. Blessed eternity will be yours, but not without your final contribution. Your life is the price of this honor. Open the book and begin your journey to eternal happiness, your journey to vanquish the assassin.

Chills run a marathon down my spine. "Oscar was right," I whisper.

"Looks like it. Ivy was chosen, by someone, to kill the assassin. Whatever that means. Who exactly are the assassins, anyway?"

"It must mean Zander...and me." I can feel Ketchup press in closer to me after hearing my words. His concern is comforting, but Ivy's sights are set on Zander right now.

"The assassin. That doesn't really sound like Zander, though. Sure, your brother's not the most compassionate guy in the world, or the most interesting, but he's not an assassin. Unless you count the teams he plays against."

I look down at the original passage in the book. I know what the words mean now, but I feel like we're missing something. The clue appears in the last word. The Italian word for assassin is *Sicarius*. I recognize the code word my parents taught us from birth and suddenly feel sick. Oscar was right. If they taught us that word, they knew about all of this. Anger builds under my skin, but I force my attention back to the words.

The translation put no significance on the word when it spit it back out, but I notice that the word in the book is capitalized. Sicarius. "It's not just a noun," I say. "It's a title. Look how it's capitalized, Ketchup, like a team or a company name."

"Like a terrorist group, an enemy."

"But, that doesn't make any sense. How could there be this whole group of wackos intent on killing me and my brothers? I know there have been others in our family, but how big of a threat can we really be?"

"Van," Ketchup says slowly as he thumbs through the book, "I don't think this is just about you and your brothers. This is way too much for a couple of messed up kids. Look how old all of this stuff is. Centuries. There's more of you somewhere. There has to be. And whatever crazy group Ivy is a part of, they've been hunting these Sicarius people for centuries all over the world. If it was just one family, they would have killed them off a long time ago."

"More?" I feel a little lightheaded all of a sudden. Was that the lie my parents told that broke Oscar?

Knowing there are more of us, that could mean help, knowledge, a real life maybe. The tiniest shake of my head makes me sway. My hands grip the table for support as Ketchup wraps his arm around my shoulders. More people like me. I don't know whether to be relieved or terrified. Oscar killed our parents. Zander, he...he killed Lisa. What lives will I steal?

Visions of dozens, hundreds of people dying to feed an eternal hunger assail me without stopping. But amid the waves of death and carnage, there is a bubble of hope in my mind. If there are others, maybe they can help me learn how to control my hunger. Surely my family isn't the first ones to try and abstain. Are we?

"Van, what are we going to do? It's getting late. School will be out soon and Ivy will be meeting Zander after his practice."

I was already scared that Ivy was going to do something bad by helping Zander. Like every other answer I've gotten today, this isn't the one I wanted to hear. "Ketchup, we have to stop her."

"How? I have a feeling there's a lot more to Ivy Guerra than we thought."

"It doesn't matter. We have to stop her from killing Zander. I won't lose another brother."

My brain starts running at high speed. There has to be an answer somewhere. Spinning, I take in the room again.

Nothing. Bare walls and velvet curtains. I drop my gaze to the writing on the floor. Reaching for Ketchup, I'm about to ask him to translate the writing. His own hand gripping my arm stops me.

"Van, she isn't going to kill Zander."

Those words should be good news, but I can hear the dread in his voice. "What?"

"The book said, 'your life is the price of this honor.' It said she'd vanquish the Sicarius, but not by killing them. She's the one who has to die, not Zander."

"But…that doesn't make sense. Why would she kill herself…?" The rest of my thought trails off as realization slaps me. "No, no, no. Ketchup, she's going to make Zander kill her! He must have told her enough that she knows how to trigger his hunger so he'll lose control. She'll sacrifice herself to expose him."

"Why? What would that accomplish? It's like you said before, everyone will forget after a while. She'll be dead and gain nothing from it."

I growl at the holes in my knowledge. I know I'm right about this. There's a piece of the explanation missing. I'm sure it's in the book, but we don't have time to translate an entire book on a phone! There has to be something else. Something in this room. My eyes fall back to the writing on the floor.

"Ketchup, tell me what that says. Hurry!"

Maybe it's nothing, but it was important enough to turn into a work of art on the floor of Ivy's personal suicide temple.

"Okay," he says after a minute, "here's what it says. *One*

life for the destruction of many. Expose the Sicarius to seal his family's fate."

The air seems to grow thick around me. It slides down my throat and chokes me. Somehow, I manage to force my voice through the cloying panic. "If Ivy makes Zander kill her, these psychos will know that my family are these Sicarius things. They'll come, and they'll kill the rest of us, just to make sure we don't hurt anyone else."

"Van, that is the stupidest plan I've ever heard," Ketchup says. "Why go through the trouble of having one of their own people commit suicide? I mean, it sounds like Zander has already given Ivy plenty of reason to convince her that he's one of these Sicarius people. So why not just come and kill him and his family? Why waste the life of one of their own?"

I shake my head, confused as well. "I don't know. This group is old. These traditions seem to go back for hundreds of years."

"Tradition can't really be enough to give up your life when you don't need to," Ketchup argues. "Maybe we could convince Ivy."

Judging by her temple, I seriously doubt that. My mind replays the translation again. One sentence sticks out, possibly giving me the answer. "Maybe it's the reward," I say.

"What?"

I grab his phone and go back to the first translation. "See. It said that if she gave up her life she would be given the highest reward possible. Ketchup, I don't think this is just some group Ivy belongs to. It's more like her religion. I think she believes that if she forces Zander to kill her, she'll go to some kind of martyr's paradise and have everything she ever wanted. Isn't that why Muslim suicide bombers do what they do? The reward of forgiveness, paradise, and dark-eyed virgins?"

"If this is her religion," Ketchups says, "then I don't think we should waste any time trying to change her mind."

I nod in agreement, but am sickened at the realization that there is only one way to stop her. I thought that all I had to do to save my brother's life was stop one twisted girl. That's not even the half of it. An army of ancient sword wielding fanatics is about to find out my family's darkest secret, and we're the only ones who know. It's me and Ketchup against a centuries-old secret society of trained killers.

23

FOLLOW

don't know how I resisted telling Ivy everything last night. I had already decided that keeping her close was worth the consequences of revealing the truth. I didn't know where to start, though, so I let Ivy take the lead by asking me questions. Her first question, "How was Van able to heal herself so fast after scorching her hand on the oven?" seemed to knock some common sense back into my head. My sister's name reminded me that I wouldn't be the only one facing the consequences if I told Ivy everything and got burned.

So I tried to answer her questions as vaguely as possible. I did admit that we can both heal quickly, and that we have trouble controlling our impulses, but I tried to play it up as some of the same craziness that landed Oscar in a mental hospital. Ivy didn't completely believe me and I ended up giving her a very basic explanation of our hunger. She did seem to be satisfied with the answers she was able to get out of me and stopped pushing after a while.

I know the conversation isn't over. At some point, I'll either be forced to tell her the whole truth or walk away. I can't stand the idea of walking away from her.

Ivy thinks she can help me. No one else has been able to, but she seemed so sure of herself. She wants to help me, which feels incredibly good. It's probably wishful thinking on her part. If not…if she could really show me how to control my hunger, there might be a real possibility of me getting to live a semi-normal life. That's a huge if.

Walking quickly, almost skipping, Ivy makes her way across the parking lot to me. The struggle to control my hunger begins. Watching her come toward me sends equal amounts of anxiety and pleasure through my body. She doesn't seem to share in my nerves. Her bright smile is almost enough to chase away my dark thoughts, but not quite. The way Van flipped out when I told her about the movie keeps shoving my hope back down.

"So," Ivy says when she approaches me, "are you ready to give this a try?"

I hesitate. "Ivy, I'm not so sure a movie is a good idea. It's dark and close…"

"But we'll be surrounded by other people too, and movies are always so loud. You said noise and other people help distract you."

True. That was part of the reason my mom always kept classical music playing in our house, and why we were encouraged to try team sports rather than individual sports. But a theater might contain others that excite my hunger, and that will only make this harder. "It's still risky. I'll be right next to you, smelling and feeling you every second. It might be more than I can handle."

"You'll be fine," she reassures me. "I told you how after the break in at our apartment I was so freaked out that my mom made me do all this meditation stuff. I've gotten pretty good at it. It will help."

"Ivy..."

Giving me a stern look, Ivy says, "The only way you're ever going to be able to stay with me is if you can get used to me, right?"

I nod.

"So we have to try something or we might as well just go our separate ways now. Is that what you want?"

"No, of course not." I argue with her, but in truth, I will try anything she suggests. I have to find a way to be with Ivy without killing her.

Ivy slowly moves closer to me. The scent of her, the feel of her life force nudging my hunger tightens my muscles. She takes another step. An ache begins in the center of my chest. Ivy's plan is to desensitize me to her presence. Judging by how being close to her now feels even worse than last night, I don't have a lot of faith in her plan.

"Why don't we start out small?" Ivy suggests.

"How small?"

She smiles. "How about, what movie do you want to see?"

Thoughts start running through my head. I looked up the local movie schedule during lunch. My decision doesn't have as much to do with my movie preferences as it does my cynical outlook. "There's a documentary about some underwater cave in South America playing at the theater on San Mateo. Let's try that."

"Spelunking?" Ivy asks incredulously.

I frown at her. "This is already going to be hard enough without violence, sex, or anything else that might set me off playing on a huge screen right in front of me."

"Sorry," Ivy says, "I know this isn't about the movie. You're choice just caught me off guard. It sounds like a perfect movie for what we're doing. What time does it start?"

"Not for a few hours. Do you want to get something to eat first?"

"That sounds good."

Ivy steps around me as if it is completely natural for her to be getting into my truck, but she takes care not to touch me or get too close on her way. I am not nearly as confident as I follow suit. My steps are sluggish. In my head, Van's outrage and warnings are blaring again. I have gotten practiced at ignoring such things, and I do it again now. I have to. All my focus goes into getting into the truck next to Ivy without losing control of my hunger.

Right away, I turn on the air conditioner and the radio. The semi-physical barrier of blasting wind between us mixed with voices loud enough to drown everything else out helps... somewhat. I try not to look at Ivy as she sits very still in the passenger's seat. I shake my head against the intensity of the affect she has on me.

I really thought this would get easier.

With Ketchup, I know it has gotten more bearable to

have him around. The first day we met, when I came home to find him and Van on the porch swing with their mouths inches away from each other, much to my dismay, my main intention in approaching them had been to break up the make-out session. Van was only thirteen at the time, way too young to be starting in on that type of behavior. My goal hadn't been to ruin their relationship, but once I got within five feet of him my hunger leapt into the driver's seat and sent me lunging for his throat.

I hadn't even suspected I would react to him, so that made it worse. He had been a friend of Van's so long, he felt familiar to me because of how much she talked about him. At that moment, it didn't cross my mind that I had never officially met him. If I had remembered that, I never would have walked up so casually. Regardless, my hunger wanted him ferociously. After that initial contact, even seeing him forced me to scramble for control. I forced Van to say goodbye. She did, and I know how much it hurt her to do it. I hated myself for demanding it of her.

I've never told her, but I have been trying to make up for that day ever since. Van keeps Ketchup away from me as much as possible. My love for her can't even be expressed. She is so much better than I will ever be, but I'm trying. She has no idea that for the last three years I have found inconspicuous ways to test my ability to withstand Ketchup. If I see him in the hall at school, I will follow behind him for a few minutes. The few times we've been in semi-close contact, I push myself a little more each time to get closer to him without letting my hunger rouse. My promise to grant her one favor has intensified my efforts lately, because I know that is the one thing she wants more than any other.

The amazing thing is…it's working.

I'm still miles away from being able to sit down to a quiet family dinner with him, but it's getting better. With Ivy, though…my desire to see her blood spilled doubles every time we're together. What scares me is that I don't understand the difference between her and Ketchup. This has to work. I don't know what else to do.

"What are you thinking about?" Ivy asks over the music and air conditioner.

It's actually a question I can answer, for once. "You've probably guessed why Van and Ketchup don't date, despite the fact that they're clearly in love with each other, right?"

Ivy nods. "It's hard to invite him to family get-togethers when your big brother wants to kill him, I suppose."

"Pretty much," I say with relief. She understands.

"So, why are you thinking about Ketchup?" she asks.

"It's getting easier to be around him," I admit, "but it only seems to get harder with you."

For a moment, she's quiet. I pull into Ivy's favorite fast food place and cut the engine. The quiet suddenly imposed, with the loss of the music and blasting air, sends a shiver through me as my hunger makes a bid for control. My hands grip the steering wheel. I have to jump out of the truck to keep control. Ivy follows more slowly and remains at a distance.

"I think it's because I'm a girl."

"What?" I ask.

She looks over at me. "This…hunger, it's not just a

desire to cause pain, right? There's something else along with that, I'm guessing, because there are different ways to hurt people, different kinds of pain that hurt some people more than others."

"Yeah," I say slowly. It is almost scary how well she understands this. Not that it should be surprising—Ivy is incredibly intelligent—but it worries me that she might figure out other things as well. The fear building inside of me doesn't seem to reach Ivy. She continues with her theory.

"I bet with Van, her hunger is impatient, adrenaline driven. It wants the pain to be fast, intense, and messy. That seems to be how she reacts to a lot of situations, anyway."

Again, it's a little frightening how perceptive she is. "Yeah, Van is impulsive when it comes to her emotions and hunger."

"And you…" she starts.

My body tenses up. I'm not sure I want her to continue. More likely than not, she'll peg me spot on. I don't want to hear her assessment of me.

"With you, I suspect you're more thoughtful. You plan. It's probably like how you play football. You see the other guy coming, and you put yourself in their path. But the whole time he's running at you, you're drinking up his fear, planning how to hit him so you can get the most benefit while still injuring him the least you can. The impact is the payoff." She turns to look at me, a quiet sort of understanding in her eyes. "Am I right?"

I nod slowly. It sickens me to hear her describe how I play. I rarely think that much while playing football. I don't actively "plan" how each encounter will play out, but I realize she is exactly right. I do it on instinct now. I draw out each experience to make sure I get fed as much as possible. My shame momentarily outweighs Ivy's presence.

But she isn't finished, yet.

"I bet that's why it's different with me than it is with Ketchup. Boys fight. It's sudden and explosive. But a relationship is always a balance between pain and joy. With me, every time we're together you have to fight between desires to kill me and kiss me. You want both, but can only have one. It makes the reward, in either case, so much greater than a simple fist to the face."

My body is trembling. Everything she said is the truth. If it weren't, Lisa would still be alive. I have buried that night so deep in my mind that it rarely surfaces anymore, but Ivy's words have brought it all back. I feel myself slipping into the memory, and no amount of struggling can save me now. I feel helpless as the scents of juniper and rabbitbrush drift through my mind.

The wind had just a hint of winter chill that night. I steered the four wheeler off the path and onto a flat area, while Lisa stayed pressed against my back. Her head nestled against me, her arms securely around my waist even though we were no longer on the steep trail. She didn't stir until the engine rumbled to a stop. Even then, she seemed content to stay wrapped around me. I was the one to move first.

Turning so my back was against the handles, I pulled Lisa into my lap. She smiled and touched my face. My world had been nothing but chaos during that time. Oscar's erratic behavior had everyone scared. I had just spent two months locked up in my room because my hunger was so out of control I couldn't be trusted to be around my own family. I was so behind on my school work that I was in danger of losing eligibility to play sports. If that was taken away from me, finding an outlet for my hunger would get even harder. I felt like I would buckle constantly. Lisa was the only one who gave me any balance. She anchored me to the good still left in life. I knew it wasn't easy for her. It scarred her almost as much as it did me.

But for that one night, we had left the fear and uncertainty behind. It was only the two of us under a blanket of stars that held no judgment. I wanted to show her how much I loved her. My fingers slid across her delicate skin and tangled in her hair. She responded at once, leaning toward me and accepting my kiss. Her arms held me so gently at first. It was just meant to be a thank you for how much she had helped me through the previous difficult months, but pent up emotion made it something more.

My arms tightened around her slender body as my desire increased. Lisa's fingernails dug into my skin in her eagerness to pull me closer. My hunger had no specific desire for her, but those small pinpricks of pain roused it that night. I was too consumed to pay it much mind consciously, but my subconscious grabbed hold of my flickering hunger and nursed it, pushed me to intensify my grip, the force of my affection, the need to be sated. My hand slid up her back, holding her at the *nape of her neck. In my mind, all I could think about was how soft her lips were. There wasn't an inch of space between us, but I felt myself pulling her closer all the same. My grip grew tighter as my hunger built.*

Maybe Lisa was as caught up in the moment as I was. Maybe she didn't want to tell me I was hurting her because she didn't want me to stop kissing her. Or maybe her trust in my ability to protect her made her think I would stop myself before it went too far. I don't know what was running through her mind in those last few moments. I only know that I had no idea my hunger had taken total control of me before it was too late.

I heard her gasp a split second before my fingers crushed her windpipe.

As if the snap is truly audible in the present, my body jerks away from the sound. I stumble back, falling against the truck. My chest is heaving, hands on my knees as though I have just finished wind sprints. The patter of Ivy's sandals tapping across the pavement sends me into a panic. I dart up with every intention of getting away from her.

"Zander!" she gasps. "What's wrong?"

"I can't do this," I finally admit. "I want you so badly, but I would never forgive myself if I hurt you. It's too big of a risk. I would rather know you were safe and never get to see you again than keep you with me and end up killing you. I love you, but I can't do this."

My body sags in defeat. I can hardly breathe. My head

feels like it's going to explode. Chunks are being ripped out of my heart with every breath. How did Van do this? How did she give up Ketchup when she clearly loved him? How can she stand to be around him every day and not pull him into her arms, not indulge in the desires I know must eat at her soul?

"Zander," Ivy says softly, "close your eyes."

I look up, questioning, but she only repeats her request. I don't understand, but I do it anyway. Maybe she just doesn't want me to have to watch her walk away. My head thumps against the truck window. This was such a mistake. I hold my breath, hoping Ivy slips away quietly so I can begin my journey into the depths of misery alone.

I am not prepared at all for the sudden feel of her lips against mine.

The race between hunger and all-encompassing passion that plows through my veins leaves me frozen. I can't give in to one without the other. I can't move or think. All I can manage is to relish the feel of her mouth poised so gently against mine. It may have lasted a second, or maybe it was an hour. I don't know. But when she pulls away, I spring away from the truck to stop her. My eyes snap open to her smile.

"I love you, too," she says quietly, "and I'm not ready to walk away just yet. Are you?"

"No," I say, "but I should."

Her head shakes softly. "No, what you should do is come inside and eat, and then take me to an incredibly boring movie about scientists poking around in underwater caves."

"Ivy, I don't want to…"

"Everything will work out, Zander. Trust me." The surety in her eyes is oddly convincing.

I know what I am capable of better than she ever will, but she has such faith in me that I can't help but be drawn in by it. She can tell I've relented by the way the tension slips from my shoulders. She smiles and starts for the door of the restaurant, knowing I will follow. I think she knows I will always follow.

Z

Zander

24

UNDERSTANDING

espite the fact that I am completely unable to resist Ivy in any way, I am still not convinced this is a good idea. I buy our tickets to a movie which would normally be enough to put me to sleep, purchase popcorn and sodas at the concession stand, and balk at the door to the theater. Ivy doesn't stop to argue or convince. She steps around me with a calm expression and enters the darkened theater. Once again, I swallow the feeling that I should run, and enter the theater as well.

It isn't as dark as I anticipated. There are lights along the floor, as well as sconces every few feet on the wall. They aren't bright, but they are enough to show me that the theater is about half full. Surprising, given the topic of the movie, but I am thankful for it. Ivy is a good ten feet in front of me and I lengthen my stride to catch up with her. She is heading up the stairs, but I know better.

"Let's take the seats in the front, on the side closest to the exit," I insist.

A small frown flashes on her lips, but she nods and takes one of the seats I was pointing to. If I have to bail, I want it to be as easy as possible, with the smallest amount of people between me and the door. Not attacking Ivy is my first priority. Not causing any collateral damage is a close second.

My meltdown in the restaurant parking lot forced us to rush through our dinner. Even still, we barely made it in time for the movie. The lights dim only a few minutes after we're seated. When they do, my heart rate skyrockets. I can't see any of the other patrons. I can hear a few of them still whispering, but it isn't enough to distract me.

My foot starts tapping nervously on the floor. Ivy stays perfectly quiet and still. With less than a foot between us, it doesn't help very much. Her body heat pulses against my skin. I can hear her breathing. Her scent fills my lungs. I can feel her energy with very little effort in this dark, silent room. My hunger begins to roil and beg for nourishment.

The sudden blaring of previews startles me enough to get a firm handle on my hunger. I lend every ounce of my focus to the images dancing across the screen. I memorize the characters, the release dates, the directors, anything that will occupy my brain. Two full previews play before I feel my body begin to relax. Relief pools in my numb extremities. I remain focused on the show, but my hunger stays manageable.

At least until Ivy whispers, "I'm going to lean my head on your shoulder. Tell me if it's too much."

I nod, even though I'm not sure she can see me. I don't trust myself enough to talk at the moment. She doesn't move right away. She gives me time to prepare myself. I breathe, tense up my muscles, do everything I can think of to steady myself against her, but I still flinch when her slight weight rests on my shoulder. My hunger races toward the point of contact. It gnaws at her, fights to be released, but I manage to keep it in check.

For a long time, we stay in that position. My hunger never gives up, but I strain to keep it contained. Ivy asks again before taking it any further. "Can I hold your hand?"

My eyes widen. I honestly don't know if I can handle that. I want to feel her fingers curl around mine. "I…I don't know," I whisper back.

The narrator drones on about plankton or some other inconsequential facet of the underwater cave. The theater is quiet, but feels saturated. I feel movement to the side of me, but before I can pull away, a tiny amount of pressure from Ivy's fingers on my hand lashes me into immobility. My hunger was grumbling before. Now it is howling.

Her voice is soft and tentative as she says, "Tell me if you want me to stop."

I groan in agony. I'll never want her to stop, even if I should. That's the problem. My entire body is rigid as her fingers glide slowly across my skin. They curve around the side and gently turn my palm up. My fingers start twitching at that point. Every small spasm is a battle between my hunger and my will to keep me from crushing her hand. She doesn't move as I struggle.

My other hand grips the arm rest. I can hear the plastic cracking, but I don't let up. Slowly, my hand stops shaking. The tremors disappearing in no ways means that I have won anything. Ivy must assume it does, though, because she slides her hand the rest of the way into mine.

I lose it.

My fingers snap down over hers. She makes not a single sound, but I know my grip is way too tight. I try. I try so hard to relax my fingers. Control has abandoned me. Feeling her pulse bound against my skin is like a countdown to the real pain beginning. I can't…don't want to stop it. My brain scrambles to find something that will allow me to regain the advantage in this battle. All it can dredge up is the memory of my last moments with Lisa. My grip tightens, Ivy's knuckles grinding together under the pressure. Still no complaint from her. Just like Lisa.

Suddenly my fingers relax their stranglehold. Lisa trusted me to protect her, right up to the moment I stole her life. Ivy's faith in me is misplaced. I won't let her hope lure me into a false belief that I can control myself. I hear Ivy sigh beside me, no doubt relieved that I didn't do any serious damage to her hand.

The excess energy I'm holding onto makes its way to my leg, which starts bouncing up and down like mad. I want to get up and leave, but how many times can I run away from Ivy and expect her to follow? I am determined to make it through this movie with Ivy and everyone else in the theater, remaining alive and unhurt. If I can't do this, I know I have no chance of pulling off a real relationship with Ivy. I will have to walk away. Fear of losing her barely, barely keeps me in check.

What seems like an eternity later, Ivy attempts to rest her other hand on my arm and snuggle against me. I shake her off immediately with a hiss of agony. "No. Don't, please," I beg.

"But…" Ivy tries to argue.

"No. I can't take anymore," I say. "I'm about to lose control as it is. Just don't."

Ivy leans away from me, but she doesn't go too far. "Breathe," she whispers. "Count up to five as you inhale, and down from five as you exhale. Focus on the way your chest expands and contracts."

I try. The best I can manage is counting to a fast three at first. My body is trying too hard to maintain control over my hunger right now to do any better. But I keep at it. After fifteen minutes, I get up to a slow count of four. That seems to be my limit, and my thoughts are still focused on the way my hunger is trying to burst out of my skin and envelop Ivy rather than what my chest is doing, but I'm back to a very precarious control. I stay in this exact state for the rest of the movie.

As soon as the theater lights blink back on, I spring up from my chair and start running out of the theater. Ivy makes a few objections to my speed as I rush out, but I have to get out of this building right now, so her complaints get ignored. When we burst into the night air, I take a deep breath, hoping it will have some kind of cleansing effect. It doesn't.

The emptiness of the parking lot has an even worse influence on me. Empty, silent, and still. There is nothing here to distract me. Ivy becomes my focus even more intently than in the theater. Desperate, I start marching away from her. I have no plan. I stop a dozen times, fully intent on grabbing her again before I can make it to the truck. I get in, having no idea where Ivy is, but hopeful that she is headed as far away from me as possible. When I hear the seal of the passenger's door break, I panic.

"Get out!" I shout at her. She looks surprised, but sits down next to me. "Ivy, please, get out of the truck. I can't handle this! I have to get away from you before I hurt you. Please!"

"Zander," she says softly, "calm down. We'll get through this."

"No, we won't. I am half a second away from killing you! Get out!" My body convulses as my hunger tries to take control. "Please, Ivy, please. Get away from me."

The slow shake of her head terrifies me. "I can't, Zander. I love you. I'm not giving up."

"*I'm* giving up!" I blurt out. I won't let myself hurt her. I'll live without her, cursing my weakness for the rest of my life, but I can't do this!

"Zander, it's okay."

She starts sliding toward me. My hand darts to the door handle. I'll run. I'll leave her and run. The palm of her hand presses flat against my chest. The hunger that flashes through me in that moment is indescribable. Before I can think, my hands have abandoned the door handle and are clutching Ivy's shoulders. I am trying to push her away and pull her to her death at the same time. My heart is screaming at me to run, my hunger howling in victory, my body responding to her slow, unstoppable approach as her lips draw closer to mine.

"Ivy, don't," I beg with every last ounce of self-control I have left.

She moves toward me, or maybe I pull her closer. She touches me softly, one hand caressing my cheek. Her touch elicits a new rush of hunger. My mind is consumed almost immediately.

I can barely force myself to utter, "Please, Ivy. I'll kill you if you don't stop."

Ivy smiles and says, "I know."

Understanding scours me inside and out in a fraction of a second, but it isn't fast enough. The last thought I have before Ivy's lips press against mine and my hunger gains complete control is that Van was right.

25

PINK HAIRED KAMIKAZE CULTIST

"Ketchup," I say frantically, "this isn't working. We're wasting too much time!"

His hand wrapping around mine stops my manic pacing. It doesn't do anything for my panic. We've been to half a dozen theaters, searched their parking lots for his car, asked ticket takers if they've seen them. All with no results. The happy theater goers drift past us, taking only minimal notice of the spastic teenage girl having a meltdown in front of the ticket window. Ketchup takes us a step further and pulls me into his arms. I look up at him, hoping he has a plan.

"Van, calm down." Anxiety has his face scrunched as much as mine, despite his words, so I'm not fooled. He doesn't relent. "They probably went to dinner first. Zander may be acting like a fool when it comes to Ivy, but he's still a smart guy. He would have done everything he could have to keep her safe, starting with eating, right? You said that helps."

I nod repeatedly. "Yeah, it does. You're right. He's not stupid. Well, not that stupid. He would have planned this out carefully."

"So, where would he have gone?" Ketchup asks. "What theater would make the most sense to him?"

My nervous twitching and talking begins to calm as my brain slows and begins to work again. It helps that Ketchup is still holding me, too. I start using logic, rather than adrenaline, to find my brother.

"Okay," I say. I take a deep breath. "Zander keeps saying he can control himself around Ivy, but he obviously can't, or he wouldn't need her to help him. So that means he'd be worried about witnesses if anything went wrong."

"So he'd choose a small theater," Ketchup says. He glances at the multiplex we're standing in front of. "So, not something like this."

I shake my head in frustration. We've wasted so much time. "No, definitely not. He'd choose somewhere out of the way, with a good exit route…and if things really went bad, a place to get rid of the body."

"Seriously?"

I look up at Ketchup and shrug. "Well, he didn't exactly tell the truth about Lisa, now did he?"

Ketchup nods, but looks disturbed by his admission. He's not the only one. I believe everything Oscar said today. Zander killed Lisa, but in my heart I know it must have been an accident. He's not that person. Not yet, anyway. But if he does the same to Ivy, I have to think of all contingencies. He may call the police himself, or he may drop her in an arroyo. More likely, he'd kill himself out of guilt. I can't count on any of those for sure. I have to find him.

"He'd have to choose a movie that wasn't going to set him off," I continue.

"Can movies do that?" Ketchup asks.

I nod. "Why do you think my grandma almost never lets us watch movies? We know it's not real, but our hunger still responds to the images and emotions."

"Well, that sucks. I was going to ask you if you wanted to see the new Resident Evil movie with me."

"That would be a no," I say, finally managing to slip out of his grip.

Ketchup smiles down at me. "How about a different movie then?"

His fingers trail down my cheek softly. The gentle touch closes my eyes and sends a shiver through my body. Ketchup leans toward me and I feel myself rising to my toes to meet him. That's when warning bells start blaring through my mind. I jump out of Ketchup embrace and slap my hand over my face in shame.

Shocked by my behavior, Ketchup stands staring at me. "What did I say?"

"Ketchup," I whisper, "I'm so sorry, but this has to stop. Nothing has changed, not really."

"Everything has changed," Ketchup argues.

I shake my head, on the verge of tears. "Zander still wants to kill you."

"I've stayed away from him so far and things have worked out just fine. And besides, it's not like you have to live with him forever."

"But...I do," I say.

321

Ketchup stares at me like I'm crazy. "What? Why?"

"At the hospital, do you remember when Rita mentioned a genetic disorder?"

"Yeah," he says slowly.

"Well, it's not a genetic disorder exactly. It's part of who we are, or what we are. We can't go more than a few days without being near each other, or...or we get sick. If the separation lasts long enough, we'll die."

Ketchups leans against a nearby car and runs his hand through his hair. "But...but we could still..."

"Maybe," I admit, "but I would hate myself if I gave you false hope, only to hurt you later." I look down at the ground. I want to give in and just let myself be happy no matter how long it might last, but the pain of losing Ketchup would never be worth it. I can't hurt him. "Ketchup, we don't have time to argue about this right now."

"Fine," he snaps, "but we *are* going to discuss this."

"Later." He leaves it alone, but I fear the result of that conversation won't be what he hopes. "We need to find a movie that is going to have low attendance, less collateral damage if something goes wrong, but not so low that they'd have the whole theater to themselves. Something boring to most, but interesting to some."

Ketchup zips through movie listings on his phone. "Okay, we've got a kid movie about pirates, that Miley Cyrus movie that bombed, a documentary about cave diving..."

"Cave diving," I say.

"Really?"

I roll my eyes at Ketchup. "Yes, really. The pirate movie

was huge with little kids. Zander would never put kids at risk. He would never see a Miley Cyrus movie, either, not even if that act alone would banish this curse. Cave diving it is. What's the smallest, most out of the way theater it's playing at?"

"Twin Cinema on San Mateo."

I grab Ketchup's arm and start hauling him back to his car. "What time did that movie start?"

His eyes bounce around as he tries to read his phone while we run. "Uh, six-thirty. It's an hour and a half long."

We skid to a stop in front of his car and scramble to get in. As soon as Ketchup turns the key and the stereo lights up, my mind starts doing the math. The clock blinks seven-forty-five. The movie ends at eight, and we're all the way across town. I look up to find Ketchup staring at me. He's obviously done the math as well.

"We'll get there in time," he reassures me.

"Just hurry up and drive," is my only response.

Drive he does. Normally, I would be telling him to slow down and watch out for cops. Today, I'm urging him to step on it and looking out for police cruisers to dodge. We dart in and out of dinner-time traffic, pass on turning lanes, and even making a mad dash down a one way street going the wrong direction in order to blaze across Albuquerque as fast as possible. Tires screech as Ketchup plows into the parking lot of Twin Cinema without slowing down. Both of our bodies snap forward when the car lurches to a halt, but seconds later we're stumbling out of the car and racing for the ticket window.

The ticket person takes a step back, despite being locked behind plexiglass when we run up looking like total lunatics. "Did you see a couple come in here earlier? The guy is a big football player type with super blond hair, and the girl was short with black and pink hair."

The guy doesn't respond for a moment, obviously trying gauge whether or not we're going to cause trouble.

"Look, it's a family emergency. The big guy is my brother," I say.

The guy nods, not looking entirely convinced. "Yeah, I saw 'em. That girl was pretty hot. I remembered her hair, and that fact that they were going to see that snoozer cave movie."

"Wow, you're good," Ketchup says to me.

"Come on. We've got to find them." I turn away from the booth with a vague plan to run in and start yelling out Zander's name. The ticket guy's voice calls me back.

"That movie got out like ten minutes ago."

"Did you see them come out?" Ketchup demands.

The guy goes back to his wary stance. "No, but they probably went out the back."

Neither of us hangs around to thank the ticket guy. We bolt around the building in search of Zander, hoping like mad that he hasn't already left. "I didn't hear any screaming," I say as we run.

"That's a good sign, but where are they?"

"Zander must have known there was a back door. I bet he parked right next to it in case he had to get away fast."

We pick up speed and round the back corner of the theater. I spot Zander's monstrous truck right away. It's one of the few sitting back here. But where is he? Where's Ivy?

"Maybe they haven't come out yet?" Ketchup offers. "Girls are always stopping off at the bathroom to put on more lipstick or whatever."

Rolling my eyes, I say, "Yeah, I'm sure Ivy wanted to freshen up before dying!"

"Well, let's hear your idea."

Actually, the bathroom isn't a bad idea. I just can't figure out why nothing has happened yet. "Ketchup, maybe one of us should go back inside while the other waits…"

My words trail off when I glance back at the truck. Something about the windows looks odd. Ketchup's eyes seem to have followed mine. His whole face wrinkles in disgust. "Oh, man, are his windows all steamed up?"

I look closer and gasp. "We have to stop them!"

"What? I don't want to see that!" Ketchup says. "Besides, if they're getting all hot and heavy, isn't that a good sign?"

"No!" I screech and start dragging him to the car. "Zander's hunger, it…it…"

Ketchup waves off an explanation. "Never mind."

We sprint the short distance and slam into the car. It should have been enough to stop anything going on in there if this were a normal couple, but in the grips of his hunger, nothing will faze Zander. One look at Ivy's limp arm sticking out from under Zander is all I can see through the window, but I doubt she's going to react to anything short of a bolt of lightning.

"The doors are locked!" Ketchup shouts.

The panic on his face is clear. I gently push him out

of the way and grip the door handle. One swift jerk, and door swings open. Mine and Ketchup's hands start clawing at Zander. We're screaming at him to stop. Nothing seems to get through to him. I can't get a firm hold on my brother with Ketchup in the way. I regret the hasty shove I give him, but it lets me get my hands around Zander's shoulders. I'm strong, but so is he. It takes all my willpower and strength combined to pry him off Ivy's unmoving body.

He fights against me viciously, elbowing, throwing fists, bucking like a crazed animal. Somewhere along the way, we reach a tipping point, and both of us tumble out of the car. The crack of my head against pavement turns my vision and thoughts hazy for a moment. I'm aware enough to start struggling back to my feet. Halfway up, a massive amount of weight flattens me as Zander plows back toward the truck. That clears my head. My arms lock around his ankles and hold on for dear life. I start to panic when my brother's hands clamp down around my waist and yank me off of him like I was a kitten.

Another crack—this time not to *my* head—resounds in the empty parking lot. Zander's grip on me loosens and we both slither back to the ground. I'm the first to get up, and I'm thoroughly stunned when I see my brother unconscious at my feet. The split skin and bruise are already disappearing from his cheek, but I know the look of a mean punch too well not to see it. Shocked, my eyes drift over to Ketchup.

"Did you do that?" I ask.

He shrugs guiltily. "Sorry, Van, but I couldn't let him hurt you."

"I, um…wow, Ketchup. Thanks."

A little of his guilt slides away, and is replaced by a grin. "I've wanted to do that for three years."

"I can imagine, but he isn't going to stay like this for long. You may not want to be standing so close when he wakes up. Help me move him out of the way."

Normally, I could lug Zander a few feet on my own, but I'm too much of a wreck right now. Together, we drag him out of the way and stand over his unconscious body. He'll be fine for now. I should leave him there, go back to the truck, but I can't bring myself to do it. Ketchup's arm slips around my waist and squeezes me against him.

"What if she's dead?" he asks quietly.

A tremble that starts in my fingertips quickly begins marching toward my heart. "I don't know," I say. My voice is shaking as badly as my body. I don't know if I can face that possibility. At least I don't have to do it alone. If she is dead, Ketchup will help me figure out what to do.

"Come on," he says, and turns me back toward the truck.

Our steps are slow, terrified. When we reach the truck, my breath catches while Ketchup's flows out in a rush. The bruises on her arms are thick where he held her down. Her neck is mottled red and purple. She's so still, I'm sure she's dead. My brain and heart have completely different reactions. I think my blood has frozen, still and unmoving along with my heart. My brain is racing through possibilities as it shoves away the horror of what just happened. My hunger stays oddly buried under my shock and disgust. I refuse to let any kind of sympathy color my judgment. She wanted this. I hate her for what she did, but while that severs any feelings of guilt, it doesn't exactly help me figure out how to keep this a secret.

As I contemplate ways to get rid of a body—something I have unfortunately pondered much too deeply—Ivy's hand twitches. The scream that bursts out of my mouth brings Ketchup's arms around me in a fraction of a second.

"What happened?" he demands.

"She moved!"

"What?"

"Her hand moved. I saw it." Seeing someone I thought to be dead move part of their body scares me half to death, but hope that I didn't imagine it is ready to burst out of me. "Check her pulse," I beg Ketchup.

Like a modern Prince Charming, he saves me from having to check myself. Gently, his first two fingers press against her wrist. He pulls his hand away slowly. "She's alive," he says. The surprise in his voice is nothing compared to mine.

"Are you sure?" I can't imagine how Zander didn't kill her. We must have taken at least a minute to act after seeing his truck. That was more than enough time for him to snap her neck.

"I felt her pulse," Ketchup says, "and look at her lips. They were purple when we first pulled Zander off her. Now they're almost back to normal. What do we do?"

"I don't know," I admit. "I just can't believe she isn't dead. If it had been me…"

"But it wasn't," Ketchup says harshly, as if he doesn't want to imagine me in the same situation. He shakes off whatever mental image my words have conjured. "You said yourself,

Zander likes to plan, or whatever. I think his overthinking bought her just enough time."

I promise myself I will never say another negative word about the way his hunger leans.

The sound of jeans and sneakers rubbing against asphalt makes me jump again. I'm not alone. Ketchup whirls around in a hurry as well. I freeze at the sight of Zander stumbling upright. What will he do? Ketchup doesn't know either, but he takes a protective stance in front of me, one hand poised to push me out of the way if needed. He's sweet, but delusional. His KO punch a few minutes ago was a total fluke. If Zander is thinking clearly, I'm the one who'll be doing the protecting.

"Zander?" I probe, when he gets to his feet but doesn't say anything.

A sluggish movement brings his eyes up to mine. I can see his confusion clearly as his gaze sweeps between me and Ketchup. He takes in the truck, the backside of the theater. His eyes flick past me to the cab of the truck. His body tenses. In a second, I shove Ketchup behind me and hold up my hands, but he doesn't move.

"No, no, no," he wails. "Ivy. Where's Ivy? What happened?"

"You don't remember?" Ketchup asks.

Turning just far enough to catch his eye, I shush him emphatically. He better not forget that Ivy isn't the only one Zander wants to make a meal out of. When I turn back, my brother is shaking his head. Thankfully, he's too confused to register Ketchup's yum factor.

"What happened?" he demands.

I decide to give him the short version. "You ignored me when I said going out with Ivy was a bad idea, took her to a movie, and then proceeded to try and strangle her in your truck. Luckily, Ketchup and I figured out where you were and stopped you, although Ketchup did have to knock you out to make that happen."

"Ketchup?" he asks, clearly in denial.

"Yes, Ketchup."

He'll never live that down, but his mind has already moved on to other things. "You stopped me?" He blinks, shakes his head again. "Does that mean…is Ivy…?"

"Alive? Barely," I admit.

His sudden panicked rush nearly catches me off guard. Luckily, I move quick enough to intercept him. "Zander, no!"

"Dude, you almost killed her!" Ketchup says. "What are you thinking? Stay back!"

"Please, I have to see her," Zander begs.

I shove him hard, suddenly very angry. At him. At Ivy. At Mom and Dad. At Grandma. Fury at the lies and deceit that has led us to this moment boils over in Zander's face. "You have to see her?" I shriek. "Have you totally lost your mind? You're never going to see her again. Ever! This was all one big setup, Zander! Just like I told you it was. She wanted you in this position. She wanted you to kill her!"

I have so much more anger I want to throw at him, but the way my brother's head suddenly drops forces me to pause.

"I know," he says quietly. The anguish in his voice is thick enough to smother him.

I can't find any words to respond, but Ketchup manages

just fine. "What? You knew? And you still brought her here tonight? What the hell is wrong with you, Zander?"

"No, I didn't know before I came here!" Zander shouts. "I didn't realize until the last second. She pushed me over the edge. I tried to run, but she knew exactly how to bring out my hunger." Zander's face screws up in shame and disgust. "I tried to tell her I was going to kill her if she didn't stop, but she…she smiled, and said she knew. And I don't remember anything after that."

Part of me aches for Zander. He must have given Ivy everything she needed to twist him into a hunger-crazed maniac. I can't even begin to fathom how excruciating it must have been to feel so helpless. I've never had my hunger gain so much control over me that my own mind shut down. I hope I never do. My anger lessens in the face of his words, but Ketchup's erupts furiously.

"You want me to feel sorry for you because Ivy tricked you? You want pity because she stirred up your hunger and you lost control? Screw you, Zander!" Ketchup shouts. "Van told you over and over again, and you didn't listen. You had to have Ivy. That was all that mattered to you. Well, this isn't just about you! If you would have killed Ivy…" He's so furious he can't even talk. He takes a threatening step toward my brother, and I know I should stop him, but I don't dare interrupt this.

Ketchup shoves his finger against Zander's chest and my heart stops. I expect to feel Zander's hunger spring to life. I'm amazed when it doesn't. Zander doesn't even say a word to Ketchup's berating. Ketchup meets my brother's eyes, and I'm mildly amused to realize he does so on even ground.

When did Ketchup get so tall? I'm the only one who seems to notice.

Ketchup jabs Zander again. "I know, now, why you made Van break up with me." Ketchup waits a moment to savor Zander's surprise at that admission, but he has more to say. "Van chose you over me, because you're her brother. But what thanks does she get from you? You cast her aside for the sake of some pink-haired kamikaze cultist! You chose Ivy over your own sister, and you damn near put all of your lives at risk! I won't let your idiotic mistakes hurt Van anymore. If you would have murdered Ivy and gotten Van killed, it would have been a race between Ivy's psychotic friends and me to see who could get to you first."

What is more shocking than my normally easy going best friend threatening to kill my brother is that I totally believe he could do it. And so does Zander, apparently. He doesn't even argue. He nods, accepting the threat almost as if it was a promise he is grateful to have. That totally freaks me out. I'm about to pull these two apart when Zander's head snaps back up. To Ketchup's immense credit, he doesn't even flinch.

"Wait," Zander says, confusion wrinkling his face, "what did you mean about Ivy's friends. And why would killing Ivy get Van killed? I'd be punished, not Van."

Now I do step up and gently push Ketchup out of the way. Zander's hunger has been subdued by tonight's events, but it will come racing back soon enough.

"Zander, obviously I was right about Ivy, but you have no idea how right."

I hand him my phone, and wait quietly while he flips through the pictures I snapped of her garage before Ketchup and I bugged out of there. The weapons, the altar, the book, the word Sicarius printed in her freaky book. When he reaches the end, he starts flipping through them again, but I start talking as he does.

"I don't understand half of what we saw in there," I admit, "but it was pretty clear that Ivy belongs to some kind of ancient group intent on killing us...all of us."

Zander's head snaps up. "All of us?"

"Ivy came here as a sacrifice. She had to get one of us to kill her in order to mark our whole family for destruction. But that's not what I meant by all of us."

Zander's head shakes back and forth slowly. I nod in return.

"Zander, we're not the only ones like this. There are more of us somewhere...and I think Grandma, and Mom and Dad, have known the whole time."

I take my phone back and flip to the picture I took of our code word. Handing it back to Zander, I say, "Sicarius. It means assassin. That's what they call us. If Grandma taught us that word, she knew about whoever it is Ivy's helping. Oscar found out that Mom and Dad had been lying to us this whole time. That's why he killed them."

It's too much for him. Zander falls against the side of the truck and presses his hands to his face. "This can't be possible," he says.

I know he's reeling from everything I just dumped on him. In a few hours, I'm probably going to be curled up in a ball, banging my head against a wall when everything finally sinks in, but for now we still have work to do. I turn away from my brother to enlist Ketchup's help. We both turn to stare at Ivy.

"What do we do with her?" I ask.

Ketchup shrugs. "She's alive. You're safe…for now. That's all I care about. Let's prop her up against the theater and get out of here."

"What if we can use her somehow?"

"What, you mean like hold her for ransom so these nut jobs will leave you alone?" he asks.

I shrug. "Maybe it would work."

Ketchup pulls me against his chest. "As much as I want to keep you safe, I doubt that would work. I get the impression these aren't the type of people you negotiate with."

"You're probably right," I say with a sigh.

"So…" Ketchup starts.

His words get swallowed as Ivy moves again. My hunger rouses suddenly. Only Ketchup holding onto me keeps me from lunging forward. The rustle of her clothes snaps Zander back to reality. He's hovering beside us an instant later, staring at his once-girlfriend turned suicide artist. I don't know what to do. So I stand there staring as she pushes herself up to sitting. We all watch as her eyes blink several times, her hand reaches up to her bruised throat, and finally her eyes look up. Shock and dread spread through her features like ink in water.

The sudden whiteness in her face makes the bruises stand out even more. Her lips are still slightly blue when they fall open. "No," she wails. "No, I shouldn't still be alive."

Actual tears start falling down her cheeks. None of us are prepared for her sudden burst out of the truck. She stumbles when she lands, and I don't realize she has a phone in her hand until she rights herself and I see it shoved against her ear. I don't know who she's calling, but I lunge after her.

"*Fallimento!*" Ivy screams before I rip the phone out of her hand and crush it between my fingers.

Now that she's awake, I want answers. I grab at her again, but she's faster than I expected. I can hear sounds of help coming from behind, but I have no intention of missing her again. I dig deep for speed and burst toward her. I would have gotten her, no problem, if not for the panel van that careens around the corner and smashes into my arm. Pain explodes through my body as I crumple to the ground. I watch helplessly as the van door slides open and Ivy is swept from her feet.

26

SEMIDIO

$\mathcal{I}$ try to tell Ketchup and Zander to follow the van, but neither of them listens to me. They both fall to the ground at my feet, flinging out questions.

"I'm fine!" I shout at them. "You should have followed Ivy."

"You're more important," Zander says.

Ketchup's answering scowl gets my brother's hackles up, but I'm sure Ketchup's earlier words are still too fresh for him to argue. Zander sinks back to his shame while Ketchup tries to inspect my arm. His simple touch makes me yelp in pain.

"Don't touch it!" I snap at him.

"Sorry. I just wanted to see how bad it is."

It's bad, but I'll live. "Let Zander take care of it, please. He knows what to do."

Put out, but not stupid, Ketchup folds his arms over his chest. His eagle eye is zeroed in on my brother. He watches as Zander gently wraps his hands around my forearm. The sudden jerk and crack sends a wave of nausea through me. Ketchup nearly loses it. Only my hand grabbing a fistful of shirt and holding him back stops him from punching Zander again.

"He had to set the breaks," I hiss though the pain.

"Breaks?" Ketchup asks. "How many?"

I wince as Zander manipulates another misplaced bone. "Three, at least."

"Four," Zander corrects. "One of your fingers is broken."

Ketchup stops trying to glare my brother to death and turns all his focus on me. He shifts me gently so my head is lying in his lap. The soft stroke of his fingers on my skin leeches out the lingering pain. I sigh as my bones begin to stitch themselves back together. It still hurts like the dickens, but it is beginning to ebb. I let myself relax into Ketchup's embrace just for a little while.

"Dude, are you sucking up her pain, or whatever it is you do?" Ketchup accuses Zander, interrupting my quiet healing time.

I open my eyes to see Zander still holding onto my arm, his eyes closed. He's too absorbed to even answer Ketchup. When I see Ketchup's mouth open to demand an answer, I say, "Leave him alone, Ketchup. It's fine. It doesn't hurt me at all for him to feed on my pain. Sometimes it's the only way we can keep our hunger in check. After what he went through with Ivy, he's got to be ravenous. Be glad he's skimming off me and not you."

He shakes his head. "That's sick."

"It's what we are," I say with a sigh.

A few minutes later, my bones are back to normal. Zander can feel it as well and sits back. "Are you okay?" he asks.

"I'm fine."

Well, as fine as can be. Ketchup helps me back to standing, catching me when I nearly topple over. Healing that many broken bones is no piece of cake. He tries to sweep me into his arms like my personal white knight, but that one I do manage to resist. He continues to hold me up, but I turn my attention back to my brother. "Call Grandma and tell her what happened. I already called her earlier today and gave her the basics, but you better let her know we're all alive before she does something rash."

The look on Zander's face is almost laughable. I don't think I have ever seen him look so scared in his entire life. I have no sympathy for him at all. I motion for Ketchup to help me to the truck. He gets me there without complaint, but walking away isn't as easy for him.

"I'm fine, now. I promise. Just go home and get some sleep," I beg.

His head starts shaking. "Absolutely not. I'm coming with you."

"There is no way you're riding in the car with Zander." Ketchup tries to argue, but I put a stop to that right away. "Look, I know he's tolerated you so far tonight, but what you saw him doing with my arm, it's not a good sign for you. He's very hungry right now."

"All the more reason for me not to leave you alone with him."

I want to argue with him about this, but I can see by the look in his eyes that I am not going to win. Sighing, I give up. "Fine, follow us in your car. And when we get to the house, stay as far away from Zander as possible. I mean it."

"Fine," he says. Then he surprises me by darting in and stealing a kiss. It is so quick, but my heart rate spikes, turning my blood to champagne for a few precious seconds. His fingers slide away from me as he says, "I'm not going anywhere."

Zander stomps into the truck and yanks his door shut. The tension following him like a storm cloud is hard to miss. Something tells me this isn't just about admitting to Grandma what happened tonight. He doesn't make me pry it out of him.

"We need to go. Grandma sounded…strange. She said there's someone at the house that we need to meet."

"What did she mean by that?" I demand.

He shakes his head. "I don't know, but I doubt it's good."

"I'll meet you there," Ketchup says before darting off to his car.

The look I get from Zander threatens to be the start of a bitter fight. My whole body tightens to steel. "If you think you have any room to talk at this point, go ahead," I dare him.

Wisely, he doesn't speak. All he does is start the truck and begin speeding home. Every mile we go sends another shot of dread through me. What if Ivy's friends thought almost dying was close enough? What if they already have Grandma? We could be driving toward a trap, but what else are we going to do? Leave her there to suffer on her own? Of course not! The only comfort I can find as we drive is the unfailing presence of headlights in the rearview mirror.

I swear it's hours later before we pull into the driveway of our house. Zander and I glance over at each other when we spot a shiny black sedan parked alongside Grandma's beat up old Volvo. Seems a little bold for Ivy's type of crowd, but we really have no idea what they might do. The crunch of gravel behind us announces Ketchup's arrival, and two seconds later he's at my door. By now, I can hop down without his help, but that doesn't stop me from grabbing his hand. I am trembling as we cautiously approach the front door.

Halfway up the steps, Grandma appears at the door. "This isn't a trap," she says flatly. "I would hope my own grandchildren would have enough faith in me not to lead them to their deaths."

"We're just being careful," Zander says.

Her answering look is scathing. "Well, it's about time. I thought you'd forgotten the meaning of the word."

Not that I don't agree with her, but my heart pangs to see Zander turn in on himself. He shuffles past her red, ashamed, broken. Grandma's only reaction is to shove a little more steel down her spine. Her laser gaze turns to fasten on me. For a moment, I can't move. I love my grandma dearly, but she is the only person I am truly scared of. I can't make my feet work under her gaze. I don't know why I would be in trouble tonight, but I'm sure there's some reason. There usually is.

So when Grandma's lips start to tremble, and tears sneak past her control, I'm too stunned to react. She's the one who has to come down the steps and swallow me up in a hug.

"Are you okay?" she asks when she finally pulls back and brushes away her tears.

"Yeah," I say, still shocked. "I'm fine."

Grandma grabs my shoulders. "What were you thinking going off on your own like that?"

"I wasn't alone. I had Ketchup." I know it's a frail argument, but I appreciate how Ketchup's hand tightens around mine in solidarity.

Grandma's mouth thins, but she doesn't argue. "Get inside, Van. This night isn't over yet." She turns to Ketchup, I'm sure to send him packing.

"Mrs. Roth," Ketchup interrupts, "I'm not leaving."

It's a bold statement to make to my grandma. She does not take comments like that from anyone. So when she simply nods and walks away, I'm stunned all over again. Ketchup has to tug me forward in order to get me moving. When we walk into the house and see a suit clad man standing in our living room, I get the feeling the surprises are only beginning.

"Who are you?" Ketchup demands.

Whoever he is, he glances over at Grandma at Ketchup's outburst. "Is this Oscar?"

"No, of course not. I already told you Oscar is being held at Peak View."

The man looks back at Ketchup, his eyes hard. "Then he does not belong here."

I can feel Ketchup's entire body bunch up in anger. "Ketchup isn't going anywhere," I blurt out before he can start a fight with whoever this guy is.

"My business is with you and your siblings only."

"Well, he's as much a part of this as we are. He already knows everything we know," I argue.

The man's mouth twists into a smirk. "You know almost nothing, child."

Child? After what I've been through tonight, I'm ready to slap him for that little remark. I hold my temper for once in my life and ask, "If we know so little, then why don't you enlighten us?"

"I will, once your toy has been put away."

I expect Ketchup to take offense. I certainly do. All Ketchup does is chuckle, much to everyone's surprise. "Toy?" he says mockingly. "You're a real comedian, aren't you?"

The man bristles, but doesn't respond.

Ketchup smirks at his reaction. "Fine. You don't want to give up your secrets in front of someone who helped stop that psycho, Ivy—not to mention someone who knows enough of your secrets to start drawing some interesting conclusions and has the ability to spread what I do know—then don't."

I'm surprised when Ketchup's hand releases mine. When he slings his backpack off his shoulder, I grab his arm in panic. I don't know if he should do this. This guy may be worse than Ivy for all we know. But Ketchup ignores me and tosses the book we stole from Ivy's garage on the coffee table. Nobody misses the way the man's eyes light up hungrily.

"As you can see," Ketchup says, "we're doing a pretty good job without your help."

The man reaches for the book, but Ketchup is quick to snatch it back up.

"You have no idea what that is!" he shouts.

"Maybe not," I say, "but it's obviously important to you. So either start explaining what you're doing here, or you'll never read a single word of it."

It takes some serious effort for the man to reel his emotions back in. When he does, Zander takes the lead. "Who are you? Are you one of the people who sent Ivy after us?"

"Am I one of the Eroi?" the man scoffs. "Of course not. My name is David Monroe. I'm a Sicarius, just like you, though we don't prefer that title."

Zander and I both turn to look at our grandma. She tries to hold her ground, but in the face of our anger and blatant proof of her lies, she looks away with shame-filled eyes.

"Who are the Eroi?" I ask.

David's mouth screws up in hatred. "The Eroi are a group of fanatics whose main purpose in life is to destroy every last one of us. Eroi means hero, a self-appointed title, to be sure. They call us the Sicarius, the Assassins, because they believe all we are capable of is killing. We use a different name. We call ourselves the Semidio. Literally it means demigods, but many of us in the U.S. prefer the term Godling. We feel it describes our hunger most accurately."

After seeing Zander tonight, I have to agree about the appropriateness of the term.

Zander shows no opinion on either name, but asks, "Why did they come after us? How did they even know who we are, or where we were?"

"They came after you because the Eroi's only purpose

is to rid the world of Godlings. The young woman, in particular, came after you because she, and others like her, are promised untold rewards in the afterlife in exchange for their lives." David stares at Zander, his eyes cutting into him. "Their methods may not make logical sense to you, but logic has little to do with it. What would you be willing to do for eternal glory?"

Nobody answers his question. We all continue to stare at him, distrusting and despising him. Zander repeats one of his earlier questions. "How did they find us?"

"How the Eroi found you here, I don't know, but now that they are aware of you, staying here is out of the question."

The whole room erupts at once. Grandma is furiously dressing down the man here to steal her grandchildren. Zander is refusing to leave Oscar behind, none too pleased with the idea of bowing to this cocky, arrogant jerk, either. My voice is thrown in as well, making sure everyone knows I have no intention of uprooting my entire life for some guy claiming to know everything.

Ketchup is the only one not yelling. It takes me a few minutes to realize that, but when I do, my own voice drops out of the argument. I turn to look at him, trying to gauge what might be running through his head in that moment. When I can't figure it out, I say, "Ketchup?"

I'm not sure how he hears me over the yelling, but he does. He glances down at me in response, a look of consternation on his features. "You're not going to go, are you?"

"Not if I can help it."

He nods slowly. "But what if you have no choice?"

"I…don't know."

I can hear Grandma throwing out every argument she has, but I get the feeling nothing is going to be enough. In the midst of yelling and fighting, the weight of everything that has happened suddenly turns into an avalanche that buries me, buckling my knees and dropping me to the couch. I can feel Ketchup sit down beside me, but he's only in my periphery. Too many other distractions are flying around in my head.

This isn't just about my family. Ivy wasn't only here to uncover *our* secret. She was a trained sacrifice. A sacrifice who failed. What does that mean? Will her own people kill her for her failure? Will she be sent after some other innocent person trying to live a normal live? All my life I have wanted answers. I've wanted my curse to be explained, to be bigger than me. To mean something. I don't want to leave my friends or my job, my life…but what if this is my only chance to find out what I really am? Who I am? I don't know if I can pass that up.

I look up, and discover Ketchup's eyes waiting for me. As soon as we find each other, he sighs. "You're going to go, aren't you?"

I want to have a different answer, but I say, "I think I have to."

"I don't trust this guy," he argues.

"Neither do I, but what if he can teach me how to control my hunger?" My heart lurches as a thought occurs to me. "What if he can teach Zander?"

That grabs Ketchup's attention. I can feel his pulse speed up. It may be a false hope, or at the very most, a slim one, but it's there. Ketchup latches onto it, his voice cutting through the raging argument and leaving only silence when he turns to David and demands, "Can you show them how to keep their hunger under control?"

David's red-faced irritation drains back to a smug expression. "Of course I can."

The words poised on Zander's lips fall away.

"I can teach you to control your hunger," David promises. "I can teach you to control it, and turn it into a power you've only dreamed of."

Suddenly, Grandma looks white as a sheet, but Zander and I are both mesmerized by his promise. I have a hard time believing this curse is anything but evil, wicked in the truest sense of the word, but his promise is so hard to resist. Wicked hunger turned into wicked power. I am positive this man is no more trustworthy than Ivy was, but if he can give me back what I've lost to this curse, if he can make up for years of being ridiculed and hated, if he can give me back Oscar, and Ketchup...I'll go wherever he tells me to go.

End of Book One

ACKNOWLEDGEMENTS

Thank you to Susan Stec for reading and helping with the initial editing. Your insights were invaluable and your enthusiasm was much appreciated! Thank you to Liz Hathenbruck for reading this book and writing such a wonderful recommendation. Thank you to Betty Goodwin for helping me come up with a new name for the series when I realized the original title was already taken. Thank you to the other awesome ladies in my writing group who helped me fine tune this book and work out all the kinks.

A big thanks to the Clean Teen Publishing team, Rebecca, Courtney, Marya, and Dyan for welcoming Wicked Hunger into the CTP family. I know all of you are behind this series one hundred percent and I am so excited to be working with you. I also wanted to thank Heather Goodall for putting a final polish on Wicked Hunger and getting rid of those last few stubborn typos.

And as always, thank you to my husband Ryan for his ever insightful help with this novel and his continual support of my writing. He really is the best.

ABOUT THE AUTHOR

DelSheree Gladden lives in New Mexico with her husband and two children. The Southwest is a big influence in her writing because of its culture, beauty, and mythology. Local folklore is strongly rooted in her writing, particularly ideas of prophecy, destiny, and talents born from natural abilities. When she is not writing, DelSheree is usually reading, painting, sewing, or working as a Dental Hygienist. Her works include Escaping Fate, Twin Souls Saga, The Destroyer Trilogy, and Invisible.

OTHER BOOKS BY: DELSHEREE GLADDEN

Escaping Fate Series
Escaping Fate
Soul Stone
(Coming 2014)

Twin Souls Saga
Twin Souls
Shaxoa's Gift
Qaletaqa

The Destroyer Trilogy
Inquest
Secret of Betrayal
Darkening Chaos

The Aerling Series
Invisible
Intangible
(Coming 2014)
Invincible
(Coming 2014)

SomeOne Wicked This Way Comes Series
Wicked Hunger
Wicked Power
(Coming 2014)
Wicked Glory
(Coming 2014)

WITHDRAWN

CPSIA information can be obtained at www.ICGtesting.com
Printed in the USA
LVOW11s2246210714

395414LV00005B/359/P